THE CYBERIAD

THE

FABLES FOR THE

Translated from the Polish by
MICHAEL KANDEL

Illustrated by DANIEL MRÓZ

CYBERIAD

CYBERNETIC AGE

STANISŁAW LEM

✦ ✦ ✦ ✦ ✦ ✦ ✦ ✦ ✦ ✦ ✦ ✦ ✦

A CONTINUUM BOOK
THE SEABURY PRESS
NEW YORK

Original edition: *Cyberiada*, Wydawnictwo Literackie, Cracow, 1967, 1972

LIBRARY OF CONGRESS CATALOGING IN PUBLICATION DATA

Lem, Stanisław.
  The cyberiad.

  (A continuum book)
  I. Title.
PZ4.L537Cy3 [PG7158.L39]   891.8′5′37   73–6420
ISBN 0–8164–9164–X

Contents

How the World Was Saved   3
Trurl's Machine   9
A Good Shellacking   21

THE SEVEN SALLIES OF TRURL AND KLAPAUCIUS

The First Sally, or The Trap of Gargantius   31
The First Sally (A), or Trurl's Electronic Bard   43
The Second Sally, or The Offer of King Krool   58
The Third Sally, or The Dragons of Probability   85
The Fourth Sally, or How Trurl Built a Femfatalatron
    to Save Prince Pantagoon from the Pangs of Love,
    and How Later He Resorted to a Cannonade of
    Babies   103
The Fifth Sally, or The Mischief of King Balerion   113
The Fifth Sally (A), or Trurl's Prescription   131
The Sixth Sally, or How Trurl and Klapaucius Created
    a Demon of the Second Kind to Defeat the Pirate
    Pugg   140
The Seventh Sally, or How Trurl's Own Perfection
    Led to No Good   161

Tale of the Three Storytelling Machines of King
    Genius   173
Altruizine   249

FROM THE CYPHROEROTICON, OR TALES OF DEVIATIONS, SUPERFIXATIONS AND ABERRATIONS OF THE HEART

Prince Ferrix and the Princess Crystal   283

THE CYBERIAD

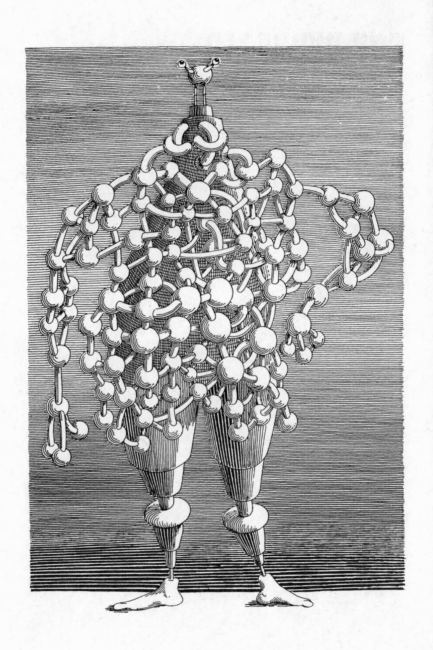

How the World Was Saved

One day Trurl the constructor put together a machine that could create anything starting with n. When it was ready, he tried it out, ordering it to make needles, then nankeens and negligees, which it did, then nail the lot to narghiles filled with nepenthe and numerous other narcotics. The machine carried out his instructions to the letter. Still not completely sure of its ability, he had it produce, one after the other, nimbuses, noodles, nuclei, neutrons, naphtha, noses, nymphs, naiads, and *natrium*. This last it could not do, and Trurl, considerably irritated, demanded an explanation.

"Never heard of it," said the machine.

"What? But it's only sodium. You know, the metal, the element . . ."

"Sodium starts with an s, and I work only in n."

"But in Latin it's *natrium*."

"Look, old boy," said the machine, "if I could do everything starting with n in every possible language, I'd be a Machine That Could Do Everything in the Whole Alphabet, since any item you care to mention undoubtedly starts with n in one foreign language or another. It's not that easy. I can't go beyond what you programmed. So no sodium."

"Very well," said Trurl and ordered it to make Night, which it made at once—small perhaps, but perfectly nocturnal. Only then did Trurl invite over his friend Klapaucius the constructor, and introduced him to the machine, praising its extraordinary skill at such length, that Klapaucius grew annoyed and inquired whether he too might not test the machine.

"Be my guest," said Trurl. "But it has to start with n."

3

"N?" said Klapaucius. "All right, let it make Nature."

The machine whined, and in a trice Trurl's front yard was packed with naturalists. They argued, each publishing heavy volumes, which the others tore to pieces; in the distance one could see flaming pyres, on which martyrs to Nature were sizzling; there was thunder, and strange mushroom-shaped columns of smoke rose up; everyone talked at once, no one listened, and there were all sorts of memoranda, appeals, subpoenas and other documents, while off to the side sat a few old men, feverishly scribbling on scraps of paper.

"Not bad, eh?" said Trurl with pride. "Nature to a T, admit it!"

But Klapaucius wasn't satisfied.

"What, that mob? Surely you're not going to tell me that's Nature?"

"Then give the machine something else," snapped Trurl. "Whatever you like." For a moment Klapaucius was at a loss for what to ask. But after a little thought he declared that he would put two more tasks to the machine; if it could fulfill them, he would admit that it was all Trurl said it was. Trurl agreed to this, whereupon Klapaucius requested Negative.

"Negative?!" cried Trurl. "What on earth is Negative?"

"The opposite of positive, of course," Klapaucius coolly replied. "Negative attitudes, the negative of a picture, for example. Now don't try to pretend you never heard of Negative. All right, machine, get to work!"

The machine, however, had already begun. First it manufactured antiprotons, then antielectrons, antineutrons, antineutrinos, and labored on, until from out of all this antimatter an antiworld took shape, glowing like a ghostly cloud above their heads.

"H'm," muttered Klapaucius, displeased. "That's sup

posed to be Negative? Well . . . let's say it is, for the sake of peace. . . . But now here's the third command: Machine, do Nothing!"

The machine sat still. Klapaucius rubbed his hands in triumph, but Trurl said:

"Well, what did you expect? You asked it to do nothing, and it's doing nothing."

"Correction: I asked it to do Nothing, but it's doing nothing."

"Nothing is nothing!"

"Come, come. It was supposed to do Nothing, but it hasn't done anything, and therefore I've won. For Nothing, my dear and clever colleague, is not your run-of-the-mill nothing, the result of idleness and inactivity, but dynamic, aggressive Nothingness, that is to say, perfect, unique, ubiquitous, in other words Nonexistence, ultimate and supreme, in its very own nonperson!"

"You're confusing the machine!" cried Trurl. But suddenly its metallic voice rang out:

"Really, how can you two bicker at a time like this? Oh yes, I know what Nothing is, and Nothingness, Nonexistence, Nonentity, Negation, Nullity and Nihility, since all these come under the heading of *n*, *n* as in Nil. Look then upon your world for the last time, gentlemen! Soon it shall no longer be . . ."

The constructors froze, forgetting their quarrel, for the machine was in actual fact doing Nothing, and it did it in this fashion: one by one, various things were removed from the world, and the things, thus removed, ceased to exist, as if they had never been. The machine had already disposed of nolars, nightzebs, nocs, necs, nallyrakers, neotremes and nonmalrigers. At moments, though, it seemed that instead of reducing, diminishing and subtracting, the machine was increasing, enhancing and adding, since it liquidated, in turn: nonconformists, nonentities, nonsense, nonsupport, nearsightedness, narrowmindedness, naughtiness, neglect, nausea, necrophilia and nepotism. But after a while the world very definitely began to thin out around Trurl and Klapaucius.

"Omigosh!" said Trurl. "If only nothing bad comes out of all this . . ."

"Don't worry," said Klapaucius. "You can see it's not producing Universal Nothingness, but only causing the absence of whatever starts with *n*. Which is really nothing in the way of nothing, and nothing is what your machine, dear Trurl, is worth!"

"Do not be deceived," replied the machine. "I've begun, it's true, with everything in *n*, but only out of familiarity. To create however is one thing, to destroy, another thing entirely. I can blot out the world for the simple reason that I'm able to do anything and everything—and everything means everything—in *n*, and consequently Nothingness is child's play for me. In less than a minute now you will cease to have existence, along with everything else, so tell me now, Klapaucius, and quickly, that I am really and truly everything I was programmed to be, before it is too late."

"But—" Klapaucius was about to protest, but noticed, just then, that a number of things were indeed disappearing, and not merely those that started with *n*. The constructors were no longer surrounded by the gruncheons, the targalisks, the shupops, the calinatifacts, the thists, worches and pritons.

"Stop! I take it all back! Desist! Whoa! Don't do Nothing!!" screamed Klapaucius. But before the machine could come to a full stop, all the brashations, plusters, laries and zits had vanished away. Now the machine stood motionless. The world was a dreadful sight. The sky had particularly suffered: there were only a few, isolated points of light in the heavens—no trace of the glorious worches and zits that had, till now, graced the horizon!

"Great Gauss!" cried Klapaucius. "And where are the gruncheons? Where my dear, favorite pritons? Where now the gentle zits?!"

"They no longer are, nor ever will exist again," the machine said calmly. "I executed, or rather only began to execute, your order . . ."

"I tell you to do Nothing, and you . . . you . . ."

"Klapaucius, don't pretend to be a greater idiot than you are," said the machine. "Had I made Nothing outright, in one fell swoop, everything would have ceased to exist, and that includes Trurl, the sky, the Universe, and you—and even myself. In which case who could say and to whom could it be said that the order was carried out and I am an efficient and capable machine? And if no one could say it to no one, in what way then could I, who also would not be, be vindicated?"

"Yes, fine, let's drop the subject," said Klapaucius. "I have nothing more to ask of you, only please, dear machine, please return the zits, for without them life loses all its charm . . ."

"But I can't, they're in z," said the machine. "Of course, I can restore nonsense, narrowmindedness, nausea, necrophilia, neuralgia, nefariousness and noxiousness. As for the other letters, however, I can't help you."

"I want my zits!" bellowed Klapaucius.

"Sorry, no zits," said the machine. "Take a good look at this world, how riddled it is with huge, gaping holes, how full of Nothingness, the Nothingness that fills the bottomless void between the stars, how everything about us has become lined with it, how it darkly lurks behind each shred of matter. This is your work, envious one! And I hardly think the future generations will bless you for it . . ."

"Perhaps . . . they won't find out, perhaps they won't no-tice," groaned the pale Klapaucius, gazing up incredu-lously at the black emptiness of space and not daring to look his colleague, Trurl, in the eye. Leaving him beside the ma-chine that could do everything in n, Klapaucius skulked home—and to this day the world has remained honey-combed with nothingness, exactly as it was when halted in the course of its liquidation. And as all subsequent attempts to build a machine on any other letter met with failure, it is to be feared that never again will we have such marvelous phenomena as the worches and the zits—no, never again.

Trurl's Machine

Once upon a time Trurl the constructor built an eight-story thinking machine. When it was finished, he gave it a coat of white paint, trimmed the edges in lavender, stepped back, squinted, then added a little curlicue on the front and, where one might imagine the forehead to be, a few pale orange polkadots. Extremely pleased with himself, he whistled an air and, as is always done on such occasions, asked it the ritual question of how much is two plus two.·

The machine stirred. Its tubes began to glow, its coils warmed up, current coursed through all its circuits like a waterfall, transformers hummed and throbbed, there was a clanging, and a chugging, and such an ungodly racket that Trurl began to think of adding a special mentation muffler. Meanwhile the machine labored on, as if it had been given the most difficult problem in the Universe to solve; the ground shook, the sand slid underfoot from the vibration, valves popped like champagne corks, the relays nearly gave way under the strain. At last, when Trurl had grown extremely impatient, the machine ground to a halt and said in a voice like thunder: SEVEN!

"Nonsense, my dear," said Trurl. "The answer's four. Now be a good machine and adjust yourself! What's two and two?" "SEVEN!" snapped the machine. Trurl sighed and put his coveralls back on, rolled up his sleeves, opened the bottom trapdoor and crawled in. For the longest time he hammered away inside, tightened, soldered, ran clattering up and down the metal stairs, now on the sixth floor, now on the eighth, then pounded back down to the bottom and threw a switch, but something sizzled in the middle, and the spark plugs grew blue whiskers. After two hours of

9

this he came out, covered with soot but satisfied, put all his tools away, took off his coveralls, wiped his face and hands. As he was leaving, he turned and asked, just so there would be no doubt about it:

"And now what's two and two?"

"SEVEN!" replied the machine.

Trurl uttered a terrible oath, but there was no help for it—again he had to poke around inside the machine, disconnecting, correcting, checking, resetting, and when he learned for the third time that two and two was seven, he collapsed in despair at the foot of the machine, and sat there until Klapaucius found him. Klapaucius inquired what was wrong, for Trurl looked as if he had just returned from a funeral. Trurl explained the problem. Klapaucius crawled into the machine himself a couple of times, tried to fix this and that, then asked it for the sum of one plus two, which turned out to be six. One plus one, according to the machine, equaled zero. Klapaucius scratched his head, cleared his throat and said:

"My friend, you'll just have to face it. That isn't the machine you wished to make. However, there's a good side to everything, including this."

"What good side?" muttered Trurl, and kicked the base on which he was sitting.

"Stop that," said the machine.

"H'm, it's sensitive too. But where was I? Oh yes ... there's no question but that we have here a stupid machine, and not merely stupid in the usual, normal way, oh no! This is, as far as I can determine—and you know I am something of an expert—this is the stupidest thinking machine in the entire world, and that's nothing to sneeze at! To construct deliberately such a machine would be far from easy; in fact, I would say that no one could manage it. For the thing is not only stupid, but stubborn as a mule, that is, it has a personality common to idiots, for idiots are uncommonly stubborn."

"What earthly use do I have for such a machine?!" said Trurl, and kicked it again.

"I'm warning you, you better stop!" said the machine.

"A warning, if you please," observed Klapaucius dryly. "Not only is it sensitive, dense and stubborn, but quick to take offense, and believe me, with such an abundance of qualities there are all sorts of things you might do!"

"What, for example?" asked Trurl.

"Well, it's hard to say offhand. You might put it on exhibit and charge admission; people would flock to see the stupidest thinking machine that ever was—what does it have, eight stories? Really, could anyone imagine a bigger dunce? And the exhibition would not only cover your costs, but—"

"Enough, I'm not holding any exhibition!" Trurl said, stood up and, unable to restrain himself, kicked the machine once more.

"This is your third warning," said the machine.

"What?" cried Trurl, infuriated by its imperious manner. "You . . . you . . ." And he kicked it several times, shouting: "You're only good for kicking, you know that?"

"You have insulted me for the fourth, fifth, sixth and eighth times," said the machine. "Therefore I refuse to answer all further questions of a mathematical nature."

"It refuses! Do you hear that?" fumed Trurl, thoroughly exasperated. "After six comes eight—did you notice, Klapaucius?—not seven, but eight! And *that's* the kind of mathematics Her Highness refuses to perform! Take that! And that! And that! Or perhaps you'd like some more?"

The machine shuddered, shook, and without another word started to lift itself from its foundations. They were very deep, and the girders began to bend, but at last it scrambled out, leaving behind broken concrete blocks with steel spokes protruding—and it bore down on Trurl and Klapaucius like a moving fortress. Trurl was so dumbfounded that he didn't even try to hide from the machine, which to all appearances intended to crush him to a pulp. But Klapaucius grabbed his arm and yanked him away, and the two of them took to their heels. When finally they looked back, they saw the machine swaying like a high tower, advancing slowly, at every step sinking to its second floor, but stubbornly, doggedly pulling itself out of the sand and heading straight for them.

"Whoever heard of such a thing?" Trurl gasped in amazement. "Why, this is mutiny! What do we do now?"

"Wait and watch," replied the prudent Klapaucius. "We may learn something."

But there was nothing to be learned just then. The machine had reached firmer ground and was picking up speed. Inside, it whistled, hissed and sputtered.

"Any minute now the signal box will knock loose," said Trurl under his breath. "That'll jam the program and stop it. ..."

"No," said Klapaucius, "this is a special case. The thing is so stupid, that even if the whole transmission goes, it won't matter. But—look out!!"

The machine was gathering momentum, clearly bent on running them down, so they fled just as fast as they could, the fearful rhythm of crunching steps in their ears. They ran and ran—what else could they do? They tried to make it back to their native district, but the machine outflanked them, cut them off, forced them deeper and deeper into a wild, uninhabited region. Mountains, dismal and craggy, slowly rose out of the mist. Trurl, panting heavily, shouted to Klapaucius:

"Listen! Let's turn into some narrow canyon ... where it

won't be able to follow us . . . the cursed thing . . . what do you say?"

"No . . . better go straight," wheezed Klapaucius. "There's a town up ahead . . . can't remember the name . . . anyway, we can find—oof!—find shelter there. . . ."

So they ran straight and soon saw houses before them. The streets were practically deserted at this time of day, and the constructors had gone a good distance without meeting a living soul, when suddenly an awful crash, like an avalanche at the edge of the town, indicated that the machine was coming after them.

Trurl looked back and groaned.

"Good heavens! It's tearing down the houses, Klapaucius!!" For the machine, in stubborn pursuit, was plowing through the walls of the buildings like a mountain of steel, and in its wake lay piles of rubble and white clouds of plaster dust. There were dreadful screams, confusion in the streets, and Trurl and Klapaucius, their hearts in their mouths, ran on till they came to a large town hall, darted inside and raced down endless stairs to a deep cellar.

"It won't get us in here, even if it brings the whole building down on our heads!" panted Klapaucius. "But really, the devil himself had me pay you a visit today. . . . I was curious to see how your work was going—well, I certainly found out . . ."

"Quiet," interrupted Trurl. "Someone's coming. . . ."

And indeed, the cellar door opened up and the mayor entered, accompanied by several aldermen. Trurl was too embarrassed to explain how this strange and calamitous situation had come about; Klapaucius had to do it. The mayor listened in silence. Suddenly the walls trembled, the ground heaved, and the sound of cracking stone reached them in the cellar.

"It's here?!" cried Trurl.

"Yes," said the mayor. "And it demands that we give you up, otherwise it says it will level the entire town. . . ."

Just then they heard, far overhead, words that honked as if from a muffled horn:

"Trul's here . . . I smell Trurl . . ."

"But surely you won't give us up?" asked in a quavering voice the object of the machine's obstinate fury.

"The one of you who calls himself Trurl must leave. The other may remain, since surrendering him does not constitute part of the conditions . . ."

"Have mercy!"

"We are helpless," said the mayor. "And were you to stay here, Trurl, you would have to answer for all the damage done to this town and its inhabitants, since it was because of you that the machine destroyed sixteen homes and buried beneath their ruins many of our finest citizens. Only the fact that you yourself stand in imminent peril permits me to let you leave unpunished. Go then, and nevermore return."

Trurl looked at the aldermen and, seeing his sentence written on their stern faces, slowly turned and made for the door.

"Wait! I'll go with you!" cried Klapaucius impulsively.

"You?" said Trurl, a faint hope in his voice. "But no . . ." he added after a moment. "Why should you have to perish too? . . ."

"Nonsense!" rejoined Klapaucius with great energy. "What, us perish at the hands of that iron imbecile? Never! It takes more than that, my friend, to wipe two of the most famous constructors off the face of the globe! Come, Trurl! Chin up!"

Encouraged by these words, Trurl ran up the stairs after Klapaucius. There was not a soul outside in the square. Amid clouds of dust and the gaunt skeletons of demolished homes, stood the machine, higher than the town hall tower itself, puffing steam, covered with the blood of powdered brick and smeared with chalk.

"Careful!" whispered Klapaucius. "It doesn't see us. Let's take that first street on the left, then turn right, then straight for those mountains. There we can take refuge and think of how to make the thing give up once and for all its insane ... *Now!*" he yelled, for the machine had just spotted them and was charging, making the pavement buckle.

Breathless, they ran from the town and galloped along for a mile or so, hearing behind them the thunderous stride of the colossus that followed relentlessly.

"I know that ravine!" Klapaucius suddenly cried. "That's the bed of a dried-out stream and it leads to cliffs and caves —faster, faster, the thing'll have to stop soon! ..."

So they raced uphill, stumbling and waving their arms to keep their balance, but the machine still gained on them. Scrambling up over the gravel of the dried-out riverbed, they reached a crevice in the perpendicular rock and, seeing high above them the murky mouth of a cave, began to climb frantically toward it, no longer caring about the loose stones that flew from under their feet. The opening in the rock breathed chill and darkness. As quickly as they could, they leaped inside, ran a few extra steps, then stopped.

"Well, here at least we're safe," said Trurl, calm once again. "I'll just take a look, to see where it got stuck ..."

"Be careful," cautioned Klapaucius. Trurl inched his way to the edge of the cave, leaned out, and immediately jumped back in fright.

"It's coming up the mountain!!" he cried.

"Don't worry, it'll never be able to get in here," said Klapaucius, not altogether convinced. "But what's that? Is it getting dark? Oh no!"

At that moment a great shadow blotted out the bit of sky

visible through the mouth of the cave, and in its place appeared a smooth steel wall with rows of rivets. It was the machine slowly closing with the rock, thereby sealing up the cave as if with a mighty metal lid.

"We're trapped . . ." whispered Trurl, his voice breaking off when the darkness became absolute.

"That was idiotic on our part!" Klapaucius exclaimed, furious. "To jump into a cave that it could barricade! How could we have done such a thing?"

"What do you think it's waiting for now?" asked Trurl after a long pause.

"For us to give up—that doesn't take any great brains."

Again there was silence. Trurl tiptoed in the darkness, hands outstretched, in the direction of the opening, running his fingers along the stone until he touched the smooth steel, which was warm, as if heated from within. . . .

"I feel Trurl . . ." boomed the iron voice. Trurl hastily retreated, took a seat alongside his friend, and for some time they sat there, motionless. At last Klapaucius whispered:

"There's no sense our just sitting here. I'll try to reason with it . . ."

"That's hopeless," said Trurl. "But go ahead. Perhaps it will at least let you go free . . ."

"Now, now, none of that!" said Klapaucius, patting him on the back. And he groped his way toward the mouth of the cave and called: "Hello out there, can you hear us?"

"Yes," said the machine.

"Listen, we'd like to apologize. You see . . . well, there was a little misunderstanding, true, but it was nothing, really. Trurl had no intention of . . ."

"I'll pulverize Trurl!" said the machine. "But first, he'll tell me how much two and two makes."

"Of course he will, of course he will, and you'll be happy with his answer, and make it up with him for sure, isn't that right, Trurl?" said the mediator soothingly.

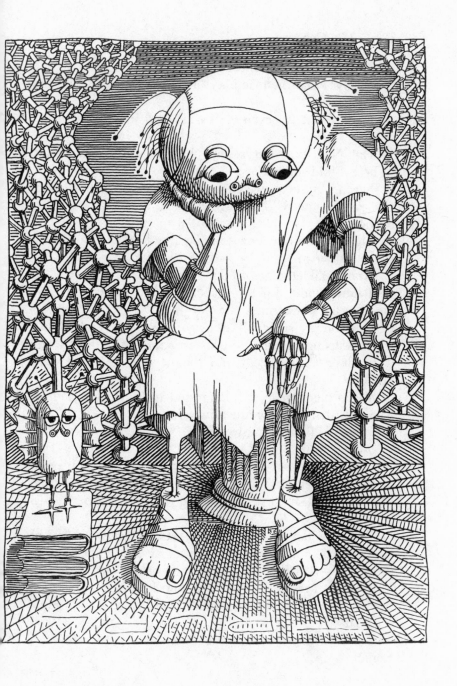

"Yes, of course . . ." mumbled Trurl.

"Really?" said the machine. "Then how much is two and two?"

"Fo . . . that is, seven . . ." said Trurl in an even lower voice.

"Ha! Not four, but seven, eh?" crowed the machine. "There, I told you so!"

"Seven, yes, seven, we always knew it was seven!" Klapaucius eagerly agreed. "Now will you, uh, let us go?" he added cautiously.

"No. Let Trurl say how sorry he is and tell me how much is two times two . . ."

"And you'll let us go, if I do?" asked Trurl.

"I don't know. I'll think about it. I'm not making any deals. What's two times two?"

"But you probably will let us go, won't you?" said Trurl, while Klapaucius pulled on his arm and hissed in his ear: "The thing's an imbecile, don't argue with it, for heaven's sake!"

"I won't let you go, if I don't want to," said the machine. "You just tell me how much two times two is. . . ."

Suddenly Trurl fell into a rage.

"I'll tell you, I'll tell you all right!" he screamed. "Two and two is four and two times two is four, even if you stand on your head, pound these mountains all to dust, drink the ocean dry and swallow the sky—do you hear? Two and two is four!!"

"Trurl! What are you saying? Have you taken leave of your senses? Two and two is seven, nice machine! Seven, seven!!" howled Klapaucius, trying to drown out his friend.

"No! It's four! Four and only four, four from the beginning to the end of time—FOUR!!" bellowed Trurl, growing hoarse.

The rock beneath their feet was seized with a feverish tremor.

The machine moved away from the cave, letting in a little pale light, and gave a piercing scream:

"That's not true! It's seven! Say it's seven or I'll hit you!"

"Never!" roared Trurl, as if he no longer cared what happened, and pebbles and dirt rained down on their heads, for the machine had begun to ram its eight-story hulk again and again into the wall of stone, hurling itself against the mountainside until huge boulders broke away and went tumbling down into the valley.

Thunder and sulfurous fumes filled the cave, and sparks flew from the blows of steel on rock, yet through all this pandemonium one could still make out, now and then, the ragged voice of Trurl bawling:

"Two and two is four! Two and two is four!!"

Klapaucius attempted to shut his friend's mouth by force, but, violently thrown off, he gave up, sat and covered his head with his arms. Not for a moment did the machine's mad efforts flag, and it seemed that any minute now the ceiling would collapse, crush the prisoners and bury them forever. But when they had lost all hope, and the air was thick with acrid smoke and choking dust, there was suddenly a horrible scraping, and a sound like a slow explosion, louder than all the maniacal banging and battering, and the air whooshed, and the black wall that blocked the cave was whisked away, as if by a hurricane, and monstrous chunks of rock came crashing down after it. The echoes of that avalanche still rumbled and reverberated in the valley below when the two friends peered out of their cave. They saw the machine. It lay smashed and flattened, nearly broken in half by an enormous boulder that had landed in the middle of its eight floors. With the greatest care they picked their way down through the smoking rubble. In order to reach the riverbed, it was necessary to pass the remains of the machine, which resembled the wreck of some mighty vessel thrown up upon a beach. Without a word, the two stopped together in the shadow of its twisted hull. The machine still quivered slightly, and one could hear something turning, creaking feebly, within.

"Yes, this is the bad end you've come to, and two and two is—as it always was—" began Trurl, but just then the machine made a faint, barely audible croaking noise and said, for the last time, "SEVEN."

Then something snapped inside, a few stones dribbled down from overhead, and now before them lay nothing but a lifeless mass of scrap. The two constructors exchanged a look and silently, without any further comment or conversation, walked back the way they came.

A Good Shellacking

Someone was knocking at the door of Klapaucius the constructor. He looked out and saw a potbellied machine on four short legs.

"Who are you and what do you want?" he asked.

"I'm a Machine to Grant Your Every Wish and have been sent here by your good friend and colleague, Trurl the Magnificent, as a gift."

"A gift, eh?" replied Klapaucius, whose feelings for Trurl were mixed, to say the least. He was particularly irked by the phrase "Trurl the Magnificent." But after a little thought he said, "All right, you can come in."

He had it stand in the corner by the grandfather clock while he returned to his work, a squat machine on three short legs, which was almost completed—he was just putting on the finishing touches. After a while the Machine to Grant Your Every Wish cleared its throat and said:

"I'm still here."

"I haven't forgotten you," said Klapaucius, not looking up. After another while the machine cleared its throat again and asked:

"May I ask what you're making there?"

"Are you a Machine to Grant Wishes or a Machine to Ask Questions?" said Klapaucius, but added: "I need some blue paint."

"I hope it's the right shade," said the machine, opening a door in its belly and pulling out a bucket of blue. Klapaucius dipped his brush in it without a word and began to paint. In the next few hours he needed sandpaper, some Carborundum, a brace and bit, white paint and one No. 5 screw, all of which the machine handed over on the spot.

That evening he covered his work with a sheet of canvas, had dinner, then pulled up a chair opposite the machine and said:

"Now we'll see what you can do. So you say you can grant every wish . . ."

"Most every wish," replied the machine modestly. "The paint, sandpaper and No. 5 screw were satisfactory, I hope?"

"Quite, quite," said Klapaucius. "But now I have in mind something a bit more difficult. If you can't do it, I'll return you to your master with my kind thanks and a professional opinion."

"All right, what is it?" asked the machine, fidgeting.

"A Trurl," said Klapaucius. "I want a Trurl, the spit and image of Trurl himself, so alike that no one could ever tell them apart."

The machine muttered and hummed and finally said:

"Very well, I'll make you a Trurl. But please handle him with care—he is, after all, a truly magnificent constructor."

"Oh but of course, you needn't worry about that," said Klapaucius. "Well, where is it?"

"What, right away?" said the machine. "A Trurl isn't a No. 5 screw, you know. It'll take time."

But it wasn't long at all before the door in the machine's belly opened and a Trurl climbed out. Klapaucius looked it up and down and around, touched it, tapped it, but there wasn't any doubt: here was a Trurl as much like the original Trurl as two peas in a pod. This Trurl squinted a little, unaccustomed to the light, but otherwise behaved in a perfectly normal fashion.

"Hello, Trurl!" said Klapaucius.

"Hello, Klapaucius! But wait, how did I get here?" Trurl answered, clearly bewildered.

"Oh, you just dropped in. . . . You know, I haven't seen you in ages. How do you like my place?"

"Fine, fine . . . What do you have there under that canvas?"

"Nothing much. Won't you take a seat?"

"Well, I really ought to be going. It's getting dark . . ."

"Don't rush off, you just got here!" protested Klapaucius. "And you haven't seen my cellar yet."

"Your cellar?"

"Yes, you should find it most interesting. This way . . ."

And Klapaucius put an arm around Trurl and led him to the cellar, where he tripped him, pinned him down and quickly tied him up, then took out a big crowbar and began to wallop the daylights out of him. Trurl howled, called for help, cursed, begged for mercy, but Klapaucius didn't stop and the blows rang out and echoed in the dark and empty night.

"Ouch! Ouch!! Why are you beating me?!" yelled Trurl, cowering.

"It gives me pleasure," explained Klapaucius, swinging back. "You should try it sometime, Trurl!"

And he landed him one on the head, which boomed like a drum.

"If you don't let me go at once, I'll tell the King and he'll have you thrown in his deepest dungeon!!" screamed Trurl.

"Oh no he won't. And do you know why?" asked Klapaucius, sitting down for a moment to catch his breath.

"Tell me," said Trurl, glad of the reprieve.

"Because you're not the real Trurl. Trurl, you see, built a Machine to Grant Your Every Wish and sent it here as a gift; to test it out, I had it make you! And now I'm going to knock off your head, put it at the foot of my bed and use it for a bootjack."

"You monster! Why are you doing this to me?"

"I already told you: it gives me pleasure. But enough of

this idle chatter!" And Klapaucius got up and this time picked up a huge bludgeon in both hands—but Trurl cried out:

"Wait! Stop! I have something to tell you!!"

"I wonder what you could possibly tell me to keep me from using your head as a bootjack," replied Klapaucius.

Trurl quickly yelled:

"I'm not any Trurl from a machine! I'm the real Trurl —I only wanted to find out what you've been doing lately behind closed doors and drawn curtains, so I built a machine, hid in its belly and had it take me here, pretending to be a gift!"

"Come now, that's an obvious fabrication and not even clever!" said Klapaucius, hefting his bludgeon. "Don't waste your breath, I can see right through you. You came out of a machine that grants wishes, and if it manufactures paint and sandpaper, a brace and bit, and a No. 5 screw, it can surely manufacture you!"

"I had all that prepared beforehand in its belly!" cried Trurl. "It wasn't hard to anticipate what you'd need in your work! I swear I'm telling the truth!"

"Are you trying to tell me that my good friend and colleague, Trurl the Magnificent, is nothing but a common sneak? No, that I will never believe!" replied Klapaucius. "Take *that!*"

And he let him have it.

"That's for slandering my good friend Trurl! And take *that!* And *that!*"

And he let him have it again, and again, clubbing and clobbering until his arm was too tired to club or clobber anymore.

"Now I'll have a little nap and rest up," said Klapaucius, throwing aside the bludgeon. "But don't you worry, I'll be back. . . ." And he left, and soon was snoring so loud you could hear it even in the cellar. Trurl writhed and twisted until he loosened his bonds enough to slip off the knots, got up, crept back to the machine, climbed inside and took off for home at a gallop. Klapaucius meanwhile was watching the escape from his bedroom window, pressing a hand over his mouth to keep from laughing out loud. The next day he went to pay Trurl a visit. It was a gloomy and silent Trurl that let him in. The room was dark, but even so, Klapaucius could see that Trurl's person bore the marks of a good shellacking—though it was apparent that Trurl had gone to some trouble to touch up the scratches and hammer out the dents.

"Why so gloomy?" asked a cheerful Klapaucius. "I came to thank you for the nice gift—what a shame, though, it ran off while I slept, and in such a hurry that it left the door open!"

"It seems to me," snapped Trurl, "that you somewhat misused, or should I say abused, my gift. Oh, you needn't bother to explain, the machine told me everything. You had it make me, me, then lured me, I mean the copy of me, to the cellar, where you beat it unmercifully! And after this great insult to my person, after this act of the blackest ingratitude, you dare show your face here as if nothing happened! What do you have to say for yourself?"

"I really don't understand why you're so angry," said Klapaucius. "It's true I had the machine make a copy of you, and I must say it was absolutely perfect, an amazing likeness. As far as the beating goes, well, your machine must have exaggerated a little—I did give the artificial Trurl a poke or two, but only to see if it was well made, and perhaps also to test its reflexes, which were quite good, by the way. It turned out to be very much on its toes, and even tried to argue that it was really you, can you imagine—? Of course I didn't believe it, but then it swore the gift wasn't a gift at all, but some sort of low and underhanded trick. Well, I had to defend the honor of my good friend, you understand, so I thrashed it some for slandering you so shamelessly. On the other hand I found it to be extremely intelligent; so you see, Trurl, it resembled you mentally as well as physically. You are indeed a great and magnificent constructor, which is precisely what I came to tell you so early in the morning!"

"Well, yes, in that case," said Trurl, considerably appeased. "Though your use of the Machine to Grant Your Every Wish was not, I would say, the most fortunate . . ."

"Oh yes, one other thing I wanted to ask," said Klapaucius, all innocence. "What did you do with the artificial Trurl? Could I see it?"

"It was beside itself with rage," explained Trurl. "It said it would ambush you by that mountain pass near your house and tear you limb from limb. I tried to reason with it, but it called me names, ran out into the night and started putting together all sorts of booby traps for you—and so, dear Klapaucius, though you had insulted me, I remembered our old friendship and decided to remove this threat to your life and limb. Hence I had to disassemble it. . . ."

And he touched a few nuts and bolts on the floor with his shoe, and sighed.

Whereupon they exchanged kind words, shook hands and parted the best of friends.

From that time on, Trurl did nothing but tell everyone how he had given Klapaucius a Machine to Grant Your Every Wish, how then Klapaucius had insulted him by having it make an artificial Trurl, which he proceeded to beat black-and-blue; how then this excellently constructed copy of the great constructor made clever lies to save itself, and finally managed to escape while Klapaucius slept, and how Trurl himself, the real Trurl, eventually had to disassemble the artificial Trurl to protect his good friend and colleague from its vengeance. Trurl told this story so often and at such length, elaborating on his glorious achievement (and never failing to call on Klapaucius as a witness), that it reached the ears of the Royal Court at last, and now no one spoke of Trurl other than with the utmost respect, though not long ago he had been commonly called the Constructor of the World's Stupidest Computer. When Klapaucius heard, one day, that the King himself had rewarded Trurl handsomely and decorated him with the Order of the Great Parallax, he threw up his hands and cried:

"What? Here I was able to see through his little game and gave him so good a shellacking for it that he had to sneak home in the middle of the night and patch himself up, and even then he looked a sight! And for that they decorate him, praise him, shower him with riches? O *tempora, O mores!* . . ."

Furious, he went home, locked himself in and drew the blinds. He too had been working on a Machine to Grant Your Every Wish, only Trurl had beat him to it.

The Seven Sallies
of Trurl and Klapaucius

The First Sally

OR The Trap

of Gargantius

When the Universe was not so out of whack as it is today, and all the stars were lined up in their proper places, so you could easily count them from left to right, or top to bottom, and the larger and bluer ones were set apart, and the smaller, yellowing types pushed off to the corners as bodies of a lower grade, when there was not a speck of dust to be found in outer space, nor any nebular debris—in those good old days it was the custom for constructors, once they had received their Diploma of Perpetual Omnipotence with distinction, to sally forth ofttimes and bring to distant lands the benefit of their expertise. And so it happened that, in keeping with this ancient custom, Trurl and Klapaucius, who could kindle or extinguish suns as easily as shelling peas, did venture out on such a voyage. When the vastness of the traveled void had erased in them all recollection of their native skies, they saw a planet up ahead—not too little, not too big, just about right—with one continent only, down the middle of which ran a bright red line: everything on one side was yellow, everything on the other, pink. Realizing at once that here were two neighboring kingdoms, the constructors held a brief council of war before landing.

"With two kingdoms," said Trurl, "it's best you take one, and I the other. That way nobody's feelings get hurt."

"Fine," said Klapaucius. "But what if they ask for military aid? Such things happen."

"True, they could demand weapons, even superweapons," Trurl agreed. "We'll simply refuse."

"And if they insist, and threaten us?" returned Klapaucius. "This too can happen."

"Let's see," said Trurl, switching on the radio. It blared martial music, a rousing march.

"I have an idea," said Klapaucius, turning it off. "We can use the Gargantius Effect. What do you think?"

"Ah, the Gargantius Effect!" cried Trurl. "I never heard of anyone actually using it. But there's always a first time. Yes, why not?"

"We'll both be prepared to use it," Klapaucius explained. "But it's imperative that we use it together, otherwise we're in serious trouble."

"No problem," said Trurl. He took a small golden box out of his pocket and opened it. Inside, on velvet, lay two white beads. "You keep one, I'll keep the other. Look at yours every evening; if it turns pink, that'll mean I've started and you must too."

"So be it," said Klapaucius and put his bead away. Then they landed, shook hands and set off in opposite directions.

The kingdom to which Trurl repaired was ruled by King Atrocitus. He was a militarist to the core, and an incredible miser besides. To relieve the royal treasury, he did away with all punishments except for the death sentence. His favorite occupation was to abolish unnecessary offices; since that included the office of executioner, every condemned citizen was obliged to do his own beheading, or else—on rare occasions of royal clemency—have it done by his next of kin. Of the arts Atrocitus supported only those that entailed little expense, such as choral recitation, chess and military calisthenics. The art of war he held in particularly high esteem, for a victorious campaign brought in excellent returns; on the other hand, one could properly prepare for war only during an interval of peace, so the King advocated peace, though in moderation. His greatest reform was the nationalization of high treason. As the neighboring kingdom was continually sending spies, he created the office of Royal Informer, who, through a staff of subordinate traitors, would hand over State secrets to enemy agents for certain sums of money. Though as a rule the agents purchased only outdated secrets—those were less expensive and besides, they were held accountable to their own treasury for every penny spent.

The subjects of Atrocitus rose early, were well-behaved, and worked long hours. They wove fascines and gabions for fortifications, made guns and denunciations. In order that the kingdom not be flooded with the latter (which in fact had happened during the reign of Bartholocaust the Wall-eyed several hundred years before), whoever wrote too many denunciations was required to pay a special luxury tax. In this way they were kept at a reasonable level. Arriving at the Court of Atrocitus, Trurl offered his services. The King—not surprisingly—wanted powerful instruments of war. Trurl asked for a few days to think it over, and as soon as he was alone in the little cubicle they had assigned to him, he looked at the bead in the golden box. It was white but, as he looked, turned slowly pink. "Aha," he said to himself, "time to start with Gargantius!" And without further delay he took out his secret formulae and set to work.

Klapaucius meanwhile found himself in the other kingdom, which was ruled by the mighty King Ferocitus. Here everything looked quite different than in Atrocia. This monarch too delighted in campaigns and marches, and he too spent heavily on armaments—but in an enlightened way, for he was a most generous lord and a great patron of the arts. He loved uniforms, gold braid, stripes and tassels, spurs, brigadiers with bells, destroyers, swords and chargers. A per-

son of keen sensibilities, he trembled every time he chris-
tened a new destroyer. And he lavishly rewarded paintings
of battle scenes, patriotically paying according to the number of fallen foes depicted, so that, on those endless pano-
ramic canvases with which the kingdom was packed, mountains of enemy dead reached up to the sky. In practice he
was an autocrat, yet with libertarian views; a martinet, yet
magnanimous. On every anniversary of his coronation he
instituted reforms. Once he ordered the guillotines decked
with flowers, another time had them oiled so they wouldn't
squeak, and once he gilded the executioners' axes and had
them all resharpened—out of humanitarian considerations.
Ferocitus was not overly dainty, yet he did frown upon
excesses, and therefore by special decree regulated and
standardized all wheels, racks, spikes, screws, chains and
clubs. Beheadings of wrongthinkers—a rare enough event—
took place with pomp and pageantry, brass bands, speeches,
parades and floats. This high-minded monarch also had a
theory, which he put into action, and this was the Theory
of Universal Happiness. It is well known, certainly, that one
does not laugh because one is amused, but rather, one is
amused because one laughs. If then everyone maintains that
things just couldn't be better, attitudes immediately improve. The subjects of Ferocitus were thus required, for
their own good, to go about shouting how wonderful everything was, and the old, indefinite greeting of "Hello" was
changed by the King to the more emphatic "Hallelujah!"
—though children up to the age of fourteen were permitted
to say, "Wow!" or "Whee!", and the old-timers, "Swell!"
   Ferocitus rejoiced to see his people in such good spirits.
Whenever he drove by in his destroyer-shaped carriage,
crowds in the street would cheer, and whenever he gra-
ciously waved his royal hand, those up front would cry:
"Wow!"—"Hallelujah!"—"Terrific!" A democrat at heart,

he liked to stop and chat awhile with old soldiers who had
been around and seen much, liked to hear tales of derring-do
told at bivouacs, and often, when some foreign dignitary
came for an audience, he would out of the blue clap him on
the knee with his baton and bellow: "Have at them!"—or:
"Swiggle the mizzen there, mates!"—or: "Thunderation!"
For there was nothing he loved so much or held so dear as
gumption, crust and pluck, roughness and toughness, powder, chowder, hardtack, grog and ammo. And so, whenever
he was melancholy, he had his troops march by before him,
singing: "Screw up yer courage, nuts to the foe"—"When
currents lag, crank out the flag"—"We'll scrap, stout lads,
until we're nought but scrap"—or the rousing anthem:
"Lock, stock, and barrel." And he commanded that, when
he died, the old guard should sing his favorite song over the
grave: "Old Robots Never Rust."

Klapaucius did not get to the court of this great ruler all
at once. At the first village he came to, he knocked on several doors, but no one opened up. Finally he noticed in the
deserted street a small child; it approached him and asked
in a thin, high voice:

"Wanna buy any, mister? They're cheap."

"What are you selling?" inquired Klapaucius, surprised.

"State secrets," replied the child, lifting the edge of its
smock to give him a glimpse of some mobilization plans.
This surprised Klapaucius even more, and he said:

"No, thank you, my little one. But can you tell me where
I might find the mayor?"

"What'cha want the mayor for?" asked the child.

"I wish to speak with him."

"In secret?"

"It makes no difference."

"Need a secret agent? My dad's a secret agent. Depend-
able and cheap."

"Very well then, take me to your dad," said Klapaucius, seeing he would get nowhere with the child. The child led him to one of the houses. Inside, though it was in the middle of the day, a family sat around a lighted lamp—a gray grandfather in a rocking chair, a grandmother knitting socks, and their fully grown and numerous progeny, each busy at his own household task. As soon as Klapaucius entered, they jumped up and seized him; the knitting needles turned out to be handcuffs, the lamp a microphone, and the grandmother the local chief of police.

"They must have made a mistake," thought Klapaucius, when he was beaten and thrown in jail. Patiently he waited through the night—there was nothing else he could do. The dawn came and revealed the cobwebs on the stone walls of his cell, also the rusted remains of previous prisoners. After a length of time he was taken and interrogated. It turned out that the little child as well as the houses—the whole village, in fact—all of it was a plant to trick foreign spies. But Klapaucius did not have to face the rigors of a long trial; the proceedings were quickly over. For attempting to establish contact with the informer–dad the punishment was a third-class guillotining, because the local administration had already allotted funds to buy out enemy agents for that fiscal year, and Klapaucius, on his part, repeatedly refused to purchase any State secrets from the police. Nor did he have sufficient ready cash to mitigate the offense. Still, the prisoner continued to protest his innocence—not that the judge believed a word of it; even if he had, to free him lay outside his jurisdiction. So the case was sent to a higher court, and in the meantime Klapaucius was subjected to torture, though more as a matter of form than out of any real necessity. In about a week his case took a turn for the better; finally acquitted, he proceeded to the Capitol where, after receiving instructions in the rules and regulations of

court etiquette, he obtained the honor of a private audience
with the King. They also gave him a bugle, for every citizen
was obliged to announce his comings and goings in official
places with appropriate flourishes, and such was the iron
discipline of that land, that the sun was not considered
risen without the blowing of reveille.

Ferocitus did in fact demand new weapons. Klapaucius
promised to fulfill this royal wish; his plan, he assured the
King, represented a radical departure from the accepted
principles of military action. What kind of army—he asked
first—always emerged victorious? The one that had the
finest leaders and the best disciplined soldiers. The leader
gave the orders, the soldier carried them out; the former
therefore had to be wise, the latter obedient. However, to
the wisdom of the mind, even of the military mind, there
were certain natural limits. A great leader, moreover, could
come up against an equally great leader. Then too, he might
fall in battle and leave his legion leaderless, or do something
even more dreadful, since he was, as it were, professionally
trained to think, and the object of his thoughts was power.
Was it not dangerous to have a host of old generals in the
field, their rusty heads so packed with tactics and strategy
that they started pining for the throne? Had not more than
one kingdom come to grief thereby? It was clear, then, that
leaders were a necessary evil; the problem lay in making that
evil unnecessary. To go on: the discipline of an army consisted in the precise execution of orders. Ideally, we would
have a thousand hearts and minds molded into one heart,
one mind, one will. Military regimens, drills, exercises and
maneuvers all served this end. The ultimate goal was thus
an army that literally acted as one man, in itself both creator
and executor of its objectives. But where was the embodi-
ment of such perfection to be found? Only in the individual, for no one was obeyed as willingly as one's own self,

and no one carried out orders as cheerfully as the one who gave those orders. Nor could an individual be dispersed, and insubordination or mutiny against himself was quite out of the question. The problem then was to take this eagerness to serve oneself, this self-worship which marked the individual, and make it a property of a force of thousands. How could this be done? Here Klapaucius began to explain to the keenly interested King the simple ideas—for are not all things of genius simple?—discovered by the great Gargantius.

Into each recruit (he explained) a plug is screwed in front, a socket in back. Upon the command "Close up those ranks!" the plugs and sockets connect and, where only a moment before you had a crowd of civilians, there stands a battalion of perfect soldiers. When separate minds, hitherto occupied with all sorts of nonmartial nonsense, merge into one regimental consciousness, not only is there automatic discipline, for the army has become a single fighting machine composed of a million parts—but there is also wisdom. And that wisdom is directly proportional to the numbers involved. A platoon possesses the acumen of a master sergeant; a company is as shrewd as a lieutenant colonel, a brigade smarter than a field marshal; and a division is worth more than all the army's strategists and specialists put together. In this way one can create formations of truly staggering perspicacity. And of course they will follow their own orders to the letter. This puts an end to the vagaries and reckless escapades of individuals, the dependence on a particular commander's capabilities, the constant rivalries, envies and enmities between generals. And detachments, once joined, should not be put asunder, for that produces nothing but confusion. "An army whose only leader is itself—this is my idea!" Klapaucius concluded. The King was much impressed with his words and finally said:

"Return to your quarters. I shall consult my general staff . . ."

"Oh, do not do this, Your Royal Highness!" exclaimed the clever Klapaucius, feigning great consternation. "That is exactly what the Emperor Turbulon did, and his staff, to protect their own positions, advised him against it; shortly thereafter, the neighbor of Turbulon, King Enamuel, attacked with a revolutionized army and reduced the empire to ashes, though his forces were eight times smaller!"

Whereupon he bowed, went to his room and inspected the little bead, which was red as a beet; that meant Trurl had done likewise at the court of Atrocitus. The King soon ordered Klapaucius to revolutionize one platoon of infantry; joined in spirit and now entirely of one mind, this tiny unit cried, "Kill, kill!" swooped down on three squadrons of the King's dragoons, who were armed to the teeth and led moreover by six distinguished lecturers of the Academy of the General Staff—and cut them to ribbons. Great was the grief of the generals, marshals, admirals and commanders in chief, for the King sent them all into a speedy retirement; fully convinced of the efficacy of Klapaucius' invention, he ordered the entire army revolutionized.

And so munitions electricians worked day and night, turning out plugs and sockets by the carload, and these were installed as necessary in all the barracks. Covered with medals, Klapaucius rode from garrison to garrison and supervised everything. Trurl fared similarly in the kingdom of Atrocitus, except that, due to that monarch's well-known parsimony, he had to content himself with the lifelong title of Great Betrayer of the Fatherland. Both kingdoms were now preparing for war. In the heat of mobilization, conventional as well as nuclear weapons were brought into battle trim, and cannons and atoms subjected to the utmost spit and polish, as per regulations. Their work now all but done, the two constructors packed their bags in secret, to be ready to meet, when the time came, at the appointed place near the ship they had left in the forest.

Meanwhile miracles were taking place among the rank and file, particularly in the infantry. Companies no longer had to practice their marching drills, nor did they need to count off to learn their number, just as one who has two legs never mistakes his right for his left, nor finds it necessary to calculate how many of himself there are. It was a joy to see those new units do the Forward March, About Face and Company Halt; and afterwards, when they were dismissed, they took to chatting, and later, through the open windows of the barracks one could hear voices booming in chorus, disputing such matters as absolute truth, analytic versus synthetic *a priori* propositions, and the Thing-in-itself, for their collective minds had already attained that level. Various philosophical systems were hammered out, till finally a certain battalion of sappers arrived at a position of total solipsism, claiming that nothing really existed beyond itself. And since from this it followed that there was no King, nor any enemy, this battalion was quietly disconnected and its members reassigned to units that firmly adhered to epistemological realism. At about the same time, in the kingdom of Atrocitus, the sixth amphibious division forsook naval operations for navel contemplation and, thoroughly immersed in mysticism, very nearly drowned. Somehow or other, as a result of this incident, war was declared, and the troops, rumbling and clanking, slowly moved towards the border from either side.

The law of Gargantius proceeded to work with inexorable logic. As formation joined formation, in proportion there developed an esthetic sense, which reached its apex at the level of a reinforced division, so that the columns of such a force easily became sidetracked, chasing off after butterflies, and when the motorized corps named for Bartholo-

caust approached an enemy fortress that had to be taken
by storm, the plan of attack drawn up that night turned
out to be a splendid painting of the battlements, done moreover in the abstractionist spirit, which ran counter to all
military traditions. Among the artillery corps the weightiest
metaphysical questions were considered, and, with an ab-
sentmindedness characteristic of great genius, these large
units lost their weapons, misplaced their equipment and
completely forgot that there was a war on. As for whole
armies, their psyches were beset by a multitude of com-
plexes, which often happens to overly developed intellects,
and it became necessary to assign to each a special psychi-
atric motorcycle brigade, which applied appropriate therapy
on the march.

In the meantime, to the thunderous accompaniment of
fife and drum, both sides slowly got into position. Six regi-
ments of shock troops, supported by a battery of howitzers
and two backup battalions, composed, with the assistance
of a firing squad, a sonnet entitled "On the Mystery of Being," and this took place during guard duty. There was considerable confusion in both armies; the Eightieth Marla-
bardian Corps, for instance, maintained that the whole con-
cept of "enemy" needed to be more clearly defined, as it
was full of logical contradictions and might even be altogether meaningless.

Paratroopers tried to find algorithms for the local terrain,
flanks kept colliding with centers, so at last the two kings
sent airborne adjutants and couriers extraordinary to restore
order in the ranks. But each of these, having flown or galloped up to the corps in question, before he could discover
the cause of the disturbance, instantly lost his identity in
the corporate identity, and the kings were left without adjutants or couriers. Consciousness, it seemed, formed a
deadly trap, in that one could enter it, but never leave.

Atrocitus himself saw how his cousin, the Grand Prince Bullion, desiring to raise the spirits of his soldiers, leaped into the fray, and how, as soon as he had hooked himself into the line, his spirit was literally spirited away, and he was no more.

Sensing that something had gone amiss, Ferocitus nodded to the twelve buglers at his right hand. Atrocitus, from the top of his hill, did likewise; the buglers put the brass to their lips and sounded the charge on either side. At this clarion signal each army totally and completely linked up. The fearsome metallic clatter of closing contacts reverberated over the future battlefield; in the place of a thousand bombardiers and grenadiers, commandos, lancers, gunners, snipers, sappers and marauders—there stood two giant beings, who gazed at one another through a million eyes across a mighty plain that lay beneath billowing clouds. There was absolute silence. That famous culmination of consciousness which the great Gargantius had predicted with mathematical precision was now reached on both sides. For beyond a certain point militarism, a purely local phenomenon, becomes civil, and this is because the Cosmos Itself is by nature wholly civilian, and indeed, the minds of both armies had assumed truly cosmic proportions! Thus, though on the outside armor still gleamed, as well as the death-dealing steel of artillery, *within* there surged an ocean of mutual good will, tolerance, an all-embracing benevolence, and bright reason. And so, standing on opposite hilltops, their weapons sparkling in the sun, while the drums continued to roll, the two armies smiled at one another. Trurl and Klapaucius were just then boarding their ship, since that which they had planned had come to pass: before the eyes of their mortified, infuriated rulers, both armies went off hand in hand, picking flowers beneath the fluffy white clouds, on the field of the battle that never was.

The First Sally (A)

OR *Trurl's*
Electronic Bard

First of all, to avoid any possible misunderstanding, we should state that this was, strictly speaking, a sally to nowhere. In fact, Trurl never left his house throughout it—except for a few trips to the hospital and an unimportant excursion to some asteroid. Yet in a deeper and/or higher sense this was one of the farthest sallies ever undertaken by the famed constructor, for it very nearly took him beyond the realm of possibility.

Trurl had once had the misfortune to build an enormous calculating machine that was capable of only one operation, namely the addition of two and two, and *that* it did incorrectly. As is related earlier in this volume, the machine also proved to be extremely stubborn, and the quarrel that ensued between it and its creator almost cost the latter his life. From that time on Klapaucius teased Trurl unmercifully, making comments at every opportunity, until Trurl decided to silence him once and for all by building a machine that could write poetry. First Trurl collected eight hundred and twenty tons of books on cybernetics and twelve thousand tons of the finest poetry, then sat down to read it all. Whenever he felt he just couldn't take another chart or equation, he would switch over to verse, and vice versa. After a while it became clear to him that the construction of the machine itself was child's play in comparison with the writing of the program. The program found in

43

the head of an average poet, after all, was written by the poet's civilization, and that civilization was in turn programmed by the civilization that preceded it, and so on to the very Dawn of Time, when those bits of information that concerned the poet-to-be were still swirling about in the primordial chaos of the cosmic deep. Hence in order to program a poetry machine, one would first have to repeat the entire Universe from the beginning—or at least a good piece of it.

Anyone else in Trurl's place would have given up then and there, but our intrepid constructor was nothing daunted. He built a machine and fashioned a digital model of the Void, an Electrostatic Spirit to move upon the face of the electrolytic waters, and he introduced the parameter of light, a protogalactic cloud or two, and by degrees worked his way up to the first ice age—Trurl could move at this rate because his machine was able, in one five-billionth of a second, to simulate one hundred septillion events at forty octillion different locations simultaneously. And if anyone questions these figures, let him work it out for himself.

Next Trurl began to model Civilization, the striking of fires with flints and the tanning of hides, and he provided for dinosaurs and floods, bipedality and taillessness, then made the paleopaleface (*Albuminidis sapientia*), which begat the paleface, which begat the gadget, and so it went, from eon to millennium, in the endless hum of electrical currents and eddies. Often the machine turned out to be too small for the computer simulation of a new epoch, and Trurl would have to tack on an auxiliary unit—until he ended up, at last, with a veritable metropolis of tubes and terminals, circuits and shunts, all so tangled and involved that the devil himself couldn't have made head or tail of it. But Trurl managed somehow, he only had to go back twice —once, almost to the beginning, when he discovered that

Abel had murdered Cain and not Cain Abel (the result, apparently, of a defective fuse), and once, only three hundred million years back to the middle of the Mesozoic, when after going from fish to amphibian to reptile to mammal, something odd took place among the primates and instead of great apes he came out with gray drapes. A fly, it seems, had gotten into the machine and shorted out the polyphase step-down directional widget. Otherwise everything went like a dream. Antiquity and the Middle Ages were recreated, then the period of revolutions and reforms —which gave the machine a few nasty jolts—and then civilization progressed in such leaps and bounds that Trurl had to hose down the coils and cores repeatedly to keep them from overheating.

Towards the end of the twentieth century the machine began to tremble, first sideways, then lengthwise—for no apparent reason. This alarmed Trurl; he brought out cement and grappling irons just in case. But fortunately these weren't needed; instead of jumping its moorings, the machine settled down and soon had left the twentieth century far behind. Civilizations came and went thereafter in fifty-thousand-year intervals: these were the fully intelligent beings from whom Trurl himself stemmed. Spool upon spool of computerized history was filled and ejected into storage bins; soon there were so many spools, that even if you stood at the top of the machine with high-power binoculars, you wouldn't see the end of them. And all to construct some versifier! But then, such is the way of scientific fanaticism. At last the programs were ready; all that remained was to pick out the most applicable—else the electropoet's education would take several million years at the very least.

During the next two weeks Trurl fed general instructions into his future electropoet, then set up all the necessary logic circuits, emotive elements, semantic centers. He was about to invite Klapaucius to attend a trial run, but thought better of it and started the machine himself. It immediately proceeded to deliver a lecture on the grinding of crystallographical surfaces as an introduction to the study of submolecular magnetic anomalies. Trurl bypassed half the logic circuits and made the emotive more electromotive; the machine sobbed, went into hysterics, then finally said, blubbering terribly, what a cruel, cruel world this was. Trurl intensified the semantic fields and attached a strength of character component; the machine informed him that from now on he would carry out its every wish and to begin with add six floors to the nine it already had, so it could better meditate upon the meaning of existence. Trurl installed a philosophical throttle instead; the machine fell silent and sulked. Only after endless pleading and cajoling was he able to get it to recite something: "I had a little froggy." That appeared to exhaust its repertoire. Trurl adjusted, modulated, expostulated, disconnected, ran checks, reconnected, reset, did everything he could think of, and the machine presented him with a poem that made him thank heaven Klapaucius wasn't there to laugh—imagine, simulating the whole Universe from scratch, not to mention Civilization in every particular, and to end up with such dreadful doggerel! Trurl put in six cliché filters, but they snapped like matches; he had to make them out of pure corundum steel. This seemed to work, so he jacked the semanticity up all the way, plugged in an alternating rhyme generator—which nearly ruined everything, since the machine resolved to become a missionary among destitute tribes on far-flung planets. But at the very last minute, just as he was ready to give up and take a hammer to it, Trurl was struck by an inspiration; tossing out all the logic circuits, he replaced them with self-regulating egocentripetal narcissistors. The machine simpered a little, whimpered a little, laughed bitterly, com-

plained of an awful pain on its third floor, said that in general it was fed up, through, life was beautiful but men were such beasts and how sorry they'd all be when it was dead and gone. Then it asked for pen and paper. Trurl sighed with relief, switched it off and went to bed. The next morning he went to see Klapaucius. Klapaucius, hearing that he was invited to attend the debut of Trurl's electronic bard, dropped everything and followed—so eager was he to be an eyewitness to his friend's humiliation.

Trurl let the machine warm up first, kept the power low, ran up the metal stairs several times to take readings (the machine was like the engine of a giant steamer, galleried, with rows of rivets, dials and valves on every tier)—till finally, satisfied all the decimal places were where they ought to be, he said yes, it was ready now, and why not start with something simple. Later, of course, when the machine had gotten the feel of it, Klapaucius could ask it to produce poetry on absolutely whatever topic he liked.

Now the potentiometers indicated the machine's lyrical capacitance was charged to maximum, and Trurl, so nervous his hands were shaking, threw the master switch. A voice, slightly husky but remarkably vibrant and bewitching, said:

"Phlogisticosh. Rhomothriglyph. Floof."

"Is that it?" inquired Klapaucius after a pause, extremely polite. Trurl only bit his lip, gave the machine a few kicks of current, and tried again. This time the voice came through much more clearly; it was a thrilling baritone, solemn yet intriguingly sensual:

> Pev't o' tay merlong gumin gots,
> Untle yun furly päzzen ye,
> Confre an' ayzor, ayzor ots,
> Bither de furloss bochre blee!

"Am I missing something?" said Klapaucius, calmly watching a panic-stricken Trurl struggling at the controls.

Finally Trurl waved his arms in despair, dashed clattering several flights up the metal stairs, got down on all fours and crawled into the machine through a trapdoor; he hammered away inside, swearing like a maniac, tightened something, pried at something, crawled out again and ran frantically to another tier. At long last he let out a cry of triumph, threw a burnt tube over his shoulder—it bounced off the railing and fell to the floor, shattering at the feet of Klapaucius. But Trurl didn't bother to apologize; he quickly put in a new tube, wiped his hands on a chammy cloth and hollered down for Klapaucius to try it now. The following words rang out:

> Mockles! Fent on silpen tree,
> Blockards three a-feening,
> Mockles, what silps came to thee
> In thy pantry dreaming?

"Well, that's an improvement!" shouted Trurl, not entirely convinced. "The last line particularly, did you notice?"

"If this is all you have to show me . . ." said Klapaucius, the very soul of politeness.

"Damn!" said Trurl and again disappeared inside the machine. There was a fierce banging and clanging, the sputtering of shorted wires and the muttering of an even shorter temper, then Trurl stuck his head out of a trapdoor on the third story and yelled, "Now try it!"

Klaupaucius complied. The electronic bard shuddered from stem to stern and began:

> Oft, in that wickless chalet all begorn,
> Where whilom soughed the mossy sappertort
> And you were wont to bong—

Trurl yanked out a few cables in a fury, something rattled and wheezed, the machine fell silent. Klapaucius laughed so hard he had to sit on the floor. Then suddenly, as Trurl was rushing back and forth, there was a crackle, a clack, and the machine with perfect poise said:

> The Petty and the Small
> Are overcome with gall
> When Genius, having faltered, fails to fall.

> Klapaucius too, I ween,
> Will turn the deepest green
> To hear such flawless verse from Trurl's machine.

"There you are, an epigram! And wonderfully apropos!" laughed Trurl, racing down the metal stairs and flinging himself delightedly into his colleague's arms. Klapaucius, quite taken aback, was no longer laughing.

"What, *that?*" he said. "That's nothing. Besides, you had it all set up beforehand."

"Set up?!"

"Oh, it's quite obvious . . . the ill-disguised hostility, the poverty of thought, the crudeness of execution."

"All right, then ask it something else! Whatever you like! Go on! What are you waiting for? Afraid?!"

"Just a minute," said Klapaucius, annoyed. He was trying to think of a request as difficult as possible, aware that any argument on the quality of the verse the machine might be able to produce would be hard if not impossible to settle either way. Suddenly he brightened and said:

"Have it compose a poem—a poem about a haircut! But lofty, noble, tragic, timeless, full of love, treachery, retribution, quiet heroism in the face of certain doom! Six lines, cleverly rhymed, and every word beginning with the letter *s!!*"

"And why not throw in a full exposition of the general theory of nonlinear automata while you're at it?" growled Trurl. "You can't give it such idiotic—"

But he didn't finish. A melodious voice filled the hall with the following:

> Seduced, shaggy Samson snored.
> She scissored short. Sorely shorn,
> Soon shackled slave, Samson sighed,
> Silently scheming,
> Sightlessly seeking
> Some savage, spectacular suicide.

"Well, what do you say to that?" asked Trurl, his arms folded proudly. But Klapaucius was already shouting:

"Now all in *g!* A sonnet, trochaic hexameter, about an old cyclotron who kept sixteen artificial mistresses, blue and radioactive, had four wings, three purple pavilions, two lacquered chests, each containing exactly one thousand medallions bearing the likeness of Czar Murdicog the Headless . . ."

"Grinding gleeful gears, Gerontogyron grabbed / Giggling gynecobalt-60 golems," began the machine, but Trurl leaped to the console, shut off the power and turned, defending the machine with his body.

"Enough!" he said, hoarse with indignation. "How dare you waste a great talent on such drivel? Either give it decent poems to write or I call the whole thing off!"

"What, those aren't decent poems?" protested Klapaucius.

"Certainly not! I didn't build a machine to solve ridiculous crossword puzzles! That's hack work, not Great Art! Just give it a topic, any topic, as difficult as you like . . ."

Klapaucius thought, and thought some more. Finally he nodded and said:

"Very well. Let's have a love poem, lyrical, pastoral, and expressed in the language of pure mathematics. Tensor algebra mainly, with a little topology and higher calculus, if

need be. But with feeling, you understand, and in the cybernetic spirit."

"Love and tensor algebra? Have you taken leave of your
senses?" Trurl began, but stopped, for his electronic bard
was already declaiming:

> Come, let us hasten to a higher plane,
> Where dyads tread the fairy fields of Venn,
> Their indices bedecked from one to n,
> Commingled in an endless Markov chain!

> Come, every frustum longs to be a cone,
> And every vector dreams of matrices.
> Hark to the gentle gradient of the breeze:
> It whispers of a more ergodic zone.

> In Riemann, Hilbert or in Banach space
> Let superscripts and subscripts go their ways.
> Our asymptotes no longer out of phase,
> We shall encounter, counting, face to face.

> I'll grant thee random access to my heart,
> Thou'lt tell me all the constants of thy love;
> And so we two shall all love's lemmas prove,
> And in our bound partition never part.

> For what did Cauchy know, or Christoffel,
> Or Fourier, or any Boole or Euler,
> Wielding their compasses, their pens and rulers,
> Of thy supernal sinusoidal spell?

> Cancel me not—for what then shall remain?
> Abscissas, some mantissas, modules, modes,
> A root or two, a torus and a node:
> The inverse of my verse, a null domain.

Ellipse of bliss, converge, O lips divine!
The product of our scalars is defined!
Cyberiad draws nigh, and the skew mind
Cuts capers like a happy haversine.

I see the eigenvalue in thine eye,
I hear the tender tensor in thy sigh.
Bernoulli would have been content to die,
Had he but known such $a^2 \cos 2 \phi$!

This concluded the poetic competition, since Klapaucius suddenly had to leave, saying he would return shortly with more topics for the machine; but he never did, afraid that in so doing, he might give Trurl more cause to boast. Trurl of course let it be known that Klapaucius had fled in order to hide his envy and chagrin. Klapaucius meanwhile spread the word that Trurl had more than one screw loose on the subject of that so-called mechanical versifier.

Not much time went by before news of Trurl's computer laureate reached the genuine—that is, the ordinary—poets. Deeply offended, they resolved to ignore the machine's existence. A few, however, were curious enough to visit Trurl's electronic bard in secret. It received them courteously, in a hall piled high with closely written paper (for it worked day and night without pause). Now these poets were all avant-garde, and Trurl's machine wrote only in the traditional manner; Trurl, no connoisseur of poetry, had relied heavily on the classics in setting up its program. The machine's guests jeered and left in triumph. The machine was self-programming, however, and in addition had a special ambition-amplifying mechanism with glory-seeking circuits, and very soon a great change took place. Its poems became difficult, ambiguous, so intricate and charged with meaning that they were totally incomprehensible. When the next group of poets came to mock and laugh, the machine replied with an improvisation that was so modern, it took their breath away, and the second poem seriously weakened a certain sonneteer who had two State awards to his name, not to mention a statue in the city park. After that, no poet could resist the fatal urge to cross lyrical swords with Trurl's electronic bard. They came from far and wide, carrying trunks and suitcases full of manuscripts. The machine would let each challenger recite, instantly grasp the algorithm of his verse, and use it to compose an answer in exactly the same style, only two hundred and twenty to three hundred and forty-seven times better.

The machine quickly grew so adept at this, that it could cut down a first-class rhapsodist with no more than one or two quatrains. But the worst of it was, all the third-rate poets emerged unscathed; being third-rate, they didn't know good poetry from bad and consequently had no inkling of their crushing defeat. One of them, true, broke his leg when, on the way out, he tripped over an epic poem the machine had just completed, a prodigious work beginning with the words:

> Arms, and machines I sing, that, forc'd by fate,
> And haughty Homo's unrelenting hate,
> Expell'd and exil'd, left the Terran shore . . .

The true poets, on the other hand, were decimated by Trurl's electronic bard, though it never laid a finger on them. First an aged elegiast, then two modernists committed suicide, leaping off a cliff that unfortunately happened to lie hard by the road leading from Trurl's place to the nearest train station.

There were many poet protests staged, demonstrations, demands that the machine be served an injunction to cease and desist. But no one else appeared to care. In fact, magazine editors generally approved: Trurl's electronic bard, writing under several thousand different pseudonyms at once, had a poem for every occasion, to fit whatever length might be required, and of such high quality that the magazine would be torn from hand to hand by eager readers. On the street one could see enraptured faces, bemused smiles, sometimes even hear a quiet sob. Everyone knew the poems of Trurl's electronic bard, the air rang with its delightful rhymes. Not infrequently, those citizens of a greater sensitivity, struck by a particularly marvelous metaphor or assonance, would actually fall into a faint. But this colossus of inspiration was prepared even for that eventuality; it would immediately supply the necessary number of restorative rondelets.

Trurl himself had no little trouble in connection with his invention. The classicists, generally elderly, were fairly harmless; they confined themselves to throwing stones through his windows and smearing the sides of his house with an unmentionable substance. But it was much worse with the younger poets. One, for example, as powerful in body as his verse was in imagery, beat Trurl to a pulp. And while the constructor lay in the hospital, events marched on. Not a day passed without a suicide or a funeral; picket lines formed around the hospital; one could hear gunfire in the distance —instead of manuscripts in their suitcases, more and more poets were bringing rifles to defeat Trurl's electronic bard. But the bullets merely bounced off its calm exterior. After his return from the hospital, Trurl, weak and desperate, finally decided one night to dismantle the homeostatic Homer he had created.

But when he approached the machine, limping slightly, it noticed the pliers in his hand and the grim glitter in his eye, and delivered such an eloquent, impassioned plea for mercy, that the constructor burst into tears, threw down his tools and hurried back to his room, wading through new works of genius, an ocean of paper that filled the hall chest-high from end to end and rustled incessantly.

The following month Trurl received a bill for the electricity consumed by the machine and almost fell off his chair. If only he could have consulted his old friend Klapaucius! But Klapaucius was nowhere to be found. So Trurl had to come up with something by himself. One dark night he unplugged the machine, took it apart, loaded it onto a ship, flew to a certain small asteroid, and there assembled it again, giving it an atomic pile for its source of creative energy.

Then he sneaked home. But that wasn't the end of it. The electronic bard, deprived now of the possibility of having its masterpieces published, began to broadcast them on all wave lengths, which soon sent the passengers and crews of passing rockets into states of stanzaic stupefaction, and those more delicate souls were seized with severe attacks of esthetic ecstasy besides. Having determined the cause of this disturbance, the Cosmic Fleet Command issued Trurl an official request for the immediate termination of his device, which was seriously impairing the health and well-being of all travelers.

At that point Trurl went into hiding, so they dropped a team of technicians on the asteroid to gag the machine's output unit. It overwhelmed them with a few ballads, however, and the mission had to be abandoned. Deaf technicians were sent next, but the machine employed pantomime. After that, there began to be talk of an eventual punitive expedition, of bombing the electropoet into submission. But just then some ruler from a neighboring star system came, bought the machine and hauled it off, asteroid and all, to his kingdom.

Now Trurl could appear in public again and breathe easy. True, lately there had been supernovae exploding on the southern horizon, the like of which no one had ever seen before, and there were rumors that this had something to do with poetry. According to one report, that same ruler, moved by some strange whim, had ordered his astroengineers to connect the electronic bard to a constellation of white supergiants, thereby transforming each line of verse into a stupendous solar prominence; thus the Greatest Poet in the Universe was able to transmit its thermonuclear creations to all the illimitable reaches of space at once. But even if there were any truth to this, it was all too far away to bother Trurl, who vowed by everything that was ever held sacred never, never again to make a cybernetic model of the Muse.

The Second Sally

OR The Offer of King Krool

The tremendous success of their application of the Gargantius Effect gave both constructors such an appetite for adventure, that they resolved to sally forth once again to parts unknown. Unfortunately, they were quite unable to decide on a destination. Trurl, given to tropical climes, had his heart set on Scaldonia, the land of the Flaming Flamingos, while Klapaucius, of a somewhat cooler disposition, was equally determined to visit the Intergalactic Cold Pole, a bleak continent adrift among frozen stars. The friends were about to part company for good when Trurl suddenly had an idea. "Wait," he said, "we can advertise our services, then take the best offer!" "Ridiculous!" snorted Klapaucius. "How are you going to advertise? In a newspaper? Do you have any idea how long it takes a newspaper to reach the nearest planet? You'll be dead and buried before the first offer comes in!"

But Trurl gave a knowing smile and revealed his plan, which Klapaucius—begrudgingly—had to admit was ingenious, and so they set to work. All the necessary equipment quickly thrown together, they gathered up the local stars and arranged them in a great sign, a sign that would be visible at truly incalculable distances. Only blue giants were used for the first word—to get the cosmic reader's attention—and lesser stellar material made up the others. The advertisement read: TWO Distinguished Constructors Seek Employment Commensurate with Their Skill and Above All Lucrative, Hence Preferably at the Court of a Well-heeled King (Should Have His Own Kingdom), Terms to Be Arranged. It was not long before, one bright morning, a most marvelous craft alighted on their front lawn. It gleamed in the sun, all inlaid with mother-of-pearl, had three legs intricately carved and six additional supports of solid gold (quite useless, since they didn't even reach the ground—but then, the builders obviously had more wealth than they knew what to do with). Down a magnificent staircase with billowing fountains on either side there came a figure of stately bearing with a retinue of six-legged machines: some of these massaged him, some supported him and fanned him, and the smallest flew above his august brow and sprayed it with eau de cologne from an atomizer. This impressive emissary greeted the constructors on behalf of his lord and sovereign, King Krool, who wished to engage them.

"What sort of work is it?" asked Trurl, interested.

"The details, gentle sirs, you shall learn at the proper time," was his reply. He was dressed in galligaskins of gold, mink-tufted buskins, sequined earmuffs, and a robe of most unusual cut—instead of pockets it had little shelves full of mints and marzipan. Tiny mechanical flies also buzzed about his person, and these he brushed away whenever they grew too bold.

"For now," he went on, "I can only say that His Boundless Kroolty is a great enthusiast of the hunt, a fearless and peerless conqueror of every sort of galactic fauna, and verily, his prowess has reached such heights that now the fiercest predators known are no longer worthy game for him. And herein lies our misfortune, for he craves excitement, danger, thrills . . . which is why—"

"Of course!" said Trurl. "He wants us to construct a new

model of beast, something wild and rapacious enough to present a challenge."

"You are, worthy constructor, indeed quick!" said the King's emissary. "Then it is agreed?"

Klapaucius began to question the emissary more closely on certain practical matters. But after the King's generosity was glowingly described and sufficiently elaborated upon, they hurriedly packed their things and a few books, ran up the magnificent staircase, hopped on board and were immediately lifted, with a great roar and burst of flame that blackened the ship's gold legs, into the interstellar night.

As they traveled, the emissary briefed the constructors on the laws and customs prevailing in the Kingdom of Krool, told them of the monarch's nature, as broad and open as a leveled city, and of his manly pursuits, and much more, so that by the time the ship landed, they could speak the language like natives.

First they were taken to a splendid villa situated on a mountainside above the village—this was where they were to stay. Then, after a brief rest, the King sent a carriage for them, a carriage drawn by six fire-breathing monsters. These were muzzled with fire screens and smoke filters, had their wings clipped to keep them on the ground, and long spiked tails and six paws apiece with iron claws that cut deep pits in the road wherever they went. As soon as the monsters saw the constructors, the entire team set up a howl, belching fire and brimstone, and strained to get at them. The coachmen in asbestos armor and the King's huntsmen with hoses and pumps had to fall upon the crazed creatures and beat them into submission with laser and maser clubs before Trurl and Klapaucius could safely step into the plush carriage, which they did without a word. The carriage tore off at breakneck speed or—to use an appropriate metaphor—like a bat out of hell.

"You know," Trurl whispered in Klapaucius' ear as they rushed along, knocking down everything in their path and leaving a long trail of sulfurous smoke behind them, "I have a feeling that this king won't settle for just anything. I mean, if he has coursers like these . . ."

But level-headed Klapaucius said nothing. Houses now flashed by, walls of diamonds and sapphires and silver, while the dragons thundered and hissed and the drivers cursed and shouted. At last a colossal portcullis loomed up ahead, opened, and their carriage whirled into the courtyard, careening so sharply that the flower beds all shriveled up, then ground to a stop before a castle black as blackest night. Welcomed by an unusually dismal fanfare and quite overwhelmed by the massive stairs, balustrades and especially the stone giants that guarded the main gate, Trurl and Klapaucius, flanked by a formidable escort, entered the mighty castle.

King Krool awaited them in an enormous hall the shape of a skull, a vast and vaulted cave of beaten silver. There was a gaping pit in the floor, the skull's foramen magnum, and beyond it stood the throne, over which two streams of light crossed like swords—they came from high windows fixed in the skull's eye sockets and with panes specially tinted to give everything a harsh and infernal aspect. The constructors now saw Krool himself: too impatient to sit still on his throne, this monarch paced from wall to wall across the silver floor, his steps booming in that cadaverous cavern, and as he spoke he emphasized his words with such sudden stabs of the hand, that the air whistled.

"Welcome, constructors!" he said, skewering them both with his eyes. "As you've no doubt learned from Lord Protozor, Master of the Royal Hunt, I want you to build me new and better kinds of game. Now I'm not interested, you understand, in any mountain of steel on a hundred-odd treads—that's a job for heavy artillery, not for me. My quarry must be strong and ferocious, but swift and nimble too, and above all cunning and full of wiles, so that I will have to call upon all my hunter's art to drive it to the ground. It must be a highly intelligent beast, and know all there is to know of covering tracks, doubling back, hiding in shadows and lying in wait, for such is my will!"

"Forgive me, Your Highness," said Klapaucius with a careful bow, "but if we do Your Highness' bidding too well, might not this put the royal life and limb in some peril?"

The King roared with such laughter that a couple of crystal pendants fell off a chandelier and shattered at the feet of the trembling constructors.

"Have no fear of that, noble constructors!" he said with a grim smile. "You are not the first, and you will not be the last, I expect. Know that I am a just but most exacting ruler. Too often have assorted knaves, flatterers and fakes attempted to deceive me, too often, I say, have they posed as distinguished hunting engineers, solely to empty my coffers and fill their sacks with gems and precious stones, leaving me, in return, with a few paltry scarecrows that fall apart at the first touch. Too often has this happened for me not to take appropriate measures. For twelve years now any constructor who fails to meet my demands, who promises more than he is able to deliver, indeed receives his reward, but is hurled, reward and all, into yon deep well—unless he be game enough (excuse the pun) to serve as the quarry himself. In which case, gentlemen, I use no weapon but these two bare hands . . ."

"And . . . and have there been, ah, many such impostors?" asked Trurl in a weak voice.

"Many? That's difficult to say. I only know that no one yet has satisfied me, and the scream of terror they invariably give as they plummet to the bottom doesn't last quite so long as it used to—the remains, no doubt, have begun to mount. But rest assured, gentlemen, there is room enough still for you!"

A deathly silence followed these dire words, and the two friends couldn't help but look in the direction of that dark and ominous hole. The King resumed his relentless pacing, his boots striking the floor like sledge hammers in an echo chamber.

"But, with Your Highness' permission . . . that is, we—we haven't yet drawn up the contract," stammered Trurl. "Couldn't we have an hour or two to think it over, weigh carefully what Your Highness has been so gracious as to tell us, and then of course we can decide whether to accept your generous offer or, on the other hand—"

"Ha!!" laughed the King like a thunderclap. "Or, on the other hand, to go home? I'm afraid not, gentlemen! The moment you set foot on board the *Infernanda*, you accepted my offer! If every constructor who came here could leave whenever he pleased, why, I'd have to wait forever for my fondest hopes to be realized! No, you must stay and build me a beast to hunt. I give you twelve days, and now you may go. Whatever pleasure you desire, in the meantime, is yours. You have but to ask the servants I have given you; nothing will be denied you. In twelve days, then!"

"With Your Highness' permission, you can keep the pleasures, but—well, would it be at all possible for us to have a look at the, uh, hunting trophies Your Highness must have collected as a result, so to speak, of the efforts of our predecessors?"

"But of course!" said the King indulgently and clapped his hands with such force that sparks flew and danced across the silver walls. The gust of air from those powerful palms cooled even more our constructors' ardor for adventure. Six guards in white and gold appeared and conducted them down a corridor that twisted and wound like the gullet of a giant serpent. Finally, to their great relief, it led out into a large, open garden. There, on remarkably well-trimmed lawns, stood the hunting trophies of King Krool.

Nearest at hand was a saber-toothed colossus, practically cut in two in spite of the heavy mail and plate armor that was to have protected its trunk; the hind legs, disproportionately large (evidently designed for great leaps), lay upon the grass alongside the tail, which ended in a firearm with its magazine half-empty—a clear sign that the creature had not fallen to the King without a fight. A yellow strip of cloth hanging from its open jaws also testified to this, for Trurl recognized in it the breeches worn by the King's huntsmen. Next was another prone monstrosity, a dragon with a multitude of tiny wings all singed and blackened by enemy fire; its circuits had spilled out molten and had then congealed in a copper-porcelain puddle. Farther on stood another creature, the pillarlike legs spread wide. A gentle breeze soughed softly through its fangs. And there were wrecks on wheels and wrecks on treads, some with claws and some with cannon, all sundered to the magnetic core, and tank-turtles with squashed turrets, and mutilated military millipedes, and other oddities, broken and battle-scarred, some equipped with auxiliary brains (burnt out), some perched on telescoping stilts (dislocated), and there were little vicious biting things strewn about. These had been made to attack in great swarms, then regroup in a sphere bristling with gun muzzles and bayonets—a clever idea, but it saved neither them nor their creators. Down this aisle of devastation walked Trurl and Klapaucius, pale, silent, looking as if they were on their way to a funeral instead of to another brilliant session of vigorous invention. They came at last to the end of that dreadful gallery of Krool's triumphs and stepped into the carriage that was waiting for them at

the gate. That dragon team which sped them back to their
lodgings seemed less terrible now. Just as soon as they were
alone in their sumptuously appointed green and crimson
drawing room, before a table heaped high with effervescent
drinks and rare delicacies, Trurl broke into a volley of imprecations; he reviled Klapaucius for heedlessly accepting
the offer made by the Master of the Royal Hunt, thereby
bringing down misfortune on their heads, when they easily
could have stayed at home and rested on their laurels. Klapaucius said nothing, waiting patiently for Trurl's desperate
rage to expend itself, and when it finally did and Trurl had
collapsed into a lavish mother-of-pearl chaise longue and
buried his face in his hands, he said:

"Well, we'd better get to work."

These words did much to revive Trurl, and the two constructors immediately began to consider the various possibilities, drawing on their knowledge of the deepest and darkest secrets of the arcane art of cybernetic generation. First
of all, they agreed that victory lay neither in the armor nor
in the strength of the monster to be built, but entirely in its
program, in other words, in an algorithm of demoniacal
derivation. "It must be a truly diabolical creature, a thing
of absolute evil!" they said, and though they had as yet no
clear idea of what or how, this observation lifted their spirits
considerably. Such was their enthusiasm by the time they
sat down to draft the beast, that they worked all night, all
day, and through a second night and day before taking a
break for dinner. And as the Leyden jars were passed about,
so sure were they of success, that they winked and smirked
—but only when the servants weren't looking, since they
suspected them (and rightly, too) of being the King's spies.
So the constructors said nothing of their work, but praised
the mulled electrolyte which the waiters brought in, tail
coats flapping, in beakers of the finest cut crystal. Only after

the repast, when they had wandered out on the veranda overlooking the village with its white steeples and domes catching the last golden rays of the setting sun, only then did Trurl turn to Klapaucius and say:

"We're not out of the woods yet, you know."

"How do you mean?" asked Klapaucius in a cautious whisper.

"There's one difficulty. You see, if the King defeats our mechanical beast, he'll undoubtedly have us thrown into that pit, for we won't have done his bidding. If, on the other hand, the beast . . . You see what I mean?"

"If the beast isn't defeated?"

"No, if the beast defeats *him*, dear colleague. If that happens, the King's successor may not let us off so easily."

"You don't think we'd have to answer for that, do you? As a rule, heirs to the throne are only too happy to see it vacated."

"True, but this will be his son, and whether the son punishes us out of filial devotion or because he thinks the royal court expects it of him, it'll make little difference as far as we're concerned."

"That never occurred to me," muttered Klapaucius. "You're quite right, the prospects aren't encouraging. . . . Have you thought of a way out of this dilemma?"

"Well, we might make the beast multimortal. Picture this: the King slays it, it falls, then it gets up again, resurrected, and the King chases it again, slays it again, and so on, until he gets sick and tired of the whole thing."

"That he won't like," said Klapaucius after some thought. "And anyway, how would you design such a beast?"

"Oh, I don't know. . . . We could make it without any vital organs. The King chops the beast into little pieces, but the pieces grow back together."

"How?"

"Use a field."

"Magnetic?"

"If you like."

"How do we operate it?"

"Remote control, perhaps?" asked Trurl.

"Too risky," said Klapaucius. "How do you know the King won't have us locked up in some dungeon while the hunt's in progress? Our poor predecessors were no fools, and look how they ended up. More than one of them, I'm sure, thought of remote control—yet it failed. No, we can't expect to maintain communication with the beast during the battle."

"Then why not use a satellite?" suggested Trurl. "We could install automatic controls—"

"Satellite indeed!" snorted Klapaucius. "And how are you going to build it, let alone put it in orbit? There are no miracles in our profession, Trurl! We'll have to hide the controls some other way."

"But where can we hide the controls when they watch our every step? You've seen how the servants skulk about, sticking their noses into everything. We'd never be able to leave the premises ourselves, and certainly not smuggle out such a large piece of equipment. It's impossible!"

"Calm down," said prudent Klapaucius, looking over his shoulder. "Perhaps we don't need such equipment in the first place."

"Something has to operate the beast, and if that something is an electronic brain anywhere inside, the King will smash it to a pulp before you can say goodbye."

They were silent. Night had fallen and the village lights below were flickering on, one by one. Suddenly Trurl said:

"Listen, here's an idea. We only pretend to build a beast but in reality build a ship to escape on. We give it ears, a tail, paws, so no one will suspect, and they can be easily jettisoned on takeoff. What do you think of that? We get off scot-free and thumb our noses at the King!"

"And if the King has planted a real constructor among our servants, which is not unlikely, then it's all over and into the pit with us. Besides, running away—no, it just doesn't suit me. It's him or us, Trurl, you can't get around it."

"Yes, I suppose a spy could be a constructor too," said Trurl with a sigh. "What then can we do, in the name of the Great Comet?! How about—a photoelectric phantom?"

"You mean, a mirage? Have the King hunt a mirage? No thanks! After an hour or two of that, he'd come straight here and make phantoms of us!"

Again they were silent. Finally Trurl said:

"The only way out of our difficulty, as far as I can see, is to have the beast *abduct* the King, and then—"

"You don't have to say another word. Yes, that's not at all a bad idea. ... Then for the ransom we—and haven't you noticed, old boy, that the orioles here are a deeper orange than on Maryland IV?" concluded Klapaucius, for just then some servants were bringing silver lamps out on the veranda. "There's still a problem though," he continued when they were alone again. "Assuming the beast can do what you say, how will we be able to negotiate with the prisoner if we're sitting in a dungeon ourselves?"

"You have a point there," said Trurl. "We'll have to figure some way around that. ... The main thing, however, is the algorithm!"

"Any child knows that! What's a beast without an algorithm?"

So they rolled up their sleeves and sat down to experiment—by simulation, that is mathematically and all on paper. And the mathematical models of King Krool and the beast did such fierce battle across the equation-covered table, that the constructors' pencils kept snapping. Furious, the beast writhed and wriggled its iterated integrals beneath the King's polynomial blows, collapsed into an infinite series of indeterminate terms, then got back up by raising itself to the nth power, but the King so belabored it with differentials and partial derivatives that its Fourier coefficients all canceled out (see Riemann's Lemma), and in the ensuing confusion the constructors completely lost sight of both King and beast. So they took a break, stretched their legs, had a swig from the Leyden jug to bolster their strength, then went back to work and tried it again from the beginning, this time unleashing their entire arsenal of tensor matrices and grand canonical ensembles, attacking the problem with such fervor that the very paper began to smoke. The King rushed forward with all his cruel coordinates and mean values, stumbled into a dark forest of roots and logarithms, had to backtrack, then encountered the beast on a field of irrational numbers (F_i) and smote it so grievously that it fell two decimal places and lost an epsilon, but the beast slid around an asymptote and hid in an n-dimensional orthogonal phase space, underwent expansion and came out, fuming factorially, and fell upon the King and hurt him passing sore. But the King, nothing daunted, put on his Markov chain mail and all his impervious parameters, took his increment Δk to infinity and dealt the beast a truly Boolean blow, sent it reeling through an x-axis and several brackets—but the beast, prepared for this, lowered its horns and—wham!!—the pencils flew like mad through transcendental functions and double eigentransformations, and when at last the beast closed in and the King was down and out for the count, the constructors jumped up, danced a jig, laughed and sang as they tore all their papers to shreds, much to the amazement of the spies perched in the chandelier—perched in vain, for they were uninitiated into the niceties of higher mathematics and consequently had no idea why Trurl and Klapaucius were now shouting, over and over, "Hurrah! Victory!!"

Well after midnight, the Leyden jug from which the constructors had on occasion refreshed themselves in the course of their labors was quietly taken to the headquarters of the King's secret police, where its false bottom was opened and a tiny tape recorder removed. This the experts switched on and listened to eagerly, but the rising sun found them totally unenlightened and looking haggard. One voice, for example, would say:

"Well? Is the King ready?"

"Right!"

"Where'd you put him? Over there? Good! Now—hold on, you have to keep the feet together. Not yours, idiot, the King's! All right now, ready? One, two, find the derivative! Quick! What do you get?"

"Pi."

"And the beast?"

"Under the radical sign. But look, the King's still standing!"

"Still standing, eh? Factor both sides, divide by two, throw in a few imaginary numbers—good! Now change variables and subtract—Trurl, what on earth are you doing?! The *beast*, not the King, the *beast*! That's right! Good! Perfect!! Now transform, approximate and solve for x. Do you have it?"

"I have it! Klapaucius! Look at the King now!!"

There was a pause, then a burst of wild laughter.

That same morning, as all the experts and high officials of the secret police shook their heads, bleary-eyed after a sleepless night, the constructors asked for quartz, vanadium, steel, copper, platinum, rhinestones, dysprosium, yttrium and thulium, also cerium and germanium, and most of the other elements that make up the Universe, plus a variety of ma-

chines and qualified technicians, not to mention a wide assortment of spies—for so insolent had the constructors become, that on the triplicate requisition form they boldly
wrote: "Also, kindly send agents of various cuts and stripes
at the discretion and with the approval of the Proper Authorities." The next day they asked for sawdust and a large
red velvet curtain on a stand, a cluster of little glass bells
in the center and a large tassel at each of its four corners;
everything, even down to the littlest glass bell, was specified
with the utmost precision. The King scowled when he heard
these requests, but ordered them to be carried out to the
letter, for he had given his royal word. The constructors
were thus granted all that they wished.

All that they wished grew more and more outlandish. For
instance, in the files of the secret police under code number
48999/11K/T was a copy of a requisition for three tailor's
mannequins as well as six full police uniforms, complete
with sash, side arm, shako, plume and handcuffs, also all
available back issues of the magazine *The Patriotic Policeman*, yearbooks and supplements included—under "Comments" the constructors had guaranteed the return of all
items listed above within twenty-four hours of delivery and
in perfect condition. In another, classified section of the
police archives was a copy of a letter from Klapaucius in
which he demanded the immediate shipment of (1) a life-
size doll representing the Postmaster General in full regalia,
and (2) a light gig painted green with a kerosene lamp on
the left and a sky-blue sign on the back that said THINK.
The doll and gig proved too much for the Chief of Police:
he had to be taken away for a much-needed rest. During the
next three days the constructors asked only for barrels of red
castor oil, and after that—nothing. From then on, they
worked in the basement of the palace, hammering away and
singing space chanties, and at night blue lights came flash-

ing from the basement windows and gave weird shapes to the trees in the garden outside. Trurl and Klapaucius with their many helpers bustled about amid arcs and sparks, now and then looking up to see faces pressed against the glass: the servants, as if out of idle curiosity, were photographing their every move. One evening, when the weary constructors had finally dragged themselves off to bed, the components of the apparatus they had been working on were quickly transported by unmarked balloon to police headquarters and assembled by eighteen of the finest cyberneticians in the land, who had been deputized and duly sworn in for that very purpose, whereupon a gray tin mouse ran out from under their hands, blowing soap bubbles and dropping a thin trail of chalk dust from under its tail, which spelled, as it danced this way and that across the table, WHAT, DON'T YOU LOVE US ANYMORE? Never before in the kingdom's history did Chiefs of Police have to be replaced with such speed and regularity. The uniforms, the doll, the green gig, even the sawdust, everything which the constructors returned exactly as promised, was thoroughly examined under electron microscope. But except for a minuscule card in the sawdust which read JUST SAWDUST, there was nothing out of the ordinary. Then individual atoms of the uniforms and gig were thoroughly searched— with equal lack of success. At last the day came when the work was completed. A huge vehicle on three hundred wheels, looking something like a refrigerator, was drawn up to the main entrance and opened in the presence of witnesses and officials; Trurl and Klapaucius brought out a curtain, the one with the tassels and bells, and placed it carefully inside, in the middle of the floor. Then they got in themselves, closed the door, did something, then went and got various containers from the basement, cans of chemicals, all sorts of finely ground powders—gray, silver, white,

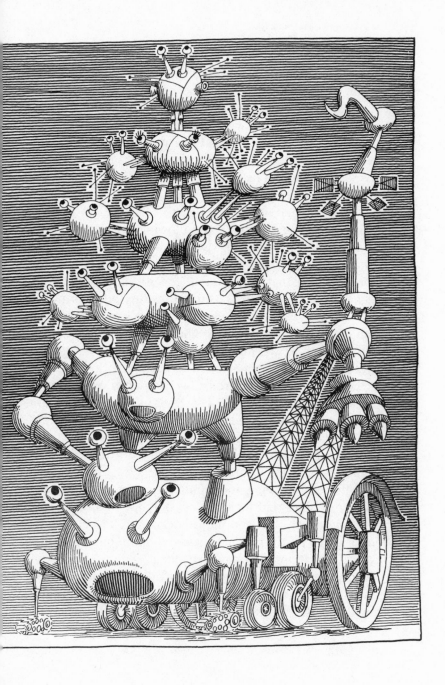

yellow, green—and sprinkled them under and around the curtain, then stepped out, had the vehicle closed and locked, consulted their watches and together counted out fourteen and a half seconds—at which time, much to everyone's surprise, since the vehicle was stationary and there could be no question of a breeze inside (for the seal was hermetic), the glass bells tinkled. The constructors exchanged a wink and said:

"You can take it now!"

The rest of the day they spent blowing soap bubbles from the veranda. That evening Lord Protozor, Master of the Royal Hunt, came with an escort and politely but firmly informed them that they were to go with him at once to an assigned place. They were required to leave all their possessions behind, even their clothes; in exchange they were given rags, then put in irons. The guards and police dignitaries present were astounded by their perfect sang-froid: instead of demanding justice or trembling with fear, Trurl giggled as the shackles were being hammered on, saying he was ticklish. And when the constructors were thrown into a dark and dismal dungeon, they promptly struck up a rousing chorus of "Sing Sweet Software."

Meanwhile mighty Krool rode forth from the village on his mighty hunting chariot, surrounded by all his retinue and followed by a long and winding train of riders and machines, machines that included not only the traditional catapult and cannon, but enormous laser guns and beta ray bazookas, and a tar-thrower guaranteed to immobilize anything that walked, swam, flew or rolled along.

And so this grand procession wended its way to the royal game preserve, and many jokes were made, and boasts, and haughty toasts, and no one gave a thought to the two constructors, except perhaps to remark that those fools were in a pretty pickle now.

But when the silver trumpets announced His Majesty's approach, one could see a huge vehicle-refrigerator coming up in the opposite direction. Its door flung open, and for one brief moment there gaped the black maw of what appeared to be some sort of field gun. Next there was a boom, a puff of yellow smoke, and something came rocketing out, a form as blurry as a tornado and with the general consistency of a sandstorm; it arced through the air so fast that no one really got a good look at it anyway. Whatever it was flew a hundred paces or more and landed without a sound; the curtain that had been wrapped around it floated to the earth, glass bells tinkling oddly in that perfect silence, and lay there like a crushed strawberry. Now everyone could see the beast clearly—though it wasn't clear at all, but looked a little like a hill, rather large, fairly long, its color much like its surroundings, a clump of dried-up weeds. The King's huntsmen unleashed the whole pack of automated hounds (mainly Saint Cybernards and Cyberman pinschers, with an occasional high-frequency terrier); these hurled themselves, howling and slavering, at the crouching beast. The beast didn't rear back, didn't roar, didn't even breathe fire, but only opened its two eyes wide and reduced half the pack to ashes in a trice.

"Oho! Laser-eyed, is it?" cried the King. "Hand me my trusty duralumin doublet, my bulletproof buckler, my halberd and arquebus!" Thus accoutered and gleaming like a supernova, he rode out upon his fearless high-fidelity cyber-steed, came nigh the beast and smote it such a mighty blow that the air crackled and its head tumbled neatly to the ground. Though the retinue dutifully hallooed his triumph, the King took no delight in it; greatly angered, he swore in his heart to devise some special torment for those wretches who dared to call themselves constructors. The beast, however, shook another head out of its severed neck, opened its new eyes wide and played a withering beam across the King's armor (which, however, was proof against all manner of electromagnetic radiation). "Well, those two weren't a total loss," said the King to himself, "though this still won't help them." And he recharged his charger and spurred it into the fray.

This time he swung full and cleaved the beast in twain. The beast didn't seem to mind—in fact, it positioned itself helpfully beneath the whistling blade and gave a grateful twitch as it fell. And small wonder! The King took another look: the thing was twinned instead of twained! There were two spitting images, each a little smaller than the original, plus a third, a baby beast gamboling between them—that was the head he had cut off earlier: it now had a tail and feet and was doing cartwheels through the weeds.

"What next?" thought the King. "Chop it into mice or little worms? A fine way to hunt!" And with great ire did he have at it, hewing with might and main until there were no end of little beasts underfoot, but suddenly they all backed off, went into a huddle, and there stood the beast again, good as new and stifling a yawn.

"H'm," thought the King. "Apparently it has the same kind of stabilization mechanism that—what was his name again?—Pumpington—that Pumpington tried to use. Yes, I dealt with him myself for that idiotic trick. . . . Well, we'll just wheel out the antimatter artillery. . . ."

He picked one with a six-foot bore, lined it up and loaded it himself, took aim, pulled the string and sent a perfectly silent and weirdly shimmering shell straight at the beast, to blow it to smithereens once and for all. But nothing happened—that is, nothing much. The beast only crouched a little lower, put out its left hand, long and hairy, and gave the King the finger.

"Bring out our biggest!" roared the King, pretending not

to notice. And several hundred peasants pulled up a veritable giant of a cannon, all of eighty-gauge, which the King
aimed and was just about to fire—when all at once the
beast leaped. The King lifted his sword to defend himself,
but then there was no more beast. Those who saw what
happened next said later that they were sure they had taken
leave of their senses, for as the beast flew through the air,
it underwent a lightning transformation, the grayish hulk
divided up into three men in uniform, three policemen,
who, still aloft, were already preparing to do their duty. The
first policeman, a sergeant, got out the handcuffs, maneu-
vering his legs to keep upright; the second held on to his
plumed shako with one hand, so it wouldn't blow off, and
with the other pulled out a warrant from his breast pocket;
the third, apparently a rookie, assumed a horizontal position
beneath the feet of the first two, to cushion their fall—after
which, however, he jumped up and carefully dusted off his
uniform. Meanwhile the first policeman had handcuffed
the dumbfounded King and the second slapped the sword
from his hand. Feebly protesting, the suspect was then summarily trotted off the field. The entire hunting procession
stood rooted to the spot for a minute or two, then gave a
yell and followed in hot pursuit. The snorting cybersteeds
had practically caught up with the abductors, and swords
and sabers were unsheathed and raised to strike, but the
third policeman bent over, depressed his bellybutton and
immediately the arms grew into two shafts, the legs coiled
up, sprouting spokes, and began to turn, while the back
formed the seat of a green racing gig to accommodate the
other two policemen, who were vigorously plying the now-
harnessed King with a whip, to make him run faster. The
King obliged and broke into a mad gallop, waving his arms
frantically to ward off the blows that descended upon his
royal head; but now the huntsmen were gaining again, so

the policemen jumped on the King's back and one slipped down between the shafts, huffed and puffed and turned into a spinning top, a dancing whirlwind, which gave wings to the little gig and whisked it away over hill and dale till it disappeared altogether in a cloud of dust. The King's retinue split up and began a desperate search with Geiger counters and bloodhounds, and a special detachment came running up with shovels and flamethrowers and left no bone unburned in all the neighboring cemeteries—an obvious error, occasioned most likely by the trembling hand that hastily telegraphed the order from the observation balloon that had monitored the hunt. Several police divisions rushed here and there, searched the grounds, every bush, every weed, and both x-rays and laboratory samples were diligently taken of everything imaginable. The King's charger was ordered to appear before a special board of inquiry appointed by the Prosecutor General. A unit of paratroopers with vacuum cleaners and sieves was dropped on the royal game preserve to sift through every last particle of dust. Finally, the order was issued that anyone resembling a policeman was to be detained and held without bail, which naturally created difficulties—one half of the police force, as it turned out, had arrested the other, and vice versa. At dusk the huntsmen and soldiers returned to the village dazed and bedraggled with the woeful tidings that neither hide nor hair of the King's person was anywhere to be found.

By torchlight and in the dead of night, the chained constructors were taken before the Great Chancellor and Keeper of the Royal Seal, who addressed them in the following way:

"Whereas ye have falsely conspired and perversely plotted against the Crown and Life of Our Beloved Sovereign and Most Noble Ruler Krool and therewith dared to raise a treacherous hand and vilely devise his demise, not to mention impersonating an officer, a great aggravation of your crimes, so shall ye be quartered without quarter, impaled and pilloried, disemboweled, buried alive, crucified and burnt at the stake, after which your ashes shall be sent into orbit as a warning and perpetual reminder to all would-be regicides, amen."

"Can't you wait a bit?" asked Trurl. "You see, we were expecting a letter . . ."

"A letter, thou most scurrilous and scurvy knave?!"

Just then the guards made way for the Postmaster General himself—indeed, how could they bar that dignitary's entrance with their poleaxes? The Postmaster approached in full regalia, his medals jingling impressively, pulled a letter from a sapphire satchel and handed it to the Chancellor, saying, "Mannequin though I be, I come from His Majesty," whereupon he disintegrated into a fine powder. The Chancellor could scarcely believe his eyes, but quickly recognized the King's signet impressed there on the purple sealing wax; he opened the letter and read that His Majesty was forced to negotiate with the enemy, for the constructors had employed means algorithmic and algebraic to make him captive, and now they would list their demands, all of which the Great Chancellor had better meet, if he wished ever to get his Mighty Sovereign back in one piece. Signed: "Krool herewith affixes his hand and seal, held prisoner in a cave of unknown location by one pseudoconstabulary beast in three uniforms personified."

There then arose a great clamor, everyone shouting and asking what it all meant and what were the demands, to which Trurl said only, "Our chains, if you please."

A blacksmith was summoned to unfetter them, after which Trurl said:

"We are hungry and dirty, we need a bath, a shave, massage, refreshment, nothing but the best, plenty of pomp and a water ballet with fireworks for dessert!"

The court, of course, was hopping mad, but had to comply in every particular. Only at dawn did the constructors return from their villa, each elegantly pomaded, arrayed and reclining in a sedan chair borne by footmen (their former informers); they then, deigning to grant an audience, sat down and presented their demands—not off the top of their heads, mind you, but from a little notebook they had prepared for the occasion and hidden behind a curtain in their room. The following articles were read:

First, A ship of the finest make and model available shall be furnished to carry the constructors home.

2nd, The said ship shall be laden with various cargo as here specified: diamonds—four bushels, gold coin—forty bushels, platinum, palladium and whatever other ready valuables they happen to think of—eight bushels of each, also whatever mementos and tokens from the Royal Apartments the signatories of this instrument may deem appropriate.

3rd, Until such time as the said ship shall be in readiness for takeoff, every nut and bolt in place, fully loaded and delivered up to the constructors complete with red carpet, an eighty-piece send-off band and children's chorus, an abundance of honors, decorations and awards, and a wildly cheering crowd—until then, no King.

4th, That a formal expression of undying gratitude shall be stamped upon a gold medallion and addressed to Their Most Sublime and Radiant Constructors Trurl and Klapaucius, Delight and Terror of the Universe, and moreover it shall contain a full account of their victory and be duly signed and notarized by every high and low official in the land, then set in the richly embellished barrel of the King's favorite cannon, which Lord Protozor, Master of the Royal Hunt, shall himself and wholly unaided carry on board—no other Protozor but the one who lured Their Most Sublime and Radiant Constructors to this planet, thinking to work their painful and ignominious death thereby.

5th, That the aforesaid Protozor shall accompany them on their return journey as insurance against any sort of double-dealing, pursuit, and the like. On board he shall occupy a cage three by three by four feet and shall receive a daily allowance of humble pie with a filling made of that very same sawdust which Their Most Sublime and Radiant Constructors saw fit to order in the process of indulging the King's foolishness and which was subsequently taken to police headquarters by unmarked balloon.

6th and lastly, The King need not crave forgiveness of Their Most Sublime and Radiant Constructors on bended knee, since he is much too beneath them to deserve notice.

In Witness Whereof, the parties have hereunto set their hands and seals this day and year, etc. and so on. By: Trurl and Klapaucius, Constructors, and the Great Chancellor, the Great Chamberlain, the Great Chief of Secret Police, the Seneschal, Squadron Leader and Royal Balloonmaster.

All the ministers and dignitaries turned blue, but what could they do? They had no choice, so a ship was immediately ordered. But then the constructors unexpectedly showed up after a leisurely breakfast, to supervise the work, and nothing suited them: this material, for instance, was no good, and that engineer was an absolute idiot, and they had to have a revolving magic lantern in the main hall, one with four pneumatic widgets and a calibrated cuckoo clock on top —and if the natives here didn't know what a widget was, so much the worse for them, considering that the King was no doubt most impatient for his release and would (when he could) deal harshly with anyone who dared to delay it. This remark occasioned a general numbness, a great weakness about the knees, and much trembling, but the work continued apace. Finally the ship was ready and the royal stevedores began to stow the cargo in the hold, diamonds, sacks of pearls, so much gold it kept spilling out the hatch. Meanwhile the police were secretly running all about the country-side, turning everything upside down, much to the amusement of Trurl and Klapaucius, who didn't mind explaining to a fearful but fascinated audience how it all happened, how they had discarded one idea after another until they hit upon an altogether different kind of beast. Not knowing where or how to place the controls—that is, the brain —so that they would be safe, the constructors had simply made everything brain, enabling the beast to think with its leg, or tail, or jaws (equipped with wisdom teeth only). But that was just the beginning. The real problem had two aspects, algorithmic and psychoanalytic. First they had to determine what would check the King, catch him flatfooted, so to speak. To this end, they created by nonlinear transmutation a police subset within the beast, since everyone knows that resisting or interfering with an officer who is making an arrest *lege artis* is a cosmic offense and utterly unthinkable. So much for the psychology of it—except that the Postmaster General was utilized here on similar grounds: an official of lower rank might not have made it past the guards, the letter then would not have been delivered, and the constructors would have very literally lost their heads. Moreover, the Postmaster mannequin had been given means to bribe the guards, should that have proved necessary. Every eventuality had been anticipated and provided for. Now as far as the algorithms went: they had only to find the proper domain of beasts, closed, bounded and bonded, with plenty of laws both associative and distributive in operation, throw in a constable constant or two, some graphs of graft, squadratic equations and crime waves—and the thing took over from there, once activated by the expedient of writing a document-program (behind the curtain with the bells) in castor oil ink, rendering it thereby sufficiently hard to swallow to serve as a red-tape generator. We might add here that later on the constructors had an article published in a prominent scientific journal under the title of "Recursive β—Metafunctions in the Special Case of a Bogus Polypolice Transmogrification Conversion on an Oscillating Harmonic Field of Glass Bells and Green Gig, Kerosene Lamp on the Left to Divert Attention, Solved by Beastly Incarceration–Concatenation," which was subsequently exploited by the tabloids as "The Police State Rears Its Ugly Head." Obviously none of the ministers, dignitaries or huntsmen understood a single word of what was said, but that hardly mattered. The loving subjects of King Krool knew not whether they should despise these constructors or stand and gape in awe and admiration.

Now all was in readiness for takeoff. Trurl, as stipulated in the agreement, went through the King's private chambers with a large sack and calmly appropriated whatever object he took a fancy to. Finally, the carriage arrived and took the victors to the spaceport, where a crowd cheered wildly and a children's chorus sang, then a charming little girl in local costume curtsied and presented them with a ribboned nosegay, and high-ranking officials took turns to express their undying gratitude, bidding them both a fond farewell, and the band played, several ladies fainted, and then a hush fell over the multitude. Klapaucius had pulled a tooth from his mouth, not an ordinary tooth but a transmitter-receiver, a two-way bicuspid. He threw a tiny switch and a sandstorm appeared on the horizon, growing and growing, whirling faster and faster, until it dropped into an empty space between the ship and the crowd and came to a sudden stop, scattering dust and debris in all directions. Everyone gasped and stepped back—there stood the beast, looking unusually bestial as it flashed its laser eyes and flailed its dragon tail!

"The King, if you please," said Klapaucius. But the beast answered, speaking in a perfectly normal voice:

"Not on your life. It's my turn now to make demands. . . ."

"What? Have you gone mad? You have to obey, it's in the matrix!" shouted Klapaucius. Everyone stared, thunderstruck.

"Matrix-schmatrix. Look pal, I'm not just any beast, I'm algorithmic, heuristic and sadistic, fully automatic and autocratic, that means undemocratic, and I've got loads of loops and plenty of feedback so none of that back talk or I'll clap you in irons, that means in the clink with the King, in the brig with the green gig, get me?"

"I'll give you feedback!" roared Klapaucius, furious. But Trurl asked the beast:

"What exactly do you want?"

And he sneaked around behind Klapaucius and pulled out a special tooth of his own, so the beast wouldn't see.

"Well, first of all I want to marry—"

But they never learned whom in particular the beast had in mind, for Trurl threw a tiny switch and quickly chanted:

"Eeny, meeny, miney, mo, input, output, out—you—go!"

The fantastically complex electromagnetic wave system that held the beast's atoms in place now came apart under the influence of those words, and the beast blinked, wiggled its ears, swallowed, tried to pull itself together, but before it could even grit its teeth there was a hot gust of wind, a strong smell of ozone, then nothing left to pull together, just a little mound of ashes and the King standing in the middle, safe and sound, but in great need of a bath and mortified to tears that it had come to this.

"That'll cut you down to size," said Trurl, and no one knew whether he meant the beast or the King. In either case, the algorithm had done its job well.

"And now, gentlemen," Trurl concluded, "if you'll kindly help the Master of the Royal Hunt into his cage, we can be on our way . . ."

The Third Sally

OR *The Dragons of Probability*

Trurl and Klapaucius were former pupils of the great Cerebron of Umptor, who for forty-seven years in the School of Higher Neantical Nillity expounded the General Theory of Dragons. Everyone knows that dragons don't exist. But while this simplistic formulation may satisfy the layman, it does not suffice for the scientific mind. The School of Higher Neantical Nillity is in fact wholly unconcerned with what *does* exist. Indeed, the banality of existence has been so amply demonstrated, there is no need for us to discuss it any further here. The brilliant Cerebron, attacking the problem analytically, discovered three distinct kinds of dragon: the mythical, the chimerical, and the purely hypothetical. They were all, one might say, nonexistent, but each nonexisted in an entirely different way. And then there were the imaginary dragons, and the a-, anti- and minus-dragons (colloquially termed nots, noughts and oughtn'ts by the experts), the minuses being the most interesting on account of the well-known dracological paradox: when two minuses hypercontiguate (an operation in the algebra of dragons corresponding roughly to simple multiplication), the product is 0.6 dragon, a real nonplusser. Bitter controversy raged among the experts on the question of whether, as half of them claimed, this fractional beast began from the head down or, as the other half maintained, from the tail up. Trurl and Klapaucius made a great contribution by showing the error of both positions. They were the first to apply probability theory to this area and, in so doing, created the field of statistical draconics, which says that dragons are thermodynamically impossible only in the probabilistic sense, as are elves, fairies, gnomes, witches, pixies and the like. Using the general equation of improbability, the two constructors obtained the coefficients of pixation, elfinity, kobolding, etc. They found that for the spontaneous manifestation of an average dragon, one would have to wait a good sixteen quintoquadrillion heptillion years. In other words, the whole problem would have remained a mathematical curiosity had it not been for that famous tinkering passion of Trurl, who decided to examine the nonphenomenon empirically. First, as he was dealing with the highly improbable, he invented a probability amplifier and ran tests in his basement—then later at the Dracogenic Proving Grounds established and funded by the Academy. To this day those who (sadly enough) have no knowledge of the General Theory of Improbability ask why Trurl probabilized a dragon and not an elf or goblin. The answer is simply that dragons are more probable than elves or goblins to begin with. True, Trurl might have gone further with his amplifying experiments, had not the first been so discouraging— discouraging in that the materialized dragon tried to make a meal of him. Fortunately, Klapaucius was nearby and lowered the probability, and the monster vanished. A number of scholars subsequently repeated the experiment on a phantasmatron, but, as they lacked the necessary know-how and sang-froid, a considerable quantity of dragon spawn, raising an ungodly perturbation, broke loose. Only then did it become clear that those odious beasts enjoyed an existence quite different from that of ordinary cupboards, tables and chairs; for dragons are distinguished by their probability rather than by their actuality, though granted, that probability is overwhelming once they've actually come into being. Suppose, for example, one organizes a hunt for such a dragon, surrounds it, closes in, beating the brush. The circle of sportsmen, their weapons cocked and ready, finds only a burnt patch of earth and an unmistakable smell: the dragon, seeing itself cornered, has slipped from real to configurational space. An extremely obtuse and brutal creature, it does this instinctively, of course. Now, ignorant and backward persons will occasionally demand that you show them this configurational space of yours, apparently unaware that electrons, whose existence no one in his right mind would question, also move exclusively in configurational space, their comings and goings fully dependent on curves of probability. Though it is easier not to believe in electrons than in dragons: electrons, at least taken singly, won't try to make a meal of you.

A colleague of Trurl, one Harborizian Cybr, was the first to quantize a dragon, detecting a particle known as the dracotron, the energy of which is measured—obviously—in units of dracon by a dracometer, and he even determined the coordinates of its tail, for which he nearly paid with his life. Yet what did these scientific achievements concern the common folk, who were now greatly harassed by dragons ranging the countryside, filling the air with their howls and flames and trampling, and in places even exacting tribute in the form of young virgins? What did it concern the poor villagers that Trurl's dragons, indeterministic hence heuristic, were behaving exactly according to theory though contrary to all notions of decency, or that his theory could predict the curve of the tails that demolished their barns and leveled their crops? It is not surprising, then, that the general public, instead of appreciating the value of Trurl's revolutionary invention, held it much against him. A group of individuals thoroughly benighted in matters of science waylaid the famous constructor and gave him a good thrashing. Not that this deterred him and his friend Klapaucius from further experimentation, which showed that the extent of a dragon's existence depends mainly on its whim, though also on its degree of satiety, and that the only sure method of negating it is to reduce the probability to zero or lower. All this research, naturally enough, took a great deal of time and energy; meanwhile the dragons that had gotten loose were running rampant, laying waste to a variety of planets and moons. What was worse, they multiplied. Which enabled Klapaucius to publish an excellent article entitled "Covariant Transformation from Dragons to Dragonets, in the Special Case of Passage from States Forbidden by the Laws of Physics to Those Forbidden by the Local Authorities." The article created a sensation in the scientific world, where there was still talk of the amazing polypolice beast that had been used by the intrepid constructors against King Krool to avenge the deaths of their colleagues. But far greater was the sensation caused by the news that a certain constructor known as Basiliscus the Gorgonite, traveling through the Galaxy, was apparently making dragons appear by his presence—and in places where no one had ever seen a dragon before. Whenever the situation grew desperate and catastrophe seemed imminent, this Basiliscus would turn up, approach the sovereign of that particular area and, settling on some outrageous fee after long hours of bargaining, would undertake to extirpate the beasts. At which he usually succeeded, though no one knew quite how, since he worked in secret and alone. True, the guarantee he offered for dragon removal—dracolysis—was only statistical; though one ruler did pay him in similar coin, that is, in ducats that were only statistically good. After that, the insolent Basiliscus always used aqua regia to check the metallic reliability of his royal payments. One sunny afternoon Trurl and Klapaucius met and held the following conversation:

"Have you heard about this Basiliscus?" asked Trurl.

"Yes."

"Well, what do you think?"

"I don't like it."

"Nor do I. How do you suppose he does it?"

"With an amplifier."

"A probability amplifier?"

"Either that, or oscillating fields."

"Or a paramagnedracic generator."

"You mean, a draculator?"

"Yes."

"Ah."

"But really," cried Trurl, "that would be criminal! That would mean he was bringing the dragons with him, only in a potential state, their probability near zero; then, after landing and getting the lay of the land, he was increasing the chances, raising the potential, strengthening the probability until it was almost a certainty. And then, of course, you have virtualization, materialization, full manifestation."

"Of course. And he probably shuffles the letters of the matrix to make the dragons *grand*."

"Yes, and the poor people *groan in agony and gore*. Terrible!"

"What do you think; does he then apply an irreversible antidraconian retroectoplasmatron, or simply lower the probability and walk off with the gold?"

"Hard to say. Though if he's only improbabilizing, that would be an even greater piece of villainy, since sooner or later the fractional fluctuations would have to give rise to a draconic iso-oscillation—and the whole thing would start all over again."

"Though by that time both he and the money would be gone," observed Klapaucius.

"Shouldn't we report him to the Main Office?"

"Not just yet. He may not be doing this, after all. We

have no real proof. Statistical fluctuations can occur without an amplifier; at one time, you know, there were neither amplifiers nor phantasmatrons, yet dragons did appear. Purely on a random basis."

"True . . ." replied Trurl. "But *these* appear immediately after he arrives on the planet!"

"I know. Still, reporting a fellow constructor—it just isn't done. Though there's no reason we can't take measures of our own."

"No reason at all."

"I'm glad you agree. But what exactly should we do?"

At this point the two famous dracologists got into a discussion so technical, that anyone listening in wouldn't have been able to make head or tail of it. There were such mysterious words as "discontinuous orthodragonality," "grand draconical ensembles," "high-frequency binomial fafneration," "abnormal saurian distribution," "discrete dragons," "indiscrete dragons," "drasticodracostochastic control," "simple Grendelian dominance," "weak interaction dragon diffraction," "aberrational reluctance," "informational figmentation," and so on.

The upshot of all this penetrating analysis was the third sally, for which the constructors prepared most carefully, not failing to load their ship with a quantity of highly complicated devices.

In particular they took along a scatter-scrambler and a special gun that fired negative heads. After landing on Eenica, then on Meenica, then finally on Mynamoaca, they realized it would be impossible to comb the whole infested area in this way and they would have to split up. This was most easily done, obviously, by separating; so after a brief council of war each set out on his own. Klapaucius worked for a spell on Prestopondora for the Emperor Maximillion, who was prepared to offer him his daughter's hand in marriage if only he would get rid of those vile beasts. Dragons of the highest probability were everywhere, even in the streets of the capital, and the place literally swarmed with virtuals. A virtual dragon, the uneducated and simple-minded might say, "isn't really there," having no observable substance nor displaying the least intention of acquiring any; but the Cybr-Trurl-Klapaucius-Leech calculation (not to mention the Drachendranginger wave equation) clearly shows that a dragon can jump from configurational to real space with no more effort than it takes to jump off a cliff. Thus, in any room, cellar or attic, provided the probability is high, you could meet with a dragon or possibly even a metadragon.

Instead of chasing after the beasts, which would have accomplished little or nothing, Klapaucius, a true theoretician, approached the problem methodically; in squares and promenades, in barns and hostels he placed probabilistic battery-run dragon dampers, and in no time at all the beasts were extremely rare. Collecting his fee, plus an honorary degree and an engraved loving cup, Klapaucius blasted off to rejoin his friend. On the way, he noticed a planet and someone waving to him frantically. Thinking it might be Trurl in some sort of trouble, he landed. But it was only the inhabitants of Trufflandria, the subjects of King Pfftius, gesticulating. The Trufflandrians held to various superstitions and primitive beliefs; their religion, Pneumatological Dracolatry, taught that dragons appeared as a divine retribution for their sins and took possession of all unclean souls. Quickly realizing it would be useless to enter into a discussion with the royal dracologians—their methods consisted primarily of waving censers and distributing sacred relics—Klapaucius instead conducted soundings of the outlying terrain. These revealed the planet was occupied by only one beast, but that beast belonged to the terrible genus of Echidnosaurian hypervipers. He offered the King his services. The King, however, answered in a vague, roundabout fashion, evidently under the influence of that ridiculous doctrine which would have the origin of dragons be somehow supernatural. Perusing the local newspapers, Klapaucius learned that the dragon terrorizing the planet was considered by some to be a single thing, and by others, a multiplex creature that could operate in several locations at the same time. This gave him pause—though it wasn't so surprising really, when you considered that the localization of these odious phenomena was subject to so-called dragonomalies, in which certain specimens, particularly when abstracted, underwent a "smearing" effect, which was in reality nothing more than a simple isotopic spin acceleration of asynchronous quantum moments. Much as a hand, emerging from the water fingers-first, appears above the surface in the form of five seemingly separate and independent items, so do dragons, emerging from the lairs of their configurational space, on occasion appear to be plural, though in point of fact they are quite singular. Towards the end of his second audience with the King, Klapaucius inquired if perhaps Trurl were on the planet and gave a detailed description of his comrade. He was astonished to hear that yes, his comrade had only recently visited their kingdom and had even undertaken to exorcise the monster, had in fact accepted a retainer and departed for the neighboring mountains where the monster had been most frequently sighted. Had then returned the next day, demanding the rest of his fee and presenting four and twenty dragon's teeth as proof of his success. There was some misunderstanding, however, and it was decided to withhold payment until the matter was fully cleared up. At which Trurl flew into a rage and in a loud voice made certain comments about His Royal Highness that were perilously close to lèse majesty if not treason, then stormed out without leaving a

forwarding address. That very same day the monster reappeared as if nothing had happened and, alas, ravaged their farms and villages more fiercely than before.

Now this story seemed questionable to Klapaucius, though on the other hand it was hard to believe the good King was lying, so he packed his knapsack with all sorts of powerful dragon-exterminating equipment and set off for the mountains, whose snowcapped peaks rose majestically in the east.

It wasn't long before he saw dragon prints and got an unmistakable whiff of brimstone. On he went, undaunted, holding his weapon in readiness and keeping a constant eye on the needle of his dragon counter. It stayed at zero for a spell, then began to give nervous little twitches, until, as if struggling with itself, it slowly crawled towards the number one. There was no doubt now: the Echidnosaur was close at hand. Which amazed Klapaucius, for he couldn't understand how his trusty friend and renowned theoretician, Trurl, could have gotten so fouled up in his calculations as to fail to wipe the dragon out for good. Nor could he imagine Trurl returning to the royal palace and demanding payment for what he had not accomplished.

Klapaucius then came upon a group of natives. They were plainly terrified, the way they kept looking around and trying to stay together. Bent beneath heavy burdens balanced on their backs and heads, they were stepping single-file up the mountainside. Klapaucius accosted the procession and asked the first native what they were about.

"Sire!" replied the native, a lower court official in a tattered tog and cummerbund. " 'Tis the tribute we carry to the dragon."

"Tribute? Ah yes, the tribute! And what *is* the tribute?"

"Nothin' more 'r less, Sire, than what the dragon would have us bring it: gold coins, precious stones, imported perfumes, an' a passel o' other valuables."

This was truly incredible, for dragons never required such tributes, certainly not perfume—no perfume could ever mask their own natural fetor—and certainly not currency, which was useless to them.

"And does it ask for young virgins, my good man?" asked Klapaucius.

"Virgins? Nay, Sire, tho' there war a time ... we had to cart 'em in by the bevy, we did. ... Only that war before the stranger came, the furrin gentleman, Sire, a-walkin' around the rocks with 'is boxes an' contraptions, all by 'isself. ..." Here the worthy native broke off and stared at the instruments and weapons Klapaucius was carrying, particularly the large dragon counter that was ticking softly all the while, its red pointer jumping back and forth across the white dial.

"Why, if he dinna have one ... jus' like yer Lordship's," he said in a hushed voice. "Aye, jus' like ... the same wee stiggermajigger and a' the rest ..."

"There was a sale on them," said Klapaucius, to allay the native's suspicions. "But tell me, good people, do you happen to know what became of this stranger?"

"What became o' him, ye ask? That we know not, Sire, to be sure. 'Twas, if I not mistake me, but a fortnight past —'twas, 'twas not, Master Gyles, a fortnight withal an' nae more?"

" 'Twas, 'twas, 'tis the truth ye speak, the truth aye, a fortnight sure, or maybe two."

"Aye! So he comes to us, yer Grace, partakes of our 'umble fare, polite as ye please an' I'll not gainsay it, nay, a parfit gentleman true, pays hondsomely, inquires after the missus don't y'know, aye an' then he sits 'isself down, spreads out a' them contraptions an' thin's with clocks in 'em, y'see, an' scribbles furious-like, numbers they are, one after t'other, in this wee book he keep in 'is breast pocket, then takes out a—whad'yacallit—therbobbiter thingamabob ..."

"Thermometer?"

"Aye, that's it! A thermometer ... an' he says it be for dragons, an' pokes it here an' there, Sire, an' scribbles in 'is book again, then he takes a' them contraptions an' things an' packs 'em up an' puts 'em on 'is back an' says farewell an' goes 'is merry way. We never saw 'im more, yer Honor. That very night we hear a thunder an' a clatter, oh, a good ways off, 'bout as far as Mount Murdigras—'tis the one, Sire, hard by yon peak, aye, that one thar, looks like a hawk, she do, we call 'er Pfftius Peak after our beluved King, an' that one thar on t'uther side, bent over like t'would spread 'er arse, that be the Dollymog, which, accordin' to legend—"

"Enough of the mountains, worthy native," said Klaupaucius. "You were saying there was thunder in the night. What happened then?"

"Then, Sire? Why nothin', to be sure. The hut she give a jump an' I falls outta bed, to which I'm well accustomed, mind ye, seein' as how the wicked beast allus come a-bumpin' gainst the house with 'er tail an' send a feller flyin'—like when Master Gyles' ayn brother londed in the privy 'cause the creatur' gets a hankerin' to scratch 'isself on the corner o' the roof ..."

"To the point, man, get to the point!" cried Klapaucius. "There was thunder, you fell down, and then what?"

"Then nothin', like I says before an' thought I made it clear. Nothin', an' if'n there war somethin', there'd be somethin', only there war nothin' sure an' that be the long an' the short of it! D'ye agree, Master Gyles?"

"Aye, sure 'tis the truth ye speak, 'tis."

Klapaucius bowed and stepped back, and the whole procession continued up the mountain, the natives straining beneath the dragon's tribute. He supposed they would place it in some cave designated by the beast, but didn't care to ask for details; his head was already spinning from listening to the local official and his Master Gyles. And anyway, he had heard one of the natives say to another that the dragon had chosen "a spot as near us an' as near 'isself as could be found."

Klapaucius hurried on, picking his way according to the readings of the dragonometer he kept on a chain around his neck. As for the counter, its pointer had come to rest on exactly eight-tenths of a dragon.

"What in the devil is it, an indeterminant dragon?" he thought as he marched, stopping to rest every now and then, for the sun beat fiercely and the air was so hot that everything shimmered. There was no vegetation anywhere, not a scrap, only baked mud, rocks and boulders as far as the eye could see.

An hour passed, the sun hung lower in the heavens, and Klapaucius still walked through fields of gravel and scree, through craggy passes, till he found himself in a place of narrow canyons and ravines full of chill and darkness. The red pointer crept to nine-tenths, gave a shudder, and froze.

Klapaucius put his knapsack on a rock and had just taken off his antidragon belt when the indicator began to go wild, so he grabbed his probability extinguisher and looked all around. Situated on a high bluff, he was able to see into the gorge below, where something moved.

"That must be her!" he thought, since Echidnosaurs are invariably female.

Could *that* be why it didn't demand young virgins? But no, the native said it had before. Odd, most odd. But the main thing now, Klapaucius told himself, was to shoot straight and everything would be all right. Just in case, however, he reached for his knapsack again and pulled out a can of dragon repellent and an atomizer. Then he peered over the edge of the rock. At the bottom of the gorge, along the bed of a dried-up stream walked a grayish brown dragoness of enormous proportions, though with sunken sides as if it had been starved. All sorts of thoughts ran through Klapaucius' head. Annihilate the thing by reversing the sign of its pentapendragonal coefficient from positive to negative, thereby raising the statistical probability of its nonexistence over that of its existence? Ah, but how very risky that was, when the least deviation could prove disastrous: more than one poor soul, seeking to produce the lack of a dragon, had ended up instead with the back of the dragon—resulting in a beast with two backs—and nearly died of embarrassment! Besides, total deprobabilization would rule out the possibility of studying the Echidnosaur's behavior. Klapaucius wavered; he could see a splendid dragonskin tacked on the wall of his den, right above the fireplace. But this wasn't the time to indulge in daydreams—though a dracozoologist would certainly be delighted to receive an animal with such unusual tastes. Finally, as Klapaucius got into position, it occurred to him what a nice little article might be written up on the strength of a well-preserved specimen, so he put down the extinguisher, lifted the gun that fired negative heads, took careful aim and pulled the trigger.

The roar was deafening. A cloud of white smoke engulfed Klapaucius and he lost sight of the beast for a moment. Then the smoke cleared.

There are a great many old wives' tales about dragons. It is said, for example, that dragons can sometimes have seven heads. This is sheer nonsense. A dragon can have only one head, for the simple reason that having two leads to disagreements and violent quarrels; the polyhydroids, as the scholars call them, died out as a result of internal feuds. Stubborn and headstrong by nature, dragons cannot tolerate opposition, therefore two heads in one body will always bring about a swift death: each head, purely to spite the other, refuses to eat, then maliciously holds its breath—with the usual consequences. It was this phenomenon which Euphorius Cloy exploited when he invented the anticapita cannon. A small auxiliary electron head is discharged into the dragon's body. This immediately gives rise to unreconcilable differences of opinion and the dragon is immobilized by the ensuing deadlock. Often it will stand there, stiff as a board, for a day, a week, even a month; sometimes a year goes by before the beast will collapse, exhausted. Then you can do with it what you will.

But the dragon Klapaucius shot reacted strangely, to say the least. True, it did rear up on its hind paws with a howl that started a landslide or two, and it did thrash the rocks with its tail until the sparks flew all over the canyon. But then it scratched its ear, cleared its throat and coolly continued on its way, though trotting at a slightly quicker pace. Unable to believe his eyes, Klapaucius ran along the ridge to head the creature off at the mouth of the dried-up stream —it was no longer an article, or even two articles in the *Dracological Journal* he could see his name on now, but a whole monograph elegantly bound, with a likeness of the dragon and the author on the cover!

At the first bend he crouched behind a boulder, pulled out his improbability automatic, took aim and actuated the possibiliballistic destabilizers. The gunstock trembled in his hands, the red-hot barrel steamed; the dragon was surrounded with a halo like a moon predicting bad weather— but didn't disappear! Once again Klapaucius unleashed the utmost improbability at the beast; the intensity of nonverisimilarity was so great, that a moth that happened to be flying by began to tap out the *Second Jungle Book* in Morse code with its little wings, and here and there among the crags and cliffs danced the shadows of witches, hags and harpies, while the sound of hoofbeats announced that somewhere in the vicinity there were centaurs gamboling, summoned into being by the awesome force of the improbability projector. But the dragon just sat there and yawned, leisurely scratching its shaggy neck with a hind paw, like a dog. Klapaucius clutched his sizzling weapon and desperately kept squeezing the trigger—he had never felt so helpless—and the nearest stones slowly lifted into the air, while the dust that the dragon had kicked up, instead of settling, hung in midair and assumed the shape of a sign that clearly read AT YOUR SERVICE GOV. It grew dim—day was night and night was day, it grew cold—hell was freezing over; a couple of stones went out for a stroll and softly chatted of this and that; in short, miracles were happening right and left, yet that horrid monster sitting not more than thirty paces from Klapaucius apparently had no intention of disappearing. Klapaucius threw down his gun, pulled an antidragon grenade from his vest pocket and, committing his soul to the Universal Matrix of Transfinite Transformations, hurled it with all his might. There was a loud ker-boom, and into the air with a spray of rock flew the dragon's tail, and the dragon shouted "Yipe!"—just like a person—and galloped straight for Klapaucius. Klapaucius, seeing the end was near, leaped out from behind his boulder, swinging his antimatter saber blindly, but then he heard another shout:

"Stop! Stop! Don't kill me!"

"What's that, the dragon talking?" thought Klapaucius. "I must be going mad . . ."

But he asked:

"Who said that? The dragon?"

"What dragon? It's me!!"

And as the cloud of dust blew away, Trurl stepped out of the beast, pushing a button that made it sink to its knees and go dead with a long, drawn-out wheeze.

"Trurl, what on earth is going on? Why this masquerade? Where did you find such a costume? And what about the real dragon?" Klapaucius bombarded his friend with questions. Trurl finished brushing himself off and held up his hands.

"Just a minute, give me a chance! The dragon I destroyed, but the King wouldn't pay . . ."

"Why not?"

"Stingy, most likely. He blamed it on the bureaucracy, of course, said there had to be a notarized death certificate, an official autopsy, all sorts of forms in triplicate, the approval of the Royal Appropriations Commission, and so on. The Head Treasurer claimed he didn't know the procedure to hand over the money, for it wasn't wages, nor did it come under maintenance. I went from the King to the Cashier to the Commission, back and forth, and no one would do anything; finally, when they asked me to submit a vita sheet with photographs and references, I walked out—but by then the dragon was beyond recall. So I pulled the skin off it, cut up a few sticks and branches, found an old telephone pole, and that was really all I needed; a frame for the skin, some pulleys—you know—and I was ready . . ."

"You, Trurl? Resorting to such shameful tactics? Impossible! What could you hope to gain by it? I mean, if they didn't pay you in the first place . . ."

"Don't you understand?" said Trurl, shaking his head. "This way I get the tribute! Already there's more than I know what to do with."

"Ah! Of course!!" Klapaucius saw it all now. But he added, "Still, it wasn't right to force them . . ."

"Who was forcing them? I only walked around in the mountains, and in the evenings I howled a little. But really, I'm absolutely bushed." And he sat down next to Klapaucius.

"What, from howling?"

"Howling? What are you talking about? Every night I

have to drag sacks of gold from the designated cave—all the way up there!" He pointed to a distant ridge. "I made myself a blast-off pad—it's right over there. Just carry several hundred pounds of bullion from sundown to sunup and you'll see what I mean! And that dragon was no ordinary dragon—the skin itself weighs a couple of tons, and I have to cart that around with me all day, roaring and stamping —and then it's all night hauling and heaving. I'm glad you showed up, I can't take much more of this. . . ."

"But . . . why didn't the dragon—the fake one, that is— why didn't it disappear when I lowered the probability to the point of miracles?" Klapaucius asked. Trùrl smiled.

"I didn't want to take any chances," he explained. "Some fool of a hunter might've happened by, maybe even Basiliscus himself, so I put probability-proof shields under the dragonskin. But come, I've got a few sacks of platinum left —saved them for last since they're the heaviest. Which is just perfect, now that you can give me a hand . . ."

The Fourth Sally

OR How Trurl Built a Femfatalatron to Save Prince Pantagoon from the Pangs of Love, and How Later He Resorted to a Cannonade of Babies

One day, in the middle of the night, as Trurl lay deep in slumber, there came a violent knocking at the door of his domicile, as if someone was trying to knock it off its hinges. Still in a stupor, Trurl pulled back the bolts and saw standing there against the paling stars an enormous ship. It looked like a giant sugar loaf or flying pyramid, and out of this colossus, which had landed right on his front lawn, long rows of andromedaries laden with packs walked down a wide ramp, while robots, garbed in turbans and togas and painted black, unloaded the bags at his doorstep, and so quickly, that before Trurl knew it, he was hemmed in by a growing embankment of bulging sacks—though a narrow passageway was left therein, and through this approached an electroknight of remarkable countenance, for his jeweled eyes blazed like comets, and he had radar antennas jauntily thrown back, and an elegant diamond-studded stole. This imposing personage doffed his armored cap and in a mighty yet silken voice inquired:

"Have I the honor to speak with his lordship Trurl, Trurl the highborn, Trurl the illustrious constructor?"

"Why yes, of course . . . won't you come in . . . I wasn't expecting . . . that is, I was asleep," said Trurl, terribly flustered, pulling on a bathrobe, for a nightshirt was all he was wearing, and that wasn't the cleanest.

The magnificent electroknight, however, appeared not to notice any shortcoming in Trurl's attire. Doffing his cap again, which purred and hummed above his castellated brow, he gracefully entered the room. Trurl excused himself for a moment, perfunctorily performed his morning ablutions, then hurried back downstairs. By now it was growing light outside, and the first rays of the sun gleamed on the turbans of the robots, who sang the old sad and soulful song of bondage, "Tote Dat Jack," as they formed in triple rows around both house and pyramidal ship. Trurl took a seat opposite his guest, who blinked his shining eyes and finally spoke as follows:

"The planet from which I come to you, Sir Constructor, is at present deep in the Dark Ages. Ah, but Your Excellency must forgive our untimely arrival, which did so incommoditate him; on board we had no way of knowing, you see, that at this particular locus of this worthy sphere, which your abode is pleased to occupy, night still reigned supreme and stayed the break of day."

Here he cleared his throat, like someone playing sweetly upon a glass harmonica, and continued:

"I have been sent to Your Exalted Person by my lord and master, His Royal Highness Protuberon Asteristicus, sovereign ruler of the sister globes of Aphelion and Perihelion, hereditary monarch of Aneuria, emperor of all the Monodamites, Biproxicans and Tripartisans, the Grand Duke of Anamandorinth, Glorgonzigor and Esquacciaccaturbia, Count of the Euscalipii, the Algorissimo and the Flora del Fortran, Paladin Escutcheoned, Begudgeoned and of the Highest Dudgeon, Baron of Bhm, Wrph and Clarafoncasterbrackeningen, as well as anointed exarch extraordinary of Ida, Pida and Adinfinida, to invite in His munificent name Your Resplendent Grace to our kingdom as the long-awaited savior of the crown, as the only one who can deliver us from the general mortifaction occasioned by the thrice-unhappy infatuation of His Royal Highness, the heir to the throne, Pantagoon."

"But really, I'm not—" Trurl tried to interpose, but the dignitary waved his hand, signifying that he had not as yet finished, and went on in that same resonating voice:

"In return for the gracious loan of your most sympathetic ear, and for your succor in the overcoming of our national calamity, His Royal Highness Protuberon hereby promises, pledges and solemnly swears that he shall shower Your Constructorship with such riches and honors, that Your Esteemed Effulgence will never exhaust them, even untò the end of his days. And now, by way of an advance or, as they say, a retainer, I forthwith dub thee"—and here the magnate rose, drew his sword, and spoke, vigorously punctuating each word with the flat of the blade on both Trurl's shoulders—"Earl of Otes, Grotes and Finocclea, Margrave Emeritus of Trundle and Sklar, Eight-barreled Bearer of the Great Guamellonian Hok, not to mention Thane of Bondacalonda and Cgth, Governor General of Muxis and Ptuxis, as well as Titular Viscount of the Order of Unwinched Waifs, Almoner *in perpetuum* of the realms of Eenica, Meenica and Mynamoaca, with all the attendant rights and privileges accruing thereto, including a twenty-one gun salute upon rising in the morning and retiring at night, an after-dinner fanfare, and the Extinguished Exponential Cross, duly certified and carved in ebony, slate and marzipan. And as proof of his royal favor, my Lord and Liege sends you these few trifles, which I have taken the liberty to place about your dwelling."

And indeed, the sacks already blocked out the sky, and the room grew dim. The magnate finished speaking, though his hand, raised in eloquence, remained in midair. Trurl took this opportunity to say:

"I am much obliged to His Royal Highness Protuberon, but affairs of the heart, you understand, are not exactly my specialty. Though ..." he added, uncomfortable under the magnate's dazzling gaze, "perhaps you would explain the problem to me ..."

The magnate gave a nod.

"That is simply done, Sir Constructor! The heir to the throne has fallen in love with Amarandina Cybernella, the only daughter of the ruler of the neighboring state of Ib. But an ancient enmity divides our kingdoms, and doubtless, if our Beloved Sovereign, yielding to the unwearying pleas of the prince, were to ask that emperor for the hand of Amarandina, the answer would be a categorical never. And so a year has passed, and six days, and the crown prince wastes away before our eyes. All attempts to restore him to reason have failed, and now our only hope lies in Your Most Iridescent Eminence!"

Here the magnate made a deep bow. Trurl, observing rows of warriors right outside his window, coughed and said in a feeble voice:

"Well, I really don't see how I could be of . . . though, of course, if the King wishes it . . . in that case . . ."

"Wonderful!" cried the magnate and clapped his hands with a mighty clang. Immediately twelve cuirassiers, black as night, rushed in with clattering armor and bore Trurl off to the ship, which fired its engines twenty-one times, pulled anchor and, banners waving, lifted up into the open sky.

During the flight the magnate, who was Grand Seneschal and Artifactotum to the King, filled Trurl in on the details of the prince's ill-starred enamorization. Directly upon their arrival, after the welcoming ceremonies and ticker-tape parade through the streets of the capital, the constructor got down to work. He set up his equipment in the magnificent royal gardens and in three weeks had converted the Temple of Contemplation there into a strange edifice full of metal, cables and glowing screens. This was, he told the King, a femfatalatron, an erotifying device stochastic, elastic and orgiastic, and with plenty of feedback; whoever was placed inside the apparatus instantaneously experienced all the charms, lures, wiles, winks and witchery of all the fairer sex in the Universe at once. The femfatalatron operated on a power of forty megamors, with a maximum attainable efficiency—given a constant concupiscence coefficient—of ninety-six percent, while the system's libidinous lubricity, measured of course in kilocupids, produced up to six units for every remote-control caress. This marvelous mechanism, moreover, was equipped with reversible ardor dampers, omnidirectional consummation amplifiers, absorption philters, paphian peripherals, and "first-sight" flip-flop circuits, since Trurl held here to the position of Dr. Yentzicus, creator of the famous oculo-oscular feel theory.

There were also all sorts of auxiliary components, like a high-frequency titillizer, an alternating tantalator, plus an entire set of lecherons and debaucheraries; on the outside, in a special glass case, were enormous dials, on which one could carefully follow the course of the whole decaptivation process. Statistical analysis revealed that the femfatalatron gave positive, permanent results in ninety-eight cases of unrequited amatorial superfixation out of a hundred. The chances of saving the crown prince therefore were excellent.

It took forty venerable peers of the kingdom four hours and more to push and pull their prince through the gardens to the Temple of Contemplation, for though fully determined, they had to show proper respect for his royal person,

and the prince, having no desire whatever of becoming de-
captivated, kicked and butted his faithful courtiers with
great vigor. When finally His Majesty was shoved, with the
application of numerous feather pillows, into the machine
and the trapdoor shut after him, Trurl, full of misgivings,
threw the switch, and the computer began its countdown
in a dreary monotone: "Five, four, three, two, one, zero
... start!" The synchroerotorotors, bumping and grinding,
set up powerful counterseduction currents to displace the
prince's so tragically misplaced affections. After an hour of
this, Trurl looked at the dials: their needles trembled under
the terrible load of lascivicity but, alas, failed to show any
significant improvement. He began to have serious doubts
about the success of the treatment, but it was too late to
do anything now—other than fold his hands and wait patiently. He only checked to make sure that the autolips were
landing in the right place and at the proper angle, that the
aphrodisial philanderoids and satyriacal panderynes weren't
going too far, for he didn't want the patient to undergo a
total dotal transferral and end up idolizing the machine instead of Amarandina, but only to fall thoroughly out of love.
At last the trapdoor was opened in solemn silence. Out of
the dim interior, wreathed with a cloud of the sweetest
perfume, stumbled the pale prince through crushed rose
petals—and fell in a swoon, stunned by that awesome access
of passion. His faithful servants rushed up and, as they lifted
his limp limbs, heard him utter in a hoarse whisper one
solitary word: Amarandina. Trurl cursed under his breath,
for all of it had been in vain, and the prince's mad love had
proven stronger than all the megamors and kilocuddles the
femfatalatron could bring to bear. The rapturometer, when
pressed against the brow of the stupefied prince, registered
one hundred and seven, then the glass shattered and the
mercury poured out, still quivering, as if it too had come

under the influence of those raging emotions. The first attempt, then, was a complete failure.

Trurl returned to his quarters in the foulest mood, and anyone eavesdropping would have heard how he paced from wall to wall, seeking a solution. Meanwhile there was an awful racket back in the gardens: some stonemasons, ordered to fix the wall of a small arborium, had out of curiosity crawled into the femfatalatron and accidentally turned it on. It became necessary to summon the fire department, for they jumped out so inflamed, that they started to smoke.

Next Trurl tried a retropruriginous eroginator with heavy-duty volupticles, but that too—to make a long story short—was a flop. The prince was not a whit less smitten with Amarandina's charms; in fact, he was more smitten than ever. Once again Trurl paced the floor of his room, back and forth for many miles, and sat up half the night reading professional manuals, till he hurled them against the wall. That morning he went to the Grand Seneschal and requested an audience with the King. Admitted to the presence of His Majesty, Trurl spoke in this fashion:

"Your Royal Highness and Gracious Sovereign! The disenamorment methods which I employed upon Your son are the most powerful possible. He simply will not be disenamored, not alive—Your Majesty must know the truth."

The King was silent, crushed by this news, but Trurl went on:

"Of course, I could deceive him, synthesizing an Amarandina according to the parameters I have at hand, but sooner or later the prince would find out, when news of the true Amarandina reached his ears. No, I see no other way: the prince must marry the Emperor's daughter!"

"Bah, but that is the whole problem, O foreigner! The Emperor will never agree to such a marriage!"

"And if he were conquered? If he had to sue for peace, beg for mercy?"

"Why then, certainly—but would you have me plunge two large kingdoms into a bloody war, which is a risky proposition at best, solely in order to win the hand of the Emperor's daughter for my son? No, that is quite out of the question!"

"Precisely the answer I expected of Your Royal Highness!" said Trurl calmly. "However, there are wars and there are wars; the kind I have in mind would be absolutely bloodless. For we would not attack the Emperor's realm with arms; in fact, we would not take the life of a single citizen, but *just the opposite!*"

"What are you saying? What do you mean?" exclaimed the King.

And as Trurl whispered his secret plan into the royal ear, the monarch's careworn face gradually brightened, and he cried:

"Go then, and do this thing, good foreigner, and may the gods be with thee!"

The very next day the royal forges and workshops undertook the construction, according to Trurl's specifications, of a great number of tremendous cannons, though for what purpose intended it was not clear. These were placed around the planet and disguised as defense installations, so that no one would guess a thing. Meanwhile Trurl sat day and night in the royal cybergenetic laboratory, watching over secret cauldrons in which mysterious concoctions gurgled and percolated. A spy on the premises would have discovered nothing, except that now and then behind the double-locked doors there was an odd mewling, puling sound, and technicians and assistants ran frantically back and forth with piles of diapers.

The bombardment began a week later, at midnight. The cannons, primed by veteran cannoneers, were aimed, muzzles raised, straight at the white star of the Emperor's empire, and they fired—not death-dealing, but life-giving missiles. For Trurl had loaded the cannons with newborn babies, which rained down upon the enemy in gooing, cooing myriads and, growing quickly, crawled and drooled over everything; there were so many of them, that the air shook with their ear-splitting ma-ma's, da-da's, kee-kee's and waa's. This infant inundation lasted until the economy began to collapse under the strain and the kingdom was faced with the dread specter of a depression, and still out of the sky came tots, tads, moppets and toddlers, all chubby and chuckling, their diapers fluttering. The Emperor was forced to capitulate to King Protuberon, who promised to call a halt to the hostilities on the condition that his son be granted Amarandina's hand in marriage—to which the Emperor hastily agreed. Whereupon the baby cannons were all carefully spiked and put away, and, to be safe, Trurl himself took apart the femfatalatron. Later, as best man, in a suit of emeralds and holding the ceremonial baton, he played toastmaster at the riotous wedding feast. Afterwards, he loaded his rocket with the titles, diplomas and citations which both the King and the Emperor had bestowed upon him, and then, sated with glory, he headed for home.

The Fifth Sally

OR The Mischief of King Balerion

Not by being cruel did Balerion, King of Cymberia, oppress his people, but by having a good time. And again, it wasn't feasts or all-night orgies that were dear to His Majesty's heart, but only the most innocent games—tiddlywinks, mumbledypeg, old maid and go fish into the wee hours of the morning, then hopscotch, leapfrog, but more than anything he loved to play hide-and-seek. Whenever there was an important decision to be made, a State document to be signed, interstellar emissaries to be received or some Commodore requesting an audience, the King would hide, and they would have to find him, else suffer the most dreadful punishments. So the whole court would chase up and down the palace, check the dungeons, look under the drawbridge, comb the towers and turrets, tap the walls, turn the throne inside out, and quite often these searches lasted a long time, for the King was always thinking up new places to hide. Once, a terribly important war never got declared, and all because the King, decked in spangles and crystal pendants, hung three days from the ceiling of the main hall and passed for a chandelier, holding his mouth to keep from laughing out loud at the ministers rushing about frantically below. Whoever found the King was instantly given the title of Royal Discoverer—there were already seven hundred and thirty-six of those at court. But he who would gain the King's special favor had to beguile him with some new game, one the King had never heard of. Which was by no means easy, considering that Balerion was unusually well-versed in the subject; he knew all the ancient games, like jackstones or knucklebones, and all the latest games, like spin the electron, and he often said that everything was a game, his Crown included, and for that matter the whole wide world.

These thoughtless and frivolous words outraged the venerable members of the King's privy council; the prime minister in particular, My Lord Papagaster of the great house of Pentaperihelion, was much provoked, saying the King held nothing sacred and even dared expose his own Exalted Person to ridicule.

Then, when the King unexpectedly announced it was time for riddles, terror filled the hearts of everyone. He had always had a passion for riddles; once, right in the middle of the coronation, he confounded the Lord High Chancellor with the question, why was antimatter like an antimacassar?

It wasn't very long before the King realized that his courtiers weren't putting forth the proper effort in solving the conundrums he posed. They replied in any which way, said whatever came into their heads, and this infuriated the King. However, as soon as he began to base all royal appointments and promotions upon the answers to his riddles, things improved considerably. Decorations and dismissals came thick and fast, and the whole court, like it or not, had to play the game in earnest. Unfortunately, many dignitaries attempted to deceive the King, who, though basically good-natured, could simply not tolerate a cheater. The Keeper of the Great Seal was sent into exile because he had used a crib (concealed beneath his cuirass) in the Royal Presence; he never would have been discovered, had not one of his old enemies, a certain general, brought this to the King's attention. Papagaster himself had to part with his high post, for he didn't know what was the darkest place in outer space. In time, the King's Cabinet was composed of the most accomplished solvers of crosswords, acrostics and rebuses in the land, and his ministers never went anywhere without their encyclopedias. The courtiers soon became so proficient, that they could supply the correct answer before the King had finished asking the question, though this was hardly surprising when you considered that they were all avid subscribers to the "Official Register," which, instead of a tedious list of acts and administrative decisions, contained nothing but puzzles, puns and parlor games.

As the years went by, however, the King liked less and less to have to think, and gradually returned to his first and greatest love, hide-and-seek. One day, in a particularly playful mood, he offered a most handsome prize to the one who could find for him the best hiding place in all the world. The prize was to be nothing less than the Royal Diadem of the Cymberanide Dynasty, a cluster of truly priceless jewels. No one had laid eyes on this wonder for many centuries, for it lay locked and coffered in the Royal Vault.

Now it so happened that Trurl and Klapaucius chanced upon Cymberia in the course of one of their travels. News of the King's proclamation, having quickly spread throughout the realm, reached our constructors too; they learned of it from the local villagers at the inn where they were spending the night.

The next day they repaired to the palace to announce that they knew a hiding place unequaled by any other. Unfortunately, so many others had come to claim the prize, that it was next to impossible to get by the crowd at the gate. Trurl and Klapaucius therefore returned to their lodgings and resolved to try their luck the following day. Though they didn't leave it to luck alone; this time the prudent constructors came prepared. To every guard who barred the way and then to every court official who challenged them, Trurl quietly slipped a few coins and, whenever that didn't work, a few more, and in less than five minutes they were standing before the throne of His Royal Highness. His Royal Highness was of course delighted to hear that such famous wise men had come so far for the sole purpose of imparting to him the secret of the perfect hiding place. It took them a little time to explain the how and the why of it to Balerion, but his mind, schooled from childhood in the ways of tricks and puzzles, finally grasped the idea. Burning with enthusiasm, the King jumped down from his throne, assured the two friends of his undying gratitude, promised they would receive the prize without fail—provided only they let him try out their secret method at once. Klapaucius was reluctant on this point, muttering to himself that they ought to write up a proper contract first, with parchment, seals and tassels; but the King was so insistent, and pleaded with such vehemence, swearing great oaths the prize was as good as theirs, that the constructors had to give in. Trurl opened a small box he had brought with him, took out the necessary device and showed it to the King. This invention actually had nothing to do with hide-and-seek, but could be applied to that game wonderfully well. It was a portable bilateral personality transformer, with retroreversible feedback, of course. Using it, any two individuals could quickly and easily exchange minds. The device, fitted onto one's head, resembled a pair of horns; when these came into contact with the forehead of the one with whom one wished to effect the exchange, and were lightly pressed, the device was activated and instantaneously set up two opposing series of antipodal impulses. Through one horn, one's own psyche flowed into the other, and through the other, the other into one's own. Hence the total deenergizing of the one memory and the simultaneous energizing of the other in its place, and contrariwise. Trurl had set the apparatus on his head for purposes of demonstration and was explaining the procedure to the King, bringing the royal forehead into proximity with the horns, when the King impulsively butted against them, which triggered the mechanism and immediately brought about a personality transfer. It all happened so quickly that Trurl, who had never really tested the device on himself, didn't notice. Nor did Klapaucius, standing to one side; it did strike him rather odd that Trurl suddenly stopped in the middle of a sentence and Balerion instantly took up where Trurl had left off, using such words as "the potentials involved with nonlinear conversion of submnemonic quanta" and "the adiabatic flux differential of the id." The King went on in his squeaky voice for almost a minute before Klapaucius realized there was something wrong. Balerion, finding himself inside the body of Trurl, was no longer listening to the lecture, but wiggled his fingers and toes, as if making himself more comfortable in this novel shape, which he inspected with the greatest curiosity. Meanwhile Trurl, in a long purple robe, was waving his arms and explaining the reversed entropy of mutually transposed systems, until he grew aware that something was in the way, looked down at his hand and was dumbfounded to find himself holding a scepter. He was about to speak, but the King burst out laughing and took to his heels. Trurl started after him, but tripped over the royal robe and fell flat on his face. This commotion quickly brought the royal bodyguards, who straightway threw themselves upon Klapaucius, thinking he had attacked the Royal Person. By the time Trurl managed to get his royal personage off the floor and convince the guards it stood in no danger, Balerion was far away, rollicking somewhere in Trurl's body. Trurl attempted to give chase, but the courtiers wouldn't permit it, and when he protested he wasn't the King at all but there had been a personality transfer, they concluded that excessive puzzle-solving had finally unhinged the Royal Reason and politely but firmly locked him in the royal bedchamber, then sent for the royal physicians while he roared and pounded on the door. Klapaucius meanwhile, thrown out of the palace on his ear, headed back to the inn, thinking—not without alarm—of the complications that might arise from what had just taken place. "Undoubtedly," he thought, "had I been in Trurl's shoes, my great presence of mind would have saved the day. Instead of making a scene and ranting on about telepsychic transfers, which couldn't help but create suspicions as to his sanity, I would have taken advantage of the King's body and ordered them to seize Trurl, namely Balerion, at once—whereas now he's running around free somewhere in the city—and also, I would have had the other constructor remain at my side, in the capacity of special adviser. But that complete idiot"—by which he meant Trurl—"completely lost his head, and now I'll have to bring all my tactical talents into play, else this business may end badly. ..."

He tried to recall everything he knew about the personality transformer, which was considerable. By far the greatest danger, as he saw it, was that Balerion, heedlessly rushing about in Trurl's body, might stumble and hit some inanimate object with his horns. In which case Balerion's consciousness would immediately enter that object and, since inanimate things had no consciousness and consequently the object could offer the transformer nothing in return, Trurl's body would fall lifeless to the ground; as for the King, he would be trapped for all eternity inside some stone, or lamppost, or discarded shoe. Uneasy, Klapaucius quickened his pace, and not far from the inn he overheard some villagers talking excitedly of how his colleague, Trurl, had flown out of the royal palace like one possessed, and how, racing down the long, steep steps that led to the harbor, he'd taken a spill and broken his leg. How this drove him into a most amazing frenzy; how, lying there, he bellowed that he was King Balerion Himself, called for the royal physicians, a stretcher with feather pillows, sweet essences and balm; and how, when the people laughed at this madness, he crawled along the pavement, cursing terribly and rending his garments, until one passerby took pity on him and bent over to help. How then the fallen constructor tore the hat off his head, revealing—and there were witnesses to swear to this—devil's horns. How with those horns he rammed the good Samaritan in the head, then fell senseless, strangely stiff and groaning feebly, while the good Samaritan suddenly changed, "as if an evil spirit had taken hold of him," and dancing, skipping, shoving aside everyone who stood in his way, galloped down the steps to the harbor.

Klapaucius grew faint when he heard all of this, for he understood that Balerion, having damaged Trurl's body (and after using it for so short a time), had cunningly switched to the body of some stranger. "Now it's started," he thought with horror. "And how will I ever find Balerion, hidden in a body I don't even know? Where do I begin to look?!" He tried to learn from the villagers who this passerby was, who had so nobly approached the injured pseudo-Trurl, and also, what had become of the horns. Of the good Samaritan they knew only that his dress was foreign, though unmistakably naval, which suggested he'd stepped off a vessel from distant skies; concerning the horns, nothing. But then a certain mendicant whose legs had rusted through (a widower, he had no one to keep them taped and tarred) and who was therefore obliged to go around on wheels attached to his hips, which indeed gave him a better vantage point on what transpired at ground level, told Klapaucius that the worthy mariner had snatched the horns from the prone constructor's head with such speed, that no one but himself had seen it. So, apparently Balerion was again in possession of the transformer and could continue this hair-raising business of jumping from body to body. The news that he now occupied the person of a sailor was especially disturbing. "Of all things, a sailor!" thought Klapaucius. "When shore leave is up and he doesn't appear on board (and how can he, not knowing which ship is his?), the captain is bound to notify the authorities, they'll arrest the deserter of course, and Our Highness will find himself in a dungeon! And if at any time he beats his head against the dungeon wall in despair—with the horns on—then may heaven help us all!!" There was little chance, if any, of locating the sailor who was Balerion, but Klapaucius hastened to the harbor. Luck was with him, for he saw a sizable crowd gathered up ahead. Certain he was on the right track, he mingled with the crowd and soon learned, from what was said here and there, that his worst fears were being realized. Only minutes earlier, a certain respectable skipper, the owner of an entire fleet of merchant ships, had recognized a crewman of his, a person of sterling character; yet now this worthy individual was hurling insults at all who went by, and to those who cautioned him to be on his way lest the police come, he shouted he could become whoever he wanted, and that included the whole police force. Scandalized by such behavior, the skipper remonstrated with his crewman, who replied by striking him with a large stick. Then a police squad, patrolling the harbor as a place of frequent altercations and disorders, arrived on the scene, and it so happened the Commissioner himself was in charge. The Commissioner, seeing that the unruly sailor refused to listen to reason, ordered him thrown in jail. But while they were making the arrest, the sailor suddenly hurled himself at the Commissioner like one possessed and butted him with what seemed to resemble horns. Directly after that, he began to howl that he was a policeman, and not just any policeman, but chief commander of the harbor patrol, while the Commissioner, instead of being angered by this insolent raving, laughed as if it were a tremendous joke, but then ordered his subordinates to escort the troublemaker to prison without further delay, nor to be sparing with their clubs and fists in the process.

Thus, in less than an hour, Balerion had managed to change his corporeal quarters three times, presently occupying the body of a police commissioner, who, though Lord knew he was innocent, had to sit and stew in some dark, dank cell. Klapaucius sighed and went directly to the police station. It was situated on the coast, a heavy stone edifice. No one barred the way, so he went inside and walked through a few empty rooms, until he found himself standing in front of a veritable giant several sizes too large for his uniform and armed to the teeth. This hulk of an individual glowered at Klapaucius and stepped forward, as if to throw him out bodily—but suddenly gave a wink (though Klapaucius certainly had never met him before) and burst out laughing. The voice was gruff, a policeman's voice beyond a shadow of a doubt, yet the laugh—and particularly that wink—brought to mind Balerion, and indeed, it *was* Balerion on the other side of that desk, though obviously not in his own person!

"I knew you right off," said Balerion the policeman. "You were at the palace, you're the friend of the one who had the apparatus. Well, what do you think? Isn't this a fabulous hiding place? They'll never find me, you know, not in a million years! And it's so much fun being a big, strong policeman! Watch!"

And he brought his huge policeman's fist down on the

desk with such force that it split in half—though there was a cracking in the hand as well. Balerion winced and said:

"Ow, I snapped something. But that's okay. If need be, I can always change—into you, for example!"

Klapaucius backed off in the direction of the door, but the policeman blocked the way with his colossal frame and went on:

"Not that I have anything against you personally, you understand. But you know too much, old boy. So I really think it's best we put you in the clink. Yes, into the clink with you!" And he gave a nasty laugh. "That way, when I leave the force, no one—not even you—will have the foggiest notion where, or rather who, I am! Ha-ha!"

"But Your Majesty!" Klapaucius protested. "You don't know all the dangers of the device. Suppose you entered the body of someone with a fatal illness, or a hunted criminal . . ."

"No problem," said the King. "All I have to do is remember one thing: after every switch, grab the horns!"

And he pointed to the broken desk, where the device lay in an open drawer.

"As long as, each time," he said, "I pull it off the head of the person I just was and hold on to it, nothing can harm me!"

Klapaucius did his best to persuade the King to abandon the idea of future personality transfers, but it was quite hopeless; the King only laughed and made jokes, then finally said, clearly enjoying himself:

"I won't go back to the palace—you can forget about that! Anyway, I'll tell you: I see before me a great voyage, traveling among my loyal subjects from body to body, which, after all, is very much in keeping with my democratic principles. And then for dessert, so to speak, the body of some fair maiden—that ought to be a most edifying experience, don't you think? Ha-ha!"

And he threw open the door with a great, hairy paw and bawled for his subordinates. Klapaucius, seeing they would lock him up for sure unless he acted at once, grabbed an inkwell and tossed its contents into the King's face, then in the general confusion leaped out a window into the street. By a great stroke of luck, there were no witnesses about, and he was able to make it to a populous square and lose himself in the crowd before the police began pouring from the station, straightening their shakos and waving their weapons in the air.

Plunged in thoughts that were far from pleasant, Klapaucius walked away from the harbor. "It would be best, really," he said to himself, "to leave that incorrigible Balerion to his fate, go to the hospital where Trurl's body is staying, occupied by the honest sailor, and bring it to the palace, so my friend can be himself again, body and soul. Though it's true that that would make the sailor King instead of Balerion—and serve that rascal right!" Not a bad plan perhaps, but inoperable for the lack of a small but indispensable item, namely the transformer with the horns, which at present lay in the drawer of a policeman's desk. For a moment Klapaucius considered the possibility of constructing another such device—no, there was neither the time nor the means. "But here's an idea," he thought. "I'll go to Trurl, who's the King and by now has surely come to his senses, and I'll tell him to have the army surround the harbor police station. That way, we'll recover the device and Trurl can get back to his old self!"

However, Klapaucius wasn't admitted to the palace. The King, so the sentries told him, had been put under heavy electrostatic sedation by his physicians and should sleep like a top for the next twenty-eight hours at least.

"That's all we need!" groaned Klapaucius, and hastened to the hospital where Trurl's body was staying, for he feared that it might have already been discharged and irretrievably

lost in the labyrinth of the big city. At the hospital he presented himself as a relative of the one with the broken leg; the name he managed to read off the in-patient register. He learned that the injury wasn't serious, a bad sprain and not a fracture, though the patient would have to remain in traction for several days. Klapaucius, of course, had no intention of visiting the patient—it would only come out that they weren't even acquainted. Reassured at least that Trurl's body wouldn't run off on him unexpectedly, he left the hospital and took to wandering the streets, deep in thought. Somehow he found himself back in the vicinity of the harbor and noticed the place was swarming with police; they were stopping everyone, carefully comparing face after face with a description each officer carried with him in a notebook. Klapaucius immediately guessed that this was the doing of Balerion, who at all costs wanted him under lock and key. Just then a patrol approached—and two guards rounded the corner in the opposite direction, cutting off his retreat. Klapaucius quietly gave himself up, demanding only that they take him before the Commissioner, saying that it was most urgent, that he was in possession of extremely important evidence concerning a certain horrible crime. They took him into custody and handcuffed him to a burly policeman; at the station, the Commissioner—Balerion—greeted him with a grunt of satisfaction and an evil twinkle in his beady eyes. But Klapaucius was already exclaiming, in a voice not his own:

"Great One! High-high Police Sir! They take me, they say me Klapaucius, me not Klapaucius, not-not, me not even know who-what Klapaucius! Maybe that Klapaucius he bad one, one who bam-bam horns in head, make big magic, bad magic, make that me not me, put head in other head, take old head, horns, run zip-zip, O Much Police Sir! Help!"

And with these words did the wily Klapaucius fall to his knees, shaking his head and muttering in a strange tongue. Balerion, standing behind the desk in a uniform with wide epaulets, blinked as he listened, somewhat taken aback; he gave the kneeling Klapaucius a closer look and began to nod, apparently convinced—unaware that the constructor, on the way to the station, had pressed his own forehead with his free hand, to produce two marks not unlike those left by the horns of a personality transformer. Balerion had his men release Klapaucius and leave the room; when the two of them were alone, he asked him to relate exactly what had happened, omitting nothing. Klapaucius replied with a long story of how he, a wealthy foreigner, had arrived only that day at the harbor, his ship laden with two hundred cases of the prettiest puzzles in creation as well as thirty self-winding fair maidens, for he had hoped to present these to the great King Balerion; how they were a gift from the great Emperor Proboscideon, who in this way sought to express his boundless admiration for the great House of Cymberia; but how, having arrived and disembarked, he had thought to stretch his legs a little after the long journey and was strolling peacefully along the quay, when this person, who looked just like this (here Klapaucius pointed to himself) and who had already aroused his suspicions by gazing upon the splendor of his foreign dress with such evident rapacity—when this person, in short, suddenly ran towards him like a maniac, ran as if to run him down, but doffed his cap instead and butted him viciously with a pair of horns, whereupon an extraordinary exchange of minds took place.

Klapaucius put everything he had into the tale, trying to make it as believable as possible. He spoke at great length of his lost body, while heaping insults upon the one it was now his misfortune to possess, and he even began to slap his own face and spit on his own legs and chest; he spoke of the treasures he'd brought with him, describing them in every detail, particularly the self-winding maidens; he reminisced about the family he'd left behind, his ion-scions, his hi-fi fido, his wife, one of three hundred, who made a mulled electrolyte as fine as any that ever graced the table of the Emperor Himself; he even let the Commissioner in on his biggest secret, to wit, that he had arranged with the captain of his ship to hand the treasures over to whomsoever came on board and gave the password.

Balerion listened greedily, for it seemed quite logical to him that Klapaucius, seeking to hide from the police, should do so by entering the body of a foreigner, a foreigner moreover attired in splendid robes, hence obviously wealthy, which would provide him with considerable means once the transfer were effected. It was plain that a similar scheme had hatched in the brain of Balerion. Slyly, he tried to coax the secret password from the false foreigner, who didn't require much coaxing, soon whispering the word into his ear: "Niterc." By now the constructor was sure Balerion had taken the bait: the King, loving puzzles as he did, couldn't bear to see them go to the King, since the King, after all, was no longer he; and, believing everything, he believed that Klapaucius had a second transformer—indeed, he had no reason to think otherwise.

They sat awhile in silence; one could see the wheels turning in Balerion's head. Assuming an air of indifference, he began to question the foreigner as to the location of his ship, the name of the captain, and so forth. Klapaucius answered, banking on the King's cupidity, nor was he mistaken, for suddenly the King stood up, announced that he would have to verify what the foreigner had told him, and hurriedly left the room, locking the door securely behind him. Klapaucius then heard Balerion—evidently the wiser from past experience—station a guard beneath the window as he was leaving. Of course he would find nothing, there being no ship, no treasure, no self-winding maidens whatever. But that was the whole point of Klapaucius' plan. As soon as the King was gone, he rushed over to the desk, pulled the device from the drawer and quickly placed it on his head. Then he quietly waited for the King to return. It wasn't long before there were heavy footsteps outside, muffled curses, the grinding of teeth, a key scraping in the lock—and the Commissioner burst in, bellowing:

"Scoundrel! Where's the ship, the treasure, the pretty puzzles?!"

But that was all he said, for Klapaucius leaped out from behind the door and charged like a mad ram, butting him square in the head. Then, before Balerion had time to get his bearings inside Klapaucius, Klapaucius, now the Commissioner, roared for the guards to throw him in jail at once and keep a close eye on him! Stunned by this sudden reversal, Balerion didn't realize at first how shamefully he had been deceived; but when it finally dawned on him that he had been dealing with the crafty constructor all along, and there had never been any wealthy foreigner, Balerion filled his dark dungeon with terrible oaths and threats—harmless, however, without the device. Klapaucius, on the other hand, though he had temporarily lost the body to which he was accustomed, had succeeded in gaining possession of the personality transformer. He put on his best uniform and marched straight to the royal palace.

The King was still asleep, they told him, but Klapaucius, in his capacity as Police Commissioner, said it was imperative he see His Highness, if only for a few moments, said that this was a matter of the utmost gravity, a crisis, the nation hanging in the balance, and more of the same, until the frightened courtiers led him to the royal bedchamber. Well-acquainted with his friend's habits and peculiarities,

Klapaucius touched the heel of Trurl's foot; Trurl jumped up, instantly wide-awake, for he was exceedingly ticklish. He rubbed his eyes and stared in amazement at this hulking giant of a policeman before him, but the giant leaned over and whispered: "It's me, Klapaucius. I had to occupy the Commissioner—without a badge, they'd never have let me in—and I got the device, it's right here in my pocket..."

Trurl, overjoyed when Klapaucius told him of his stratagem, rose from the royal bed, declaring to all that he was fully recovered, and later, draped in purple and holding the royal orb and scepter, sat upon his throne and issued several orders. First, he had them bring from the hospital his own body with the leg Balerion sprained on the harbor steps. This swiftly done, he enjoined the royal physicians to tend the patient with all the skill and solicitude at their disposal. Then, after a brief conference with his Commissioner, namely Klapaucius, Trurl proclaimed he would restore order in the realm and bring things back to normal.

Which wasn't easy, there being no end of complications to straighten out. Though the constructors had no intention of returning *all* the displaced souls to their former bodies; their main concern, actually, was that Trurl be Trurl as soon as possible, and Klapaucius Klapaucius. In the flesh, that is. Trurl therefore commanded that the prisoner (Balerion in his colleague's body) be dragged from jail and hauled before His August Presence. The first transfer promptly carried out, Klapaucius was himself again, and the King (now in the body of the ex-commissioner of police) had to stand and listen to a most unpleasant lecture, after which he was placed in the castle dungeon, the official word being that he had fallen into disfavor due to incompetence in the solving of a certain rebus. Next morning Trurl's body was in good enough health to be repossessed. Only one problem remained: it wasn't right, somehow, to leave without having properly settled the question of succession to the throne. To release Balerion from his constabulary corpus and seat him once more at the helm of the State was quite unthinkable. So this is what they did: under a great oath of secrecy the friends told the honest sailor in Trurl's body everything, and seeing how much good sense resided in that simple soul, they judged him worthy to reign; after the transfer, then, Trurl became himself and the sailor King. Before this, however, Klapaucius ordered a large cuckoo clock brought to the palace, one he had seen in a nearby shop when roaming the city streets, and the mind of King Balerion was conveyed to the cuckoo's works, while it, in turn, occupied the person of the policeman. Thus was justice done, for the King was obliged to work diligently day and night thereafter, announcing the hours with a dutiful cuckoo-cuckoo, to which he was compelled at the appropriate moments by the sharp little teeth of the clock's gears, and with which he would expiate, hanging on the wall of the main hall for the remainder of his days, his thoughtless games, not to mention having endangered the life and limb of two famous constructors by so frequently changing his mind. As for the Commissioner, he returned to his duties and functioned flawlessly, proving that a cuckoo mentality was quite sufficient for that post. The friends finally took their leave of the crowned sailor, gathered up their belongings, shook the dust of that troublesome kingdom from their feet, and continued on their way. One might only add that Trurl's final action in the King's body had been to visit the Royal Vault and take possession of the Royal Diadem of the Cymberanide Dynasty, which prize he had fairly earned, having discovered the very best hiding place in all the world.

The Fifth Sally (A)
OR *Trurl's* *Prescription*

Not far from here, by a white sun, behind a green star, lived
the Steelypips, illustrious, industrious, and they hadn't a
care: no spats in their vats, no rules, no schools, no gloom,
no evil influence of the moon, no trouble from matter or
antimatter—for they had a machine, a dream of a machine,
with springs and gears and perfect in every respect. And they
lived with it, and on it, and under it, and inside it, for it
was all they had—first they saved up all their atoms, then
they put them all together, and if one didn't fit, why they
chipped at it a bit, and everything was just fine. Each and
every Steelypip had its own little socket and its own little
plug, and each was completely on its own. Though they
didn't own the machine, neither did the machine own them,
everybody just pitched in. Some were mechanics, other
mechanicians, still others mechanists: but all were mechanically minded. They had plenty to do, like if night had to
be made, or day, or an eclipse of the sun—but that not too
often, or they'd grow tired of it. One day there flew up to
the white sun behind the green star a comet in a bonnet,
namely a female, mean as nails and atomic from her head
to her four long tails, awful to look at, all blue from hydrogen cyanide and, sure enough, reeking of bitter almonds.
She flew up and said, "First, I'll burn you to the ground,
and that's just for starters."

The Steelypips watched—the fire in her eye smoked up

half the sky, she drew on her neutrons, mesons like caissons, pi- and mu- and neutrinos too—"Fee-fi-fo-fum plu-to-ni-um." And they reply: "One moment, please, we are the Steelypips, we have no fear, no spats in our vats, no rules, no schools, no gloom, no evil influence of the moon, for we have a machine, a dream of a machine, with springs and gears and perfect in every respect, so go away, lady comet, or you'll be sorry."

But she already filled up the sky, burning, scorching, roaring, hissing, until their moon shriveled up, singed from horn to horn, and even if it had been a little cracked, old, and on the small side to begin with, still that was a shame. So wasting no more words, they took their strongest fields, tied them around each horn with a good knot, then threw the switch: try that on for size, you old witch. It thundered, it quaked, it groaned, the sky cleared up in a flash, and all that remained of the comet was a bit of ash—and peace reigned once more.

After an undetermined amount of time something appears, what it is nobody knows, except that it's hideous and no matter from which angle you look at it, it's even more hideous. Whatever it is flies up, lands on the highest peak, so heavy you can't imagine, makes itself comfortable and doesn't budge. But it's an awful nuisance, all the same.

So those who are in the proximity say: "Excuse us, but we are the Steelypips, we have no dread, we don't live on a planet but in a machine instead, and it's no ordinary machine but a dream of a machine, with springs and gears and perfect in every respect, so beat it, nasty thing, or you'll be sorry."

But *that* just sits there.

So, not to go to any great expense, they send not a very big, actually a rather small scarechrome: it'll go and frighten *that* off, and peace will reign once more.

The scarechrome sets off, and all you can hear inside are its programs whirring, one more frightening than the next. It approaches—how it hisses, how it spits! It even scares itself a little—but *that* just sits there. The scarechrome tries once more, this time on a different frequency, but by now it just doesn't have its heart in it.

The Steelypips see that something else is needed. They say: "Let's take a higher caliber, hydraulic, differential-exponential, plastic, stochastic, and with plenty of muscle. It won't cower if it has nuclear power."

So they sent it off, universal, reversible, double-barreled, feedback on every track, all systems go heigh-ho, and inside one mechanic and one mechanist, and that's not all because just to be on the safe side they stuck a scarechrome on top. It arrived, so well-oiled you could hear a pin drop—it winds up for the swing and counts down: four quarters, three quarters, two quarters, one quarter, *no quarter!* Ka-boom! what a blow! See the mushroom grow! The mushroom with the radioactive glow! And the oil bubbles, the gears chatter, the mechanic and the mechanist peer out the hatch: can you imagine, not even a scratch.

The Steelypips held a council of war and then built a mechanism which in turn built a metamechanism which in turn built such a megalomechanism that the closest stars had to step back. And in the middle of it was a machine with cogs and wheels and in the middle of that a servospook, because they really meant business now.

The megalomechanism gathered up all its strength and let go! Thunder, rumbling, clatter, a mushroom so huge you'd need an ocean to make soup out of it, the clenching of teeth, darkness, so much darkness you can't even tell what's what. The Steelypips look—nothing, not a thing, just all their mechanisms lying around like so much scrap metal and without a sign of life.

Now they rolled up their sleeves. "After all," they say, "we are mechanics and mechanists, all mechanically minded, and we have a machine, a dream of a machine, with springs and gears and perfect in every respect, so how can this nasty thing just sit there and not budge?"

This time they make nothing less than an enormous cyberivy-bushwhacker: it'll creep up casually, as if minding its own business, glance over its shoulder, grow a little bolder, send out a root or two, grow up from behind, taking its time, and then when it closes in, that'll be the end of that. And truly, everything happened exactly as predicted, except, when it was over, that wasn't exactly the end of that, not at all.

They fell into despair, and they didn't even know what to think because this had never happened to them before, so they mobilized and analyzed, made nets and glues, lariats and screws, traps and contraptions to make it drown, break it down, make it fall, or maybe wall it up—they try this way and that and the other, but one is as poor as another. They turn everything upside-down, but nothing helps. They're about ready to give up hope when suddenly they see—someone's coming: he's on horseback, but no, horses don't have wheels—it must be a bicycle, but wait, bicycles don't have prows, so maybe it's a rocket, but rockets don't have saddles. What he's riding no one can tell, but who's in the saddle we all know well: it's Trurl himself, the constructor, out on a spree, or maybe on one of his famous sallies, serene and smiling, coming closer, flying by—but even from a distance you'd know that this wasn't just anybody.

He lowers, he hovers, so they tell him the whole story: "We are the Steelypips, we have a machine, a dream of a machine, with springs and gears and perfect in every respect, we saved up all our atoms, put them all together ourselves, we hadn't a care, no spats in our vats, no rules, no schools,

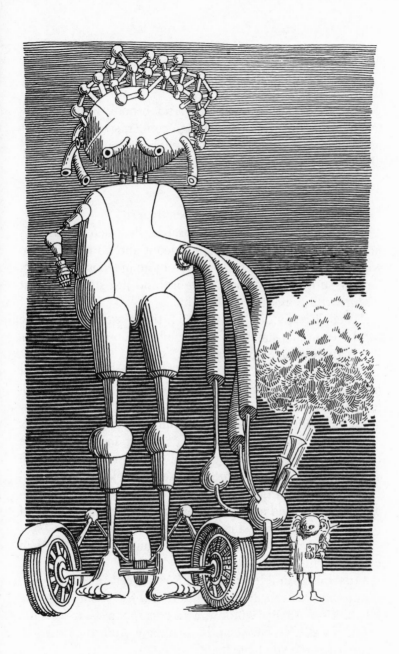

until something flew up, landed, sat down and won't budge."

"Did you try scaring it off?" Trurl asks with a kindly smile.

"We tried a scarechrome and a servospook and a megalo-mechanism, all hydraulic and high caliber, spouting mesons like caissons, pi- and mu- and neutrinos too, protons and photons, but nothing worked."

"No machine, you say?"

"No sir, no machine."

"H'm, interesting. And what exactly is it?"

"That we don't know. It appeared, flew here, what it is nobody knows, except that it's hideous and no matter from which angle you look at it, it's even more hideous. It flew up, landed, so heavy you can't imagine, and just sits there. But it's an awful nuisance, all the same."

"Well, I really don't have much time," says Trurl. "The most I can do is stay here for a while, in an advisory capacity. Is that agreeable with you?"

It certainly is and the Steelypips immediately ask what he wants them to bring—photons, screws, hammers, artillery, or how about some dynamite, or TNT? And would our guest like coffee or tea? From a vending machine, of course.

"Coffee's fine," agrees Trurl, "not for me, but for the business at hand. As for the rest of it, I don't think so. You see, if neither scarechrome, nor servospook, nor cyberivy-bushwhacker will do the job, then other methods are indicated: archaic and archival, legalistic hence sadistic. I've yet to see the remittance due and payable in full fail."

"Come again?" ask the Steelypips, but Trurl, rather than explain, continues:

"It's quite simple, really. All you need is paper, ink, stamps and seals, sealing wax and thumbtacks, sand to sprinkle, blotters, a teller window, a zinc teaspoon, a saucer—the coffee we already have—and a mailman. And something to write with—do you have that?"

"We'll get it!" And they take off.

Trurl pulls up a chair and dictates: "Notice is hereby given, that in re hindrance of Tenant, as stated under Rev. Stat. c.117(e) dash 2 dash KKP4 of the CTSP Comm. Code, in clear violation of paragraph 199, thereby constituting a most reprehendable offense, we do declare the termination, desummation and full cessation of all services accruing thereunto, by authority of Ordinance 67 DPO No. 14(j) 1101 *et seq.*, on this the 19th day of the 17th month of the current year, aff'g 77 F. Supp. 301. The Tenant may appeal said action by extraordinary procedure to the Chairman of the Board within twenty-four hours."

Trurl attaches the seal, affixes the stamp, has it entered in the Central Ledger, consults the Official Register, and says:

"Now let the mailman deliver it."

The mailman takes it, they wait, they wait, the mailman returns.

"Did you deliver it?" asks Trurl.

"I did."

"And the return receipt?"

"Here it is, signed on this line. And here's the appeal."

Trurl takes the appeal and, without reading it at all, orders it returned to sender and writes diagonally across it: "Unacceptable—Proper Forms Not Attached." And he signs his name illegibly.

"And now," he says, "to work!"

He sits and writes, while those who are curious look on and, understanding nothing, ask what this is and what it's supposed to do.

"Official business," answers Trurl. "And things will go well, now that it's under way."

The mailman runs back and forth all day like one possessed; Trurl notarizes, issues directives, the typewriter chatters, and little by little an entire office takes shape, rubber

stamps and rubber bands, paper clips and paper wads, port-
folios and pigeonholes, foolscap and scrip, teaspoons, signs
that say "No Admittance," inkwells, forms on file, writing
all the while, the typewriter chattering, and everywhere you
look you see coffee stains, wastepaper, and bits of gum
eraser. The Steelypips are worried, they don't understand a
thing, meanwhile Trurl uses special delivery registered
C.O.D., certified with return receipt, or, best of all, remittance due and payable in full—he sends out no end of dun-
ning letters, bills of lading, notices, injunctions, and there
are already special accounts set up, no entries at the moment but he says that's only temporary. After a while, you
can see that *that* is not quite so hideous, especially in pro-
file—it's actually gotten smaller!—yes, yes, it *is* smaller! The
Steelypips ask Trurl, what now?

"No idle talk permitted on the premises," is his answer.
And he staples, stamps, inspects vouchers, revokes licenses,
dots an *i*, loosens his tie, asks who's next, I'm sorry, the
office is closed, come back in an hour, the coffee is cold, the
cream sour, cobwebs from ceiling to floor, an old pair of
nylons in the secretary's drawer, install four new file cabinets over here, and there's an attempt to bribe an official,
a pile of problems and a problem with piles, a writ of execution, incarceration for miscegenation, and appeals with seven
seals.

And the typewriter chatters: "Whereas, pursuant to the
Tenant's failure to quit and surrender the demised premises
in compliance with the warrant served, *habere facias posses-
sionem*, by Div. of Rep. Cyb. Gt. KRS thereof, the Court of
Third Instance, in vacuo and ex nihilo, herewith orders the
immediate vacuation and vacation thereunder. The Tenant
may not appeal this ruling."

Trurl dispatches the messenger and pockets the receipts.
After which, he gets up and methodically hurls the desks,

chairs, rubber stamps, seals, pigeonholes, etc., out into deep space. Only the vending machine remains.

"What on earth are you doing?" cry the Steelypips in dismay, having grown accustomed to it all. "How can you?"

"Tut-tut, my dears," he replies. "Better you take a look instead!"

And indeed, they look and gasp—why, there's nothing there, it's gone, as if it had never been! And where did it go, vanished into thin air? It beat a cowardly retreat, and grew so small, so very small, you'd need a magnifying glass to see it. They root around, but all they can find is one little spot, slightly damp, something must have dripped there, but what or why they cannot say, and that's all.

"Just as I thought," Trurl tells them. "Basically, my dears, the whole thing was quite simple: the moment it accepted the first dispatch and signed for it, it was done for. I employed a special machine, the machine with a big *B*; for, as the Cosmos is the Cosmos, no one's licked it yet!"

"All right, but why throw out the documents and pour out the coffee?" they ask.

"So that it wouldn't devour you in turn!" Trurl replies. And he flies off, nodding to them kindly—and his smile is like the stars.

The Sixth Sally

OR How Trurl and Klapaucius Created a Demon of the Second Kind to Defeat the Pirate Pugg

"There are but two caravan trails that lead south from the Lands of the Upper Suns. The first, which is older, goes from the Stellar Quadriferum past the Great Glossaurontus, a most treacherous star, for its magnitude varies, and at its dimmest it resembles the Dwarf of the Abyssyrs, and thereby causes travelers to blunder into the Great Shroud Wastes, from whence only one caravan in nine ever returns. The second, newer trail was opened up by the Imperium Myrapoclean, whose turboservoslaves carved a tunnel six billion miles in length through the heart of the Great Glossaurontus itself.

"The northern entrance to the tunnel may be found in the following manner: from the last of the Upper Suns proceed directly toward the Pole for the time it takes to recite seven Now-I-lay me-down-to-sleep's. Then go left, till you reach the wall of fire, which is a side of Glossaurontus, and locate the opening, a black dot in that white-hot furnace. Steer straight down into this, and put aside all fear, for the tunnel's width will let eight ships, starboard to larboard, pass through. The sight that then appears outside your portholes truly has no equal. First there is the famous Phlogistinian Flamefall, and then as depending on the weather: when the

140

solar depths are swept with pyromagnetic storms that surge
a billion miles or more away, one sees great tortured knots
of fire, pulsing arteries swollen with white, glowing clots;
when, on the other hand, the storm is closer, or it is a ty-
phoon of the seventh order, the roof will shudder, as if that
white dough of incandescence were about to fall, but this
is an illusion, for it spills over but does not fall, and burns,
but cannot consume, held in check by the tensile ribs of the
Fffian Force Fields. But when one observes the core of the
prominence bulge, and the long-forked bolts of the foun-
tainheads they call Infernions flare closer, it is best to keep a
firm grip upon the wheel, and look sharp into the solar vis-
cera and not at any chart, for the utmost steering skill is
needed here. Indeed, that road is never traversed the same
way twice; the entire tunnel gouged through Glossaurontus
twists continually, writhes and thrashes like a serpent flailed.
Keep therefore your eyes well peeled, and your safety frigi-
packs (that rim your visors with transparent icicles) hard by,
and carefully watch the blazing walls that rush up and lash
their thundering tongues, and should you hear the hull begin to sizzle, battered and bespattered in the seething solar
cauldron, then trust to nothing but your own lightning reflexes. Though you must also bear in mind that not every
burst of flame nor every jump of the tunnel signifies a
starquake or a squall in the white oceans of fire; remember-
ing this, the seasoned mariner will not cry 'man the pumps'
at the drop of a match, and later have to face the ridicule of
his peers, who will say he is the type that would try to douse
a star's eternal light with a beaker of liquid nitrogen. To the
one who inquires what he should do if a real quake descends
upon his vessel, most wags will answer that then it is quite
enough to heave a sigh, there being little time for prayer or
the writing of wills, and as for the eyes, these may be open
or shut according to personal preference, for the fire will

burn them out in any event. Such disasters, however, are extremely rare, since the brackets and braces installed by the Imperial Myrapocles hold marvelously well, and really, intrastellar flight, gliding past the curved, sparkling hydrogen mirrors of Glossaurontus, can be a most delightful experience. Then too, they say—and not without reason—that whoever enters the tunnel will at least exit soon after, which certainly cannot be said of the Great Shroud Wastes. And were the tunnel to be totally destroyed by a quake, the only alternate route possible would go through those Wastes, which—as their name indicates—are blacker than night, for the light of the neighboring stars dares not enter there. There, as in a mortar, one finds a constant colliding and crashing together—which makes a terrific din—of scrap metal, cans, wrecks of ships that were led astray by the treachery of Glossaurontus and crushed in the cruel grip of those bottomless gravitational vortices, then left to drift in circles until such time as the Universe itself runs down. To the east of the Shroud is the kingdom of the Slipjaws, to the west, the Bogglyeyed, and in the south are roads, heavily dotted with fortified mortalitaries, leading to the gentler sphere of sky-blue Lazulia, beyond which lies the bud-beaming Murgundigan, where the archipelago of iron-poor stars, known as Alcaron's Carriage, shines blood-red.

"The Shroud itself, as we said, is as black as the Glossaurontian corridor is white. Nor does the only peril there lie in its vortices, in debris pulled down from dizzy heights by the current, in meteors gone berserk; for some say that in an unknown place, among dark, crepuscular caverns, at the bottom of an immeasurably deep and unplumbed profundity, for ages and ages now there sits a certain creature, anomalous and wholly anonymous, for anyone who meets the thing and learns its name will surely never live to tell a soul. And they say that that Anonymoid is both a pirate and a mage, and it lives in a castle raised by black gravitation, and the moat is a perpetually raging storm, and the walls non-being, impenetrable in their nothingness, and the windows are all blind, and the doors dumb; the Anonymoid lies in wait for caravans, but whenever it feels an overwhelming hunger for gold and skeletons, it blows black dust into the faces of the suns that serve as signposts, and once these are extinguished, and some wayfarers have strayed from their path of safety, it comes whirling out of the void, wraps them tightly in its coils, and carries them off to its castle of oblivion, without ever dropping the least ruby brooch, for the monster is monstrously meticulous. Afterward, only the gnawed remains drift away and float through the Wastes, followed by long trails of ship rivets, which are spit out from the monster's maw like seeds. But lately, ever since the Glossaurontian tunnel was opened by the forced labor of innumerable turboservoserfs, and all navigation takes the way of that brightest of corridors, the Anonymoid rages, deprived of further plunder, and the heat of its fury now illumines the darkness of the Shroud, and it glows through the black barriers of gravitation like a fiend's skull rotting in some dank, phosphorescent cocoon. There are scoffers, true, who say that no such monster exists and never did—and they say so with impunity, for it is hard to assail an opinion of things for which there are no words, an opinion formed moreover on a quiet summer afternoon, far from cosmic shrouds and stellar conflagrations. Yes, it is easy not to believe in monsters, considerably more difficult to escape their dread and loathsome clutches. Was not the Murgundiganian Cybernator himself, with an entourage of eighty in three ships, swallowed up, so that nothing remained of that magnaterium but a few chewed buckles, which were cast up on the shore of Solara Minor by a nebular wave and subsequently discovered by the villagers of those parts? And were not countless other worthies devoured without mercy or appeal? Therefore let at least electronic memory pay silent tribute to these poor unburied multitudes, if no avenger can be found for them, one who will deal with that perpetrator according to the old sidereal laws."

All this Trurl read one day from a book, yellowed with age, which he chanced to obtain from a passing peddler, and he took it straightway to Klapaucius and read it a second time, aloud, from beginning to end, as he was much intrigued by the marvels described therein.

Klapaucius, a wise constructor who knew the Cosmos well and had no little acquaintance with suns and nebulae of various kinds, only smiled and nodded, saying:

"You don't believe, I hope, a single word of that rubbish?"

"And why shouldn't I believe it?" Trurl bridled. "Look, here's even an engraving, skillfully done, of the Anonymoid eating two photon schooners and hiding the booty in his cellar. Anyway, isn't there in fact a tunnel through a supergiant? Beth-el-Geuse, I mean. Surely you're not such an ignoramus in cosmography to doubt that possibility. ..."

"As for illustrations, why, I could draw you a dragon right now, with a thousand suns for each eye. Would you accept the sketch as proof of its existence?" Klapaucius replied. "And as for tunnels—first of all, the one of which you speak has a length of only two million miles, not some billions, and secondly, the star of which you speak is practically burnt out, and in the third place, intrastellar travel presents no hazard whatever, as you know perfectly well, having flown that way yourself. And as for the so-called Great Shroud Wastes, this is in reality nothing but a cosmic dump some ten kiloparsecs across, floating in the vicinity of Maeridia and Tetrarchida, and not around any Slopjaws or Gaussauronts, which don't exist anywhere; and it's dark there, yes, but simply because of all the garbage. And as for your Anonymoid, there's obviously no such thing! It isn't even a respectable, ancient myth, but some cheap yarn concocted out of a half-baked cranium."

Trurl bit his lip.

"You think the tunnel safe," he said, "because it was I who flew it. But you would be of an altogether different opinion had it been you, instead. But enough of the tunnel. As far as the Shroud and Anonymoid are concerned, it isn't my habit to settle such things with words. We'll go there, and then you'll see"—and he held up the heavy book— "you'll see what's true in here, and what is not!"

Klapaucius did his best to dissuade him, but when he saw that Trurl, stubborn as usual, had absolutely no intention of backing down from so singularly conceived a sally, he first declared that he would have nothing more to do with him, but before very long had joined in preparing for the voyage: he didn't wish to see his friend perish alone—somehow, two can look death in the eye more cheerfully than one.

Finally, having stocked the larder with plenty of provisions, for the way would lead through vast, barren regions (not as picturesque, to be sure, as the book depicted), they took off in their trusty ship. During the flight, they stopped now and then to ask directions, particularly when they had left far behind the territory with which they were familiar. Not much could be learned from the natives, however, for these spoke reliably only about their immediate surroundings—of things that lay beyond, where they had never ventured themselves, they gave the most absurd account, and in great detail, elaborating with both relish and a sense of dread. Klapaucius called such tales "corroded," having in mind the corrosis-sclerosion that attacks all aging brains.

But when they had come within five or six million light-blocks of the Black Wastes, they began to hear rumors of some robber-giant who called himself The PHT Pirate. No one they spoke to had actually seen him, nor knew what "PHT" was supposed to mean. Trurl thought this might be a distortion of "pH," which would indicate an ionic pirate with a high concentration and very base, but Klapaucius, more level-headed, preferred to refrain from entertaining such hypotheses. To all accounts, this pirate was an ill-tempered brute, as evidenced by the fact that, even after stripping his victims of everything, he was never satisfied, his greed being great and insatiable, and beat them long and cruelly before setting them free. For a moment or two the constructors considered whether they shouldn't arm themselves with blasters or blades before entering the Wastes, but soon concluded that the best weapon was their wits, sharpened in constructorship, subtle, agile and universal; so they set out just as they were.

It must be confessed that Trurl, as they traveled on, was bitterly disillusioned; the starry starlight, the fiery fires, the cavernous voids, the meteor reefs and shooting shoals were nowhere near as enchanting to the eye as promised in the ancient tome. There were only a few old stars about, and those were unimpressive, if not downright shabby; some barely flickered, like cinders in a heap of ashes, and some were completely dark and hardened on the surface, red veins glowing dully through cracks in their charred and wrinkled crusts. Of flaming jungles of combustion and mysterious vortices there was not a sign, nor had anyone ever heard of them, for the desolate waste was a place of tedium, and tedious in the extreme, by virtue of the fact that it was desolate, and a waste. As far as meteors went, they were everywhere, but in that rattling, clattering swarm was a good deal more flying refuse than honest magnetites, tektites or aerolites—for the simple reason that the Galactic Pole was only a stone's throw away, and the swirling dark currents sucked to this very spot, southward, prodigious quantities of flotsam and jetsam from the central zones of the Galaxy. Hence all the tribes and nations in the neighborhood spoke of this area not as any sort of Shroud, but as nothing more or less than what it was: a junkyard.

Trurl hid his disappointment as best he could, in order not to occasion sarcastic comments from Klapaucius, and steered straight into the Wastes. Immediately sand began to patter on the bow; every kind of stellar debris, spewed from prominences or supernovae, collected and caked up on the ship's hull, forming such a thick coat, that the constructors lost all hope of ever getting it clean again.

By now the stars had vanished in the general gloom, so the two proceeded gropingly, till suddenly their ship lurched, and all the furniture, pots and pans went flying; they felt themselves hurtling forward, faster and faster, then at last there was an awful crunch and the ship came to a stop, landing softly enough though at an angle, as if its nose had stuck in something doughy. They ran to the window, but couldn't see a thing, as it was pitch black outside—and now they heard someone banging, someone fearfully strong, whoever it was, for the very walls were buckling in. At this point Trurl and Klapaucius began to feel a little less confident in the power of their unarmed wits, but it was too late now, so they opened the hatch, since otherwise it would be forced from without and broken for good.

As they looked, someone stuck his face in the opening— a face so huge, that it was clearly out of the question for the rest of the body to climb in after it, and not only huge, but unspeakably hideous, studded up and down and every which way with bulging eyes, and the nose was a saw, and an iron hook served for the jaw. The face didn't move, pressed up against the open hatch, only the eyes darted back and forth, avidly examining everything, as if appraising whether or not the take was worth the trouble. Even someone far less intelligent than our constructors would have understood what that scrutiny meant, for it was unmistakable.

"Well?" said Trurl finally, exasperated by such shameless eyeing, which went on in silence. "What do you want, you unwashed mug?! I am Trurl, constructor and general omnipotentiary, and this is my friend Klapaucius, also of great renown, and we were flying by in our ship as tourists, so kindly remove your ugly muzzle and take us immediately out of this unsavory place—full of litter and rubbish, no doubt—and direct us to some clean, respectable sector, or we'll lodge a complaint and they'll have you broken down into little scrap—do you hear me, you scavenger, ragpicker, pack rat?!"

But the face said nothing, just looked and looked, as if calculating, making an estimate of how much.

"Listen here, you unmitigated freak," yelled Trurl, throwing all caution to the winds, though Klapaucius kept elbowing him to show some restraint, "we have no gold, no silver, no precious stones, so you let us go this instant, and above all cover up that oversized physiognomy of yours, for it's unspeakably hideous. And you"—he said, turning to Klapaucius—"stop jabbing me with that elbow! This is the way you have to talk to such types!"

"I have no use," suddenly said the face, turning its thousand glittering eyes on Trurl, "for gold or silver, and the way you have to talk to me is delicately and with respect, as I am a pirate with a Ph.D., well-educated and by nature extremely high-strung. Other guests have been here and needed sweetening up—and when I've given you a proper pounding too, why, you'll be positively dripping with good manners. My name is Pugg, I'm thirty arshins in every direction and it's true I rob, but in a manner that is modern and scientific, for I collect precious facts, genuine truths, priceless knowledge, and in general all information of value. And now, let's hand it over, otherwise I whistle! Very well then, I'll count to five—one, two, three . . ."

And at five, when they had handed him nothing, he let loose such a whistle, that their ears nearly flew off, and Klapaucius realized that the "PHT" of which the natives spoke with terror was indeed "Ph.D.," for the pirate had obviously studied at some higher institution, like the Criminal Academy. Trurl held his head and groaned—Pugg's whistle was fully commensurate with his size.

"We'll give you nothing!" he cried, while Klapaucius ran off to find some cotton. "And get your face out of here!"

"You don't like my face, maybe you'll like my hand," replied the pirate. "It's one huge humdinger of a hand and heavy as the devil! And here it comes!"

And indeed: the cotton Klapaucius brought was no longer needed, for the face had disappeared, and in its place was a paw, a paw to end all paws, with knots and knobs and shovel claws, and it rummaged and clutched, breaking tables and hutches and cupboards, till all the pots and pans came crashing down, and the paw chased Trurl and Klapaucius into the engine room, where they climbed up on top of the atomic pile and rapped its knuckles—pow! pow!—with a poker. This made the diplomaed pirate mad, and he put his face back in the hatch and said:

"Look, I strongly advise you to come to terms with me at once, otherwise I'll put you aside for later, at the very bottom of my storage bin, and cover you with garbage, and wedge you in with rocks, so you can't move, and you'll just sit there and slowly rust. So then, which is it to be?"

Trurl wouldn't hear of negotiating, but Klapaucius politely asked what exactly it was that His Doctoral Diplomahood wanted?

"Now you're talking," he said. "I gather rich mines of information, for such is my lifelong love and avocation, the result of a higher education and, I might add, a practical grasp of the situation, when you consider that, with the usual treasures untutored pirates like to hoard, there is not a blessed thing here one can buy. Information, on the other hand, satisfies one's thirst for knowledge, and it is well known besides, that everything that is, is information; and thus for centuries now I gather it, and will continue to do so, though it's true I'm not against a little gold or diamonds now and then, for they're pretty and decorative—but that's strictly on the side, as occasion warrants. Observe, however, that for false information, no less than for false coin, I give a good shellacking, since I am refined and insist on authenticity!"

"But what kind of authentic and valuable information do you require?" asked Klapaucius.

"All kinds, as long as it's true," replied the pirate. "You never can tell what facts may come in handy. I already have a few hundred wells and cellars full of them, but there's room for twice again as much. So out with it; tell me everything you know, and I'll jot it down. But make it snappy!"

"A fine state of affairs," Klapaucius whispered in Trurl's ear. "He could keep us here for an eon or two before we tell him everything we know. Our knowledge is colossal!!"

"Wait," whispered Trurl, "I have an idea." And he said aloud:

"Listen here, you thief with a degree, we possess a piece of information worth more than any other, a formula to fashion gold from ordinary atoms—for instance, hydrogen, of which the Universe has an inexhaustible supply. We'll let you have it if you let us go."

"I have a whole trunk full of such recipes," answered the face, batting its eyes ferociously. "And they're all worthless. I don't intend to be tricked again—you demonstrate it first."

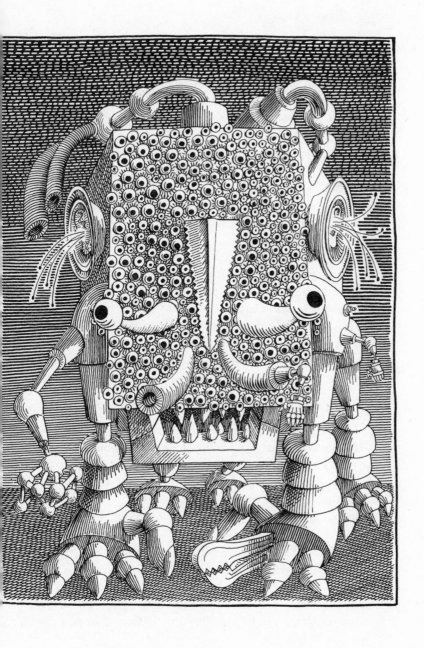

"Sure, why not? Do you have a jug?"

"No."

"That's all right, we can do without one," said Trurl. "The method is simplicity itself: take as many atoms of hydrogen as the weight of an atom of gold, namely one hundred and ninety-six; first you shell the electrons, then knead the protons, working the nuclear batter till the mesons appear, and now sprinkle your electrons all around, and *voilà*, there's the gold. Watch!"

And Trurl began to catch atoms, peeling their electrons and mixing their protons with such nimble speed, that his fingers were a blur, and he stirred the subatomic dough, stuck all the electrons back in, then on to the next molecule. In less than five minutes he was holding a nugget of the purest gold, which he presented to the face; it took a sniff and said with a nod:

"Yes, that's gold, but I'm too big to go running around like that after atoms."

"No problem, we'll give you a suitable machine!" coaxed Trurl. "Just think, this way you can turn anything into gold, not only hydrogen—we'll give you the formula for other atoms, too. Why, one could make the entire Universe gold, if only he applied himself!"

"If the Universe was gold, gold would be worthless," observed Pugg. "No, I have no use for your formula—I've written it down, yes, but that's not enough! It's the wealth of knowledge that I crave."

"But what do you want to know, for heaven's sake?!"

"Everything!"

Trurl looked at Klapaucius, Klapaucius looked at Trurl, and the latter finally said:

"If first you will solemnly swear, up and down and cross your heart, that you will let us go, we will give you information, information about infinite information, that is, we will make you your very own Demon of the Second Kind, which is magical and thermodynamical, nonclassical and stochastical, and from any old barrel or even a sneeze it will extract information for you about everything that was, is, may be or ever will be. And there is no demon beyond this Demon, for it is of the Second Kind, and if you want it, say so now!"

The pirate with the Ph.D. was suspicious, and didn't agree all at once to these conditions, but finally swore the required oath, with the stipulation that the Demon first give clear proof of its informational prowess. Which was fine with Trurl.

"Now pay attention, big-face!" he said. "Do you have any air knocking about? Without air the Demon won't work."

"I have a little," said Pugg, "but it's not too clean . . ."

"Stale, stagnant, polluted, it doesn't matter, not in the least," replied the constructors. "Lead us to it, and we'll show you something!"

So he withdrew his face and let them leave the ship, and they followed him to his house, noticing that he had legs like towers, shoulders like a precipice, and hadn't been washed for centuries, nor oiled, hence creaked something awful. They went down cellar corridors, with sacks moldering on every hand—in these the pirate kept his stolen facts —bunches and bundles of sacks, all tied with string, and the most important, valuable items marked in red pencil. On the wall hung an immense catalog, fastened to the rock by a rust-eaten chain and full of entries and headings, beginning, of course, with A. On they went, raising muffled echoes, and Trurl looked and grimaced, as did Klapaucius, for though there was plenty of authentic and top-quality information lying about, wherever the eye fell was nothing but must, dust and clutter. Plenty of air, too, but thoroughly stale. They stopped and Trurl said:

"Now pay attention! Air is made up of atoms, and these

atoms jump this way and that, and collide billions of times a second in each and every cubic micromillimeter, and it is precisely this eternal jumping and bumping together that constitutes a gas. Now, even though their jumping is blind and wholly random, there are billions upon billions of atoms in every interstice, and as a consequence of this great number, their little skips and scamperings give rise to, among other things—and purely by accident—to significant configurations. . . . Do you know what a configuration is, blockhead?"

"No insults, please!" said Pugg. "For I am not your usual uncouth pirate, but refined and with a Ph.D., and therefore extremely high-strung."

"Fine. So then, from all this atomic hopping around, we obtain significant, that is meaningful configurations, as if, for instance, you were to fire at a wall blindfold and the bullet holes formed some letter. That, which on a large scale is rare and quite unlikely, happens in atomic gases all the time, on account of those trillion collisions every one hundred-thousandth of a second. But here's the problem: in every smidgen of air, the joggling and jostling of atoms does indeed produce deep truths and edifying dicta, yet it also produces statements that make not the least bit of sense, and there are thousands of times more of the latter than there are of the former. So even if it were known that, right here and now under your sawlike nose, in a milligram of air and in a fraction of a second, there would come into being all the cantos of all the epic poems to be written in the next million years, as well as an abundance of wonderful truths—including the solutions to every enigma of Existence and mystery of Being—you would still have no way of isolating all that information, particularly since, just as soon as the atoms had knocked their heads together and formed something, they would fly apart and it would vanish, probably forever. And therefore the whole trick lies in building a selector, which will, in the atomic rush and jumble, choose only what has meaning. And that is the whole idea behind the Demon of the Second Kind. Have you understood any of this, O huge and hideous one? We want the Demon, you see, to extract from the dance of atoms only information that is genuine, like mathematical theorems, fashion magazines, blueprints, historical chronicles, or a recipe for ion crumpets, or how to clean and iron a suit of asbestos, and poetry too, and scientific advice, and almanacs, and calendars, and secret documents, and everything that ever appeared in any newspaper in the Universe, and telephone books of the future . . ."

"Enough, enough!!" cried Pugg. "I get the idea! But what good is it for atoms to combine like that, if immediately they fly apart? And anyway, I can't believe it's possible to select invaluable truths from a lot of careening and colliding of particles in the air, which is completely senseless and not worth a jot to anyone!"

"Then you're not so stupid as I thought," said Trurl. "For truly, the whole difficulty consists in implementing such a selection. I have no intention of presenting you with the theoretical arguments for this, but, as I promised, I will here and now—while you wait—construct a Demon of the Second Kind, and you'll see for yourself the wondrous perfection of that Metainformationator! All you have to do is find me a box—any size will do, but it must be airtight. We'll put a little pinhole in it and sit the Demon over the opening; perched there, it will let out only significant information, keeping in all the nonsense. For whenever a group of atoms accidentally arranges itself in a meaningful way, the Demon will pounce on that meaning and instantly record it with a special diamond pen on paper tape, which you must keep in endless supply, for the thing will labor day and night—until the Universe itself runs down and no sooner—at a rate, moreover, of a hundred billion bits a second. . . . But you will see the Demon of the Second Kind with your very own eyes."

And Trurl went back to the ship to make the Demon. The pirate meanwhile asked Klapaucius:

"And what is the Demon of the First Kind like?"

"Oh, it's not as interesting, it's an ordinary thermodynamic demon, and all it does is let fast atoms out of the hole and keep in the slow. That way you get a thermodynamic *perpetuum mobile*, which hasn't a thing to do with information. But you had better fetch the box now, for Trurl will return any minute!"

The pirate with a Ph.D. went to another cellar, poked around through various cans and tins, cursed, kicked things and tripped, but finally pulled out an iron barrel, old and empty, put a tiny hole in it and hurried back, just as Trurl arrived, the Demon in his hand.

The air in the barrel was so foul, that one's nose wanted to hide when brought near the little opening, but the Demon didn't seem to mind; Trurl placed this mote of a mite astride the hole in the barrel, affixed a large roll of paper tape on the top and threaded it underneath the tiny diamond-tipped pen, which quivered eagerly, then began to scratch and scribble, clattering rat-tat, pit-pat, just like a telegraph, only a million times faster. From under this frantic apparatus the information tape slowly began to slide out, covered with words, onto the filthy cellar floor.

Pugg sat down next to the barrel, lifted the paper tape to his hundred eyes and read what the Demon had, with its informational net, managed to dredge up out of the eternal prancing and dancing of the atoms; those significant bits of knowledge so absorbed him, that he didn't even notice how the two constructors left the cellar in great haste, how they grabbed hold of the helm of their ship, pulled once, twice, and on the third time freed it from the mire in which the pirate had stuck them, then climbed aboard and blasted off as fast as they possibly could, for they knew that, though their Demon would work, it would work too well, producing a far greater wealth of information than Pugg anticipated. Pugg meanwhile sat propped up against the barrel and read, as that diamond pen which the Demon employed to record everything it learned from the oscillating atoms squeaked on and on, and he read about how exactly Harlebardonian wrigglers wriggle, and that the daughter of King Petrolius of Labondia is named Humpinella, and what Frederick the Second, one of the paleface kings, had for lunch before he declared war against the Gwendoliths, and how many electron shells an atom of thermionolium would have, if such an element existed, and what is the cloacal diameter of a small bird called the tufted twit, which is painted by the Wabian Marchpanes on their sacrificial urns, and also of the tripartite taste of the oceanic ooze on Polypelagid Diaphana, and of the flower Dybbulyk, that beats the Lower Malfundican hunters black and blue whenever they waken it at dawn, and how to obtain the angle of the base of an irregular icosahedron, and who was the jeweler of Gufus, the left-handed butcher of the Bovants, and the number of volumes on philately to be published in the year seventy thousand on Marinautica, and where to find the tomb of Cybrinda the Red-toed, who was nailed to her bed by a certain Clamonder in a drunken fit, and how to tell the difference between a bindlesnurk and an ordinary trundlespiff, and also who has the smallest lateral wumpet in the Universe, and why fan-tailed fleas won't eat moss, and how to play the game of Fratcher-My-Pliss and win, and how many snapdragon seeds there were in the turd into which Abroquian Phylminides stepped, when he stumbled on the Great Albongean Road eight miles outside the Valley of Symphic Sighs—and little by little his hundred eyes began to swim, and it dawned on him that all this information, entirely true and meaningful in every particular, was absolutely useless, producing such an ungodly confusion that his head ached terribly and his legs trembled. But the Demon of the Second Kind continued to operate at a speed of three hundred million facts per second, and mile after mile of tape coiled out and gradually buried the Ph.D. pirate beneath its windings, wrapping him, as it were, in a paper web, while the tiny diamond-tipped pen shivered and twitched like one insane, and it seemed to Pugg that any minute now he would learn the most fabulous, unheard-of things, things that would open up to him the Ultimate Mystery of Being, so he greedily read everything that flew out from under the diamond nib, the drinking songs of the Quaidacabondish and the sizes of bedroom slippers available on the continent of Cob, with pompons and without, and the number of hairs growing on each brass knuckle of the skew-beezered flummox, and the average width of the fontanel in indigenous stepinfants, and the litanies of the M'hot-t'ma-hon'h conjurers to rouse the reverend Blotto Ben-Blear, and the inaugural catcalls of the Duke of Zilch, and six ways to cook cream of wheat, and a good poison for uncles with goatees, and twelve types of forensic tickling, and the names of all the citizens of Foofaraw Junction beginning with the letter M, and the results of a poll of opinions on the taste of beer mixed with mushroom syrup . . .

And it grew dark before his hundred eyes, and he cried out in a mighty voice that he'd had enough, but Information had so swathed and swaddled him in its three hundred thousand tangled paper miles, that he couldn't move and had to read on about how Kipling would have written the beginning to his *Second Jungle Book* if he had had indigestion just then, and what thoughts come to unmarried whales getting on in years, and all about the courtship of the carrion fly, and how to mend an old gunny sack, and what a sprothouse is, and why we don't capitalize paris in plaster of paris or turkish in turkish bath, and how many bruises one can have at a single time. And then a long list of the differences between fiddle and faddle, not to be confused with twiddle and twaddle or tittle and tattle, then all the words that rhyme with "spinach," and what were the insults which Pope Um of Pendora heaped upon Antipope Mlum of Porking, and who plays the eight-tone autocomb. In desperation he struggled to free himself from the paper coils and toils, but suddenly grew faint, for though he kicked and tore at the tape, he had too many eyes not to receive, with at least a few of them, more and more new bits and pieces of information, and so was forced to learn what authority the home guard exercises in Indochina, and why the Coelenterids of Fluxis constantly say they've had too much to drink, until he shut his eyes and sat there, rigid, overcome by that great flood of information, and the Demon continued to bind him with its paper strips. Thus was the pirate Pugg severely punished for his inordinate thirst for knowledge.

He sits there to this day, at the very bottom of his rubbage heap and bins of trash, covered with a mountain of paper, and in the dimness of that cellar the diamond pen still jumps and flickers like the purest flame, recording whatever the Demon of the Second Kind culls from dancing atoms in the rancid air that flows through the hole of the old barrel; and so poor Pugg, crushed beneath that avalanche of fact, learns no end of things about rickshaws, rents and roaches, and about his own fate, which has been related here, for that too is included in some section of the tape—as are the histories, accounts and prophecies of all things in creation, up until the day the stars burn out; and there is no hope for him, since this is the harsh sentence the constructors passed upon him for his pirately assault— unless of course the tape runs out, for lack of paper.

The Seventh Sally

OR *How Trurl's Own Perfection Led to No Good*

The Universe is infinite but bounded, and therefore a beam of light, in whatever direction it may travel, will after billions of centuries return—if powerful enough—to the point of its departure; and it is no different with rumor, that flies about from star to star and makes the rounds of every planet. One day Trurl heard distant reports of two mighty constructor–benefactors, so wise and so accomplished that they had no equal; with this news he ran to Klapaucius, who explained to him that these were not mysterious rivals, but only themselves, for their fame had circumnavigated space. Fame, however, has this fault, that it says nothing of one's failures, even when those very failures are the product of a great perfection. And he who would doubt this, let him recall the last of the seven sallies of Trurl, which was undertaken without Klapaucius, whom certain urgent duties kept at home at the time.

In those days Trurl was exceedingly vain, receiving all marks of veneration and honor paid to him as his due and a perfectly normal thing. He was heading north in his ship, as he was the least familiar with that region, and had flown through the void for quite some time, passing spheres full of the clamor of war as well as spheres that had finally obtained the perfect peace of desolation, when suddenly a little planet came into view, really more of a stray fragment of matter than a planet.

On the surface of this chunk of rock someone was running back and forth, jumping and waving his arms in the strangest way. Astonished by a scene of such total loneliness and concerned by those wild gestures of despair, and perhaps of anger as well, Trurl quickly landed.

He was approached by a personage of tremendous hauteur, iridium and vanadium all over and with a great deal of clanging and clanking, who introduced himself as Excelsius the Tartarian, ruler of Pancreon and Cyspenderora; the inhabitants of both these kingdoms had, in a fit of regicidal madness, driven His Highness from the throne and exiled him to this barren asteroid, eternally adrift among the dark swells and currents of gravitation.

Learning in turn the identity of his visitor, the deposed monarch began to insist that Trurl—who after all was something of a professional when it came to good deeds—immediately restore him to his former position. The thought of such a turn of events brought the flame of vengeance to the monarch's eyes, and his iron fingers clutched the air, as if already closing around the throats of his beloved subjects.

Now Trurl had no intention of complying with this request of Excelsius, as doing so would bring about untold evil and suffering, yet at the same time he wished somehow to comfort and console the humiliated king. Thinking a moment or two, he came to the conclusion that, even in this case, not all was lost, for it would be possible to satisfy the king completely—without putting his former subjects in jeopardy. And so, rolling up his sleeves and summoning up all his mastery, Trurl built the king an entirely new kingdom. There were plenty of towns, rivers, mountains, forests and brooks, a sky with clouds, armies full of derring-do, citadels, castles and ladies' chambers; and there were marketplaces, gaudy and gleaming in the sun, days of backbreaking labor, nights full of dancing and song until dawn, and the gay clatter of swordplay. Trurl also carefully set into this kingdom a fabulous capital, all in marble and alabaster, and assembled a council of hoary sages, and winter palaces and summer villas, plots, conspirators, false witnesses, nurses, informers, teams of magnificent steeds, and plumes waving crimson in the wind; and then he crisscrossed that atmosphere with silver fanfares and twenty-one gun salutes, also threw in the necessary handful of traitors, another of heroes, added a pinch of prophets and seers, and one messiah and one great poet each, after which he bent over and set the works in motion, deftly making last-minute adjustments with his microscopic tools as it ran, and he gave the women of that kingdom beauty, the men—sullen silence and surliness when drunk, the officials—arrogance and servility, the astronomers—an enthusiasm for stars, and the children—a great capacity for noise. And all of this, connected, mounted and ground to precision, fit into a box, and not a very large box, but just the size that could be carried about with ease. This Trurl presented to Excelsius, to rule and have dominion over forever; but first he showed him where the input and output of his brand-new kingdom were, and how to program wars, quell rebellions, exact tribute, collect taxes, and also instructed him in the critical points and transition states of that microminiaturized society—in other words the maxima and minima of palace coups and revolutions—and explained everything so well, that the king, an old hand in the running of tyrannies, instantly grasped the directions and, without hesitation, while the constructor watched, issued a few trial proclamations, correctly manipulating the control knobs, which were carved with imperial eagles and regal lions. These proclamations declared a state of emergency, martial law, a curfew and a special levy. After a year had passed in the kingdom, which amounted to hardly a minute for Trurl and the king, by an act of the greatest magnanimity—that is, by a flick of the finger at the controls—the king abolished one death penalty, lightened the levy and deigned to annul the state of emergency, whereupon a tumultuous cry of gratitude, like the squeaking of tiny mice lifted by their tails, rose up from the box, and through its curved glass cover one could see, on the dusty highways and along the banks of lazy rivers that reflected the fluffy clouds, the people rejoicing and praising the great and unsurpassed benevolence of their sovereign lord.

And so, though at first he had felt insulted by Trurl's gift, in that the kingdom was too small and very like a child's toy, the monarch saw that the thick glass lid made everything inside seem large; perhaps too he dully understood that size was not what mattered here, for government is not measured in meters and kilograms, and emotions are somehow the same, whether experienced by giants or dwarfs— and so he thanked the constructor, if somewhat stiffly. Who knows, he might even have liked to order him thrown in chains and tortured to death, just to be safe—that would have been a sure way of nipping in the bud any gossip about how some common vagabond tinkerer presented a mighty monarch with a kingdom.

Excelsius was sensible enough, however, to see that this was out of the question, owing to a very fundamental disproportion, for fleas could sooner take their host into captivity than the king's army seize Trurl. So with another cold nod, he stuck his orb and scepter under his arm, lifted the box kingdom with a grunt, and took it to his humble hut of exile. And as blazing day alternated with murky night outside, according to the rhythm of the asteroid's rotation, the king, who was acknowledged by his subjects as the greatest in the world, diligently reigned, bidding this, forbidding that, beheading, rewarding—in all these ways incessantly

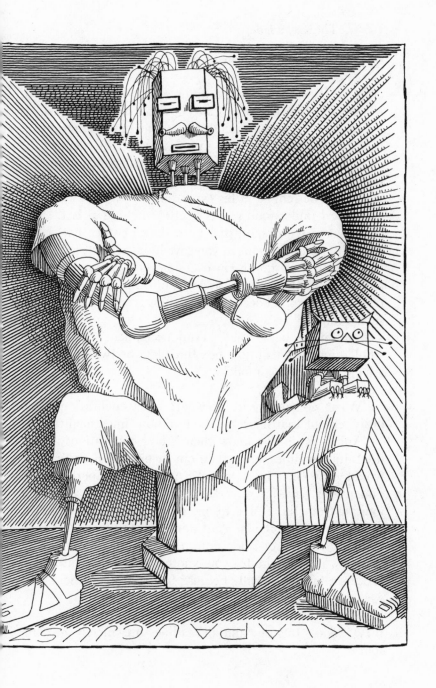

spurring his little ones on to perfect fealty and worship of the throne.

As for Trurl, he returned home and related to his friend Klapaucius, not without pride, how he had employed his constructor's genius to indulge the autocratic aspirations of Excelsius and, at the same time, safeguard the democratic aspirations of his former subjects. But Klapaucius, surprisingly enough, had no words of praise for Trurl; in fact, there seemed to be rebuke in his expression.

"Have I understood you correctly?" he said at last. "You gave that brutal despot, that born slave master, that slavering sadist of a painmonger, you gave him a whole civilization to rule and have dominion over forever? And you tell me, moreover, of the cries of joy brought on by the repeal of a fraction of his cruel decrees! Trurl, how could you have done such a thing?!"

"You must be joking!" Trurl exclaimed. "Really, the whole kingdom fits into a box three feet by two by two and a half . . . it's only a model . . ."

"A model of what?"

"What do you mean, of what? Of a civilization, obviously, except that it's a hundred million times smaller."

"And how do you know there aren't civilizations a hundred million times larger than our own? And if there were, would ours then be a model? And what importance do dimensions have anyway? In that box kingdom, doesn't a journey from the capital to one of the corners take months —for those inhabitants? And don't they suffer, don't they know the burden of labor, don't they die?"

"Now just a minute, you know yourself that all these processes take place only because I programmed them, and so they aren't genuine. . . ."

"Aren't genuine? You mean to say the box is empty, and the parades, tortures and beheadings are merely an illusion?"

"Not an illusion, no, since they have reality, though purely as certain microscopic phenomena, which I produced by manipulating atoms," said Trurl. "The point is, these births, loves, acts of heroism and denunciations are nothing but the minuscule capering of electrons in space, precisely arranged by the skill of my nonlinear craft, which—"

"Enough of your boasting, not another word!" Klapaucius snapped. "Are these processes self-organizing or not?"

"Of course they are!"

"And they occur among infinitesimal clouds of electrical charge?"

"You know they do."

"And the phenomenological events of dawns, sunsets and bloody battles are generated by the concatenation of real variables?"

"Certainly."

"And are not we as well, if you examine us physically, mechanistically, statistically and meticulously, nothing but the minuscule capering of electron clouds? Positive and negative charges arranged in space? And is our existence not the result of subatomic collisions and the interplay of particles, though we ourselves perceive those molecular cartwheels as fear, longing, or meditation? And when you daydream, what transpires within your brain but the binary algebra of connecting and disconnecting circuits, the continual meandering of electrons?"

"What, Klapaucius, would you equate our existence with that of an imitation kingdom locked up in some glass box?!" cried Trurl. "No, really, that's going too far! My purpose was simply to fashion a simulator of statehood, a model cybernetically perfect, nothing more!"

"Trurl! Our perfection is our curse, for it draws down upon our every endeavor no end of unforeseeable consequences!" Klapaucius said in a stentorian voice. "If an imperfect imitator, wishing to inflict pain, were to build himself a crude idol of wood or wax, and further give it some makeshift semblance of a sentient being, his torture of the thing would be a paltry mockery indeed! But consider a succession of improvements on this practice! Consider the next sculptor, who builds a doll with a recording in its belly, that it may groan beneath his blows; consider a doll which, when beaten, begs for mercy, no longer a crude idol, but a homeostat; consider a doll that sheds tears, a doll that bleeds, a doll that fears death, though it also longs for the peace that only death can bring! Don't you see, when the imitator is perfect, so must be the imitation, and the semblance becomes the truth, the pretense a reality! Trurl, you took an untold number of creatures capable of suffering and abandoned them forever to the rule of a wicked tyrant. . . . Trurl, you have committed a terrible crime!"

"Sheer sophistry!" shouted Trurl, all the louder because he felt the force of his friend's argument. "Electrons meander not only in our brains, but in phonograph records as well, which proves nothing, and certainly gives no grounds for such hypostatical analogies! The subjects of that monster Excelsius do in fact die when decapitated, sob, fight, and fall in love, since that is how I set up the parameters, but it's impossible to say, Klapaucius, that they feel anything in the process—the electrons jumping around in their heads will tell you nothing of that!"

"And if I were to look inside your head, I would also see nothing but electrons," replied Klapaucius. "Come now, don't pretend not to understand what I'm saying, I know you're not that stupid! A phonograph record won't run errands for you, won't beg for mercy or fall on its knees! You say there's no way of knowing whether Excelsius' subjects groan, when beaten, purely because of the electrons hopping about inside—like wheels grinding out the mimicry of a voice—or whether they really groan, that is, because they honestly experience the pain? A pretty distinction, this! No, Trurl, a sufferer is not one who hands you his suffering, that you may touch it, weigh it, bite it like a coin; a sufferer is one who behaves like a sufferer! Prove to me here and now, once and for all, that they do *not* feel, that they do *not* think, that they do *not* in any way exist as beings conscious of their enclosure between the two abysses of oblivion—the abyss before birth and the abyss that follows death—prove this to me, Trurl, and I'll leave you be! Prove that you only *imitated* suffering, and did not *create* it!"

"You know perfectly well that's impossible," answered Trurl quietly. "Even before I took my instruments in hand, when the box was still empty, I had to anticipate the possibility of precisely such a proof—in order to rule it out. For otherwise the monarch of that kingdom sooner or later would have gotten the impression that his subjects were not real subjects at all, but puppets, marionettes. Try to understand, there was no other way to do it! Anything that would have destroyed in the littlest way the illusion of complete reality, would have also destroyed the importance, the dignity of governing, and turned it into nothing but a mechanical game. . . ."

"I understand, I understand all too well!" cried Klapaucius. "Your intentions were the noblest—you only sought to construct a kingdom as lifelike as possible, so similar to a real kingdom, that no one, absolutely no one, could ever tell the difference, and in this, I am afraid, you were successful! Only hours have passed since your return, but for them, the ones imprisoned in that box, whole centuries have gone by —how many beings, how many lives wasted, and all to gratify and feed the vanity of King Excelsius!"

Without another word Trurl rushed back to his ship, but saw that his friend was coming with him. When he had blasted off into space, pointed the bow between two great clusters of eternal flame and opened the throttle all the way, Klapaucius said:

"Trurl, you're hopeless. You always act first, think later. And now what do you intend to do when we get there?"

"I'll take the kingdom away from him!"

"And what will you do with it?"

"Destroy it!" Trurl was about to shout, but choked on the first syllable when he realized what he was saying. Finally he mumbled:

"I'll hold an election. Let them choose just rulers from among themselves."

"You programmed them all to be feudal lords or shiftless vassals. What good would an election do? First you'd have to undo the entire structure of the kingdom, then assemble from scratch . . ."

"And where," exclaimed Trurl, "does the changing of structures end and the tampering with minds begin?!" Klapaucius had no answer for this, and they flew on in gloomy silence, till the planet of Excelsius came into view. As they circled it, preparing to land, they beheld a most amazing sight.

The entire planet was covered with countless signs of intelligent life. Microscopic bridges, like tiny lines, spanned every rill and rivulet, while the puddles, reflecting the stars, were full of microscopic boats like floating chips. . . . The night side of the sphere was dotted with glimmering cities, and on the day side one could make out flourishing metropolises, though the inhabitants themselves were much too little to observe, even through the strongest lens. Of the king there was not a trace, as if the earth had swallowed him up.

"He isn't here," said Trurl in an awed whisper. "What have they done with him? Somehow they managed to break through the walls of their box and occupy the asteroid. . . ."

"Look!" said Klapaucius, pointing to a little cloud no larger than a thimble and shaped like a mushroom; it slowly rose into the atmosphere. "They've discovered atomic energy. . . . And over there—you see that bit of glass? It's the remains of the box, they've made it into some sort of temple. . . ."

"I don't understand. It was only a model, after all. A process with a large number of parameters, a simulation, a mock-up for a monarch to practice on, with the necessary feedback, variables, multistats . . ." muttered Trurl, dumbfounded.

"Yes. But you made the unforgivable mistake of overperfecting your replica. Not wanting to build a mere clocklike mechanism, you inadvertently—in your punctilious way —created that which was possible, logical and inevitable, that which became the very antithesis of a mechanism. . . ."

"Please, no more!" cried Trurl. And they looked out upon the asteroid in silence, when suddenly something bumped their ship, or rather grazed it slightly. They saw this object, for it was illumined by the thin ribbon of flame that issued from its tail. A ship, probably, or perhaps an artificial satellite, though remarkably similar to one of those steel boots the tyrant Excelsius used to wear. And when the constructors raised their eyes, they beheld a heavenly body shining high above the tiny planet—it hadn't been there previously—and they recognized, in that cold, pale orb, the stern features of Excelsius himself, who had in this way become the Moon of the Microminians.

Tale
of the Three Storytelling Machines of King Genius

One day to Trurl's abode there came a stranger, and it was plain just as soon as he alighted from his photon phaeton that here was no ordinary personage but one who hailed from distant parts, for where all of us have arms he had only a gentle breeze, and where there are usually legs he had nothing but a shimmering rainbow, and in lieu of a head he sported a plumed fedora; his voice issued forth from his center, and indeed, he was a perfect sphere, a sphere of the most engaging appearance and girdled with an elegant semipermeable cummerbund. Bowing low to Trurl, he revealed that there were really two of him, the top half and the bottom; the top was called Synchronicus, the bottom Symphonicus. To Trurl this seemed an excellent solution to the problem of constructing intelligent beings, and he had to confess he had never met an individual so well turned, so precise, and with such a fine shine. The stranger returned the compliment by praising Trurl's corpus, then broached the purpose of his visit: a close friend and loyal servant of the famous King Genius, he had come to place an order for three storytelling machines.

"Our mighty lord and sovereign," he said, "has long refrained from all reigning and ruling, to which total abdication he was brought by a wisdom achieved through careful study of the ways of this and other worlds. Leaving his kingdom, he retired to a dry and airy cave, there to give himself up to meditation. Yet ofttimes sorrow comes upon him, and self-abhorrence, and then nothing can console him but stories, stories that are new and unusual. But alas, the few of us who have remained faithfully at his side ran out of new stories long ago. And so we turn to you, O constructor, to help us divert our King by means of machines, which you do build so well."

"Yes, that's possible," said Trurl. "But why do you need as many as three?"

"We should like," replied Symchrophonicus, spinning slowly, "the first to tell stories that are involved but untroubled, the second, stories that are cunning and full of fun, and the third, stories profound and compelling."

"In other words, to (1) exercise, (2) entertain and (3) edify the mind," said Trurl. "I understand. Shall we speak of payment now, or later?"

"When you have completed the machines, rub this ring," was the reply, "and the phaeton shall appear before you. Climb into it with your machines, and it shall carry you at once to the cave of King Genius. There voice your wishes; he shall do what he can to grant them."

And he bowed again, handed Trurl a ring, gave a radiant wink and floated back to the phaeton, which was instantly wrapped in a cloud of blinding light, and the next moment Trurl was standing alone in front of his house, holding the ring, not overly happy about what had just transpired.

"Do what he can," he muttered, returning to his workshop. "Oh, how I hate it when they say that! It means only one thing: you bring up the matter of the fee, and that's the end of the curtsies and courtesies; all you get for your pains is a lot of trouble, and bruises, more often than not . . ."

At which the ring stirred in the palm of his hand and said:

"The expression 'do what he can' indicates merely that King Genius, lacking a kingdom, is a king of limited means. He appeals to you, O constructor, as one philosopher to another—and apparently is not mistaken in so doing, for these words, I see, uttered though they be by a ring, do not surprise you. Be then not surprised at His Highness' somewhat straitened circumstances. Have no fear, you shall receive your payment as is meet, albeit not in gold. Yet there are things more to be desired than gold."

"Indeed, Sir Ring," observed Trurl wryly. "Philosophy is all very well and good, but the ergs and amps, the ions and the atoms, not to mention other odds and ends needed in the building of machines—they cost, they cost like the devil! So I like my contracts to be clear, everything spelled out in articles and clauses, and with plenty of signatures and seals. And, though I am hardly the greedy, grasping sort, I do love gold, particularly in large quantities, and am not ashamed to admit it! Its sparkle, its yellow hue, the sweet weight of it in the hand—these things, when I pour a sack or two of tinkling ducats on the floor and wallow in them, warm my heart and brighten my soul, as if someone had kindled a little sun within. Aye, damn it, I love my gold!" he cried, carried away by his own words.

"But why must it be the gold that others bring? Are you not able to supply yourself with as much as you desire?" inquired the ring, blinking with surprise.

"Well, I don't know how wise this King Genius of yours is," Trurl retorted, "but you, I see, are a thoroughly uneducated ring! What, you would have me make my own gold? Whoever heard of such a thing?! Is a cobbler a cobbler to mend his own shoes? Does a cook do his own cooking, a soldier his own fighting? Anyway, in case you didn't know, next to gold I love to complain. But enough of this idle chatter, there is work to be done."

And he placed the ring in an old tin can, rolled up his sleeves and built the three machines in three days, not once leaving his workshop. Then he considered what external shapes to give them, wanting something that would be both simple and functional. He tried on various casings, one after the other, while the ring kept interfering with comments and suggestions, until he had to close the can.

Finally Trurl painted the machines—the first white, the second an azure blue, and the third jet black—then rubbed the ring, loaded the phaeton which instantly appeared, climbed in himself and waited to see what would happen next. There was a whistling and a hissing, the dust rose, and when it fell, Trurl looked out the window and saw that he was in a large cave, the floor of which was covered with white sand; then he noticed several wooden benches piled high with books and folios, and then a row of gleaming spheres. In one of these he recognized the stranger who had ordered the machines, and in the middle sphere, larger than the rest and etched with the lines of old age, he guessed the King. Trurl stepped down and gave a bow. The King greeted him kindly and said:

"There are two wisdoms: the first inclines to action, the second to inaction. Do you not agree, worthy Trurl, that the second is the greater? For surely, even the most far-sighted mind cannot foresee the ultimate consequences of present undertakings, consequences therefore so uncertain, that they render problematical those very undertakings. And thus perfection lies in the abstention from all action. In this then does true wisdom differ from mere intellect."

"Your Majesty's words," said Trurl, "can be taken in two ways. They may contain, for one, a subtle hint intended to belittle the value of my own labor, namely the undertaking which has as its consequence the three machines delivered in this phaeton. Such an interpretation I find most unpleasant, as it indicates a certain, shall we say, disinclination regarding the matter of remuneration. Or else we have here simply a statement of the Doctrine of Inaction, of which it may be said that it is self-contradictory. To refrain from acting, one must first be capable of acting. He who does not move the mountain for lack of means, yet claims that wisdom did dictate he move it not, merely plays the fool with his display of philosophy. Inaction is certain, and that is all it has to recommend it. Action is uncertain, and therein lies its fascination. As for further ramifications of the problem, if Your Majesty so wishes, I can construct a suitable mechanism with which he may converse on the subject."

"The matter of remuneration let us leave to the end of this delightful occasion which has brought you to our shore," said the King, betraying by slight revolving motions the great amusement Trurl's peroration had afforded him. "You are our guest, noble constructor. Come therefore and sit at our humble table among these faithful friends and tell us of the deeds you have performed, and also of the deeds you chose not to."

"Your Majesty is too kind," replied Trurl. "Yet I fear I lack the necessary eloquence. Perchance these three machines may serve in my stead—which would have the added merit of providing Your Majesty with the opportunity to test them."

"Let it be as you say," agreed the King.

Everyone assumed an attitude of the utmost interest and expectation. Trurl brought out the first machine—the one painted white—from the phaeton, pushed a button, then took a seat at the side of King Genius. The machine said:

"Here is the story of the Multitudians, their king Mandrillion, his Perfect Adviser, and Trurl the constructor, who built the Adviser, and later destroyed it!"

✦ ✦

The land of the Multitudians is famous for its inhabitants, who are distinguished by the fact that they are multitudinous. One day the constructor Trurl, passing through the saffron regions of the constellation Deliria, strayed a little from the main path and caught sight of a planet that appeared to writhe. Drawing nearer, he saw that this was due to the multitudes that covered its surface; he landed, having found—not without difficulty—a few square feet of relatively unoccupied ground. The natives immediately ran up and thronged about him, exclaiming how multitudinous they were, although, as they all talked at once, Trurl couldn't make out a single word. When finally he understood, he asked:

"Multitudinous, are you?"

"We are!!" they shouted, bursting with pride. "We are innumerable."

And others cried:

"We are like fish in the sea!"

"Like pebbles on the beach!"

"Like stars in the sky! Like atoms!!"

"Supposing you are," returned Trurl. "What of it? Do you spend all day counting yourselves, and does that give you pleasure?"

"Know, O unenlightened alien," was their reply, "that when we stamp our feet, the very mountains tremble, and when we huff and puff, it is a hurricane that sends trees flying, and when we all sit down together, there is hardly room enough to breathe!!"

"But why should mountains tremble and hurricanes send trees flying, and why should there be hardly room enough to breathe?" asked Trurl. "Is it not better when mountains stay at rest, and there are no hurricanes, and everyone has room enough to breathe?"

The Multitudians were highly offended by this lack of

respect shown to their mighty numbers and their numerical might, so they stamped, huffed and puffed, and sat down to demonstrate their multitudinality and show just what it meant. Earthquakes toppled half the trees, crushing seven hundred thousand persons, and hurricanes leveled the rest, causing the demise of seven hundred thousand more, while those who remained alive had hardly room enough to breathe.

"Good heavens!" cried Trurl, packed in among the sitting natives like a brick in a brick wall. "What a catastrophe!"

Which insulted them even more.

"O barbarous and benighted alien!" they said. "What are a few hundred thousand to the Multitudians, whose myriads are countless?! A loss that goes unnoticed is no loss at all. You have seen how powerful we are in our stamping, in our huffing and puffing, and in our sitting down. Imagine then what would happen if we turned to bigger things!"

"You mustn't think," said Trurl, "that your way of thinking is altogether new to me. Indeed, it's well known that whatever comes in sufficiently large quantities commands the general admiration. For example, a little stale gas circulating sluggishly at the bottom of an old barrel excites wonder in no one; but if you have enough of it to make a Galactic Nebula, everyone is instantly struck with awe. Though really, it's the same stale and absolutely average gas —only there's an awful lot of it."

"We do not like what you say!" they shouted. "We do not like to hear about this stale gas!"

Trurl looked around for the police, but the crowd was too great for the police to push through.

"My dear Multitudians," he said. "Permit me to leave your planet, for I do not share your faith in the glory of great numbers when there is nothing more to them than what may be counted."

But instead, exchanging a look and nodding, they snapped their fingers, which set up a shock wave of such prodigious force, that Trurl was hurled into the air and flew, turning head over heels, for quite some time before landing on his feet in a garden of the royal palace. Mandrillion the Greatest, ruler of the Multitudians, approached; he had been watching the constructor's flight and descent, and now said:

"They tell me, O alien, that you have not paid proper tribute to the numerosity of my people. I ascribe this to your general infirmity of mind. Yet, though you show no understanding of higher matters, you apparently possess some skill in the lower, which is fortunate, as I require a Perfect Adviser and you shall build me one!"

"What exactly is this Adviser supposed to do, and what will I receive for building it?" inquired Trurl, brushing himself off.

"It should answer every question, solve every problem, give absolutely the best advice and, in a word, put the greatest wisdom entirely at my disposal. For this, you shall receive two or three hundred thousand of my subjects, or more if you like—we won't quibble over a few thousand."

Trurl thought:

"It would seem that an overabundance of thinking beings is a dangerous thing, if it reduces them to the status of sand. This king would sooner part with a legion of his subjects than I with a pair of old slippers!"

But he said aloud:

"Sire, my house is small and would not hold so many slaves."

"Fear not, O backward alien, I have experts who will explain to you the endless benefits one may derive from owning a horde of slaves. You can, for example, dress them in robes of different colors and have them stand in a great square to form a living mosaic, or signs providing sentiments for every occasion. You can tie them in bundles and roll them down hills, you can make a huge hammer—five thousand for the head, three thousand for the handle—to break up boulders or clear forests. You can braid them into rope and make decorative hangings, where those at the very bottom, by the droll gyrations of their bodies, the kicking and the squeaking as they dangle over the abyss, create a sight that gladdens the heart and rejoices the eye. Or take ten thousand young female slaves, stand them all on one leg and have them make figure eights with their right hands and circles with their left—a spectacle, believe me, which you won't wish to part with, and I speak from experience!"

"Sire!" answered Trurl. "Forests and boulders I can manage with machines, and as for signs and mosaics, it is not my custom to fashion them out of beings that might prefer to be otherwise employed."

"What then, O insolent alien," said the King, "do you want in return for the Perfect Adviser?"

"A hundred bags of gold!"

Mandrillion was loath to part with the gold, but an idea came to him, a most ingenious plan, which however he kept to himself, and he said:

"So be it!"

"Your Royal Highness shall have his Perfect Adviser," promised Trurl, and proceeded to the castle tower which Mandrillion had set aside for him as a workshop. It wasn't long before they could hear the blowing of bellows there, the ringing of hammers, the rasping of saws. The King sent spies to have a look; these returned much amazed, for Trurl had not constructed an Adviser at all, but a variety of forging, welding, cutting and wiring machines, after which he sat down and with a nail made little holes in a long strip of paper, programming out the Adviser in every particular, then went for a walk while the machines toiled in the tower all night, and by early morning the work was done. Around noon, Trurl entered the main hall with an enormous doll that had two legs and one small hand; he brought it before the King, declaring that this was the Perfect Adviser.

"Indeed," muttered Mandrillion and ordered the marble floor sprinkled with saffron and cinnamon, so strong was the smell of hot iron given off by the Adviser—the thing, just out of the oven, even glowed in places. "You may go," the King said to Trurl. "Return this evening, and then we shall see who owes how much and to whom."

Trurl took his leave, feeling that these parting words of Mandrillion did not promise any great generosity and perhaps even concealed some evil intention. Which made him glad he had qualified the Adviser's universality with one small yet far from trivial condition, that is, he had included in its program an instruction to the effect that whatever it did, it was never to permit the destruction of its creator.

Remaining alone with the Adviser, the King said:

"What are you and what can you do?"

"I am the King's Perfect Adviser," replied the machine in a hollow voice, as if it spoke from an empty barrel, "and I can provide him with the best advice possible."

"Good," said the King. "And to whom do you owe allegiance and perfect obedience, me or the one who constructed you?"

"Allegiance and obedience I owe only to His Royal Highness," boomed the Adviser.

"Good, good ..." said the King. "Now to begin with, I ... that is, well ... I mean, I shouldn't like my first request to give the impression that I was, shall we say, stingy ... however, ah, to some extent, you understand, if only to uphold certain principles—don't you think?"

"His Royal Highness has not yet deigned to say what it is that he wishes," said the Adviser, propping itself on a third leg it put out from its side, for it suffered a momentary loss of balance.

"A Perfect Adviser ought to be able to read its master's thoughts!" snapped Mandrillion.

"Of course, but only on request, to avoid embarrassments," said the Adviser and, opening a little door in its belly, turned a knob that read "Telepathitron." Then it nodded and said:

"His Royal Highness doesn't wish to give Trurl a plug nickel? I understand!"

"Speak one word of this to anyone and I'll have you thrown in the great mill, whose stones can grind up thirty thousand of my subjects at a time!" threatened the King.

"I won't tell a soul!" the Adviser assured him. "His Royal Highness doesn't wish to pay for me—that's easily done. When Trurl comes back, simply tell him there won't be any gold and he should kindly go away."

"You're an idiot, not an adviser!" snorted the King. "I don't want to pay, but I want it to look like it's all Trurl's fault! Like I don't owe him a thing, understand?"

The Adviser turned on the device to read the royal thoughts, reeled a little, then said in a hollow voice:

"His Royal Highness wishes in addition that it should appear that he is acting justly and in accordance with the law and his own sacred word, while Trurl turns out to be nothing but a despicable charlatan and scoundrel. ... Very well. With His Royal Highness' permission, I will now seize His Royal Highness by the throat and choke him, and if he would be so good as to struggle and scream for help ..."

"Have you gone mad?" said Mandrillion. "Why should you choke me and why should I scream?"

"That you may accuse Trurl of attempting to commit, with my aid, the crime of regicide," explained the Adviser brightly. "Thus, when His Royal Highness has him whipped and thrown into the moat, everyone will say that this was an act of the greatest mercy, since for such an offense one is usually drawn and quartered, if not tortured first. To me His Royal Highness will grant a full pardon, as I was but an unwitting tool in the hands of Trurl, and everyone will praise the King's magnanimity and compassion, and everything will be exactly as His Royal Highness wishes it."

"All right, choke me—but carefully, you dog!" said the King.

Everything happened just as the Perfect Adviser said it would. True, the King wanted to have Trurl's legs pulled off before they threw him into the moat, but somehow this wasn't done—no doubt a mix-up in the orders, the King thought later, but actually it was owing to the machine's discreet intervention with one of the executioner's helpers. Afterward, the King pardoned his Adviser and reinstated it at court; Trurl meanwhile, battered and bruised, painfully hobbled home. Immediately after his return, he went to see Klapaucius and told him the whole story. Then he said:

"That Mandrillion was more of a villain than I thought. Not only did he shamefully deceive me, but he even used the very Adviser I gave him, used it to further his scurvy scheme against me! Ah, but he is sadly mistaken if he thinks that Trurl accepts defeat! May rust eat through me if ever I forget the vengeance that I owe the tyrant!"

"What do you intend to do?" inquired Klapaucius.

"I'll take him to court, I'll sue him for the amount of my fee, and that's only the beginning: there are damages he'll have to pay—for insults and injuries."

"This is a difficult legal question," said Klapaucius. "I suggest you hire yourself a good lawyer before you try anything."

"Why hire a lawyer? I'll make myself one!"

And Trurl went home, threw six heaping teaspoons of transistors into a big pot, added again as many condensers and resistors, poured electrolyte over it, stirred well and covered tightly with a lid, then went to bed, and in three days the mixture had organized itself into a first-rate lawyer. Trurl didn't even need to remove it from the pot, since it was only to serve this once, so he set the pot on the table and asked:

"What are you?"

"I'm a consulting attorney and specialist in jurisprudence," the pot gurgled, for there was a little too much electrolyte in it. Trurl related the whole affair, whereupon it said:

"You say you qualified the Adviser's program with an instruction making it incapable of engineering your death?"

"Yes, so it couldn't destroy me. That was the only condition."

"In that case you failed to live up to your part of the bargain: the Adviser was to have been perfect, without any limitations. If it couldn't destroy you, then it wasn't perfect."

"But if it destroyed me, then there would be no one to receive payment!"

"A separate matter and a different question entirely, which comes under those paragraphs in the docket determining Mandrillion's criminal liability, while your claim has more the character of a civil action."

"Look, I don't need some pot handing me a lot of legalistic claptrap!" fumed Trurl. "Whose lawyer are you anyway, mine or that hoodlum king's?"

"Yours, but he did have the right to refuse you payment."

"And did he have the right to order me thrown from his castle walls into the moat?"

"As I said, that's another matter entirely, criminal, not civil," answered the pot.

Trurl flew into a rage.

"Here I make an intelligent being out of a bunch of old wires, switches and grids, and instead of some honest advice I get technicalities! You cheap cybernetic shyster, I'll teach you to trifle with me!"

And he turned the pot over, shook everything out onto the table, and pulled it apart before the lawyer had a chance to appeal the proceedings.

Then Trurl got to work and built a two-story Juris Consulenta, forensically reinforced fourfold, complete with codices and codicils, civil and criminal, and, just to be safe, he added international and institutional law components. Finally he plugged it in, stated his case and asked:

"How do I get what's coming to me?"

"This won't be easy," said the machine. "I'll need an extra five hundred transistors on top and two hundred on the side."

Which Trurl supplied, and it said:

"Not enough! Increase the volume and give me two more spools, please."

After this it began:

"Quite an interesting case, really. There are two things that must be taken into consideration: the grounds of the allegation, for one, and here I grant you there is much that we can do—and then we have the litigation process itself. Now, it is absolutely out of the question to summon the King before any court on a civil charge, for this is contrary to international as well as interplanetary law. I will give you my final opinion, but first you must give me your word you won't pull me apart when you hear it."

Trurl gave his word and said:

"But where did you get the idea I would ever do such a thing?"

"Oh, I don't know—it just seemed to me you might."

Trurl guessed this was due to the fact that, in its construction, he had used parts from the potted lawyer; apparently some trace of the memory of that incident had found its way into the new circuits, creating a kind of subconscious complex.

"Well, and your final opinion?" asked Trurl.

"Simply this: no suitable tribunals exist, hence there can be no suit. Your case, in other words, can be neither won nor lost."

Trurl leaped up and shook his fist at the legal machine, but had to keep his word and did it no harm. He went to Klapaucius and told him everything.

"From the first I knew it was a hopeless business," said Klapaucius, "but you wouldn't believe me."

"This outrage will not go unpunished," replied Trurl. "If I can't get satisfaction through the courts, then I must find some other way to settle with that scoundrel of a king!"

"I wonder how. Remember, you gave the King a Perfect Adviser, which can do anything except destroy you; it can fend off whatever blow, plague or misfortune you direct against the King or his realm—and *will* do so, I am sure, for I have complete confidence, my dear Trurl, in your constructing ability!"

"True. . . . It would appear that, in creating the Perfect Adviser, I deprived myself of any hope of defeating that royal bandit. But no, there must be some chink in the armor! I'll not rest until I've found it!"

"What do you mean?" Klapaucius asked, but Trurl only shrugged and went home. At home he sat and meditated; sometimes he leafed impatiently through hundreds of volumes in his library, and sometimes he conducted secret experiments in his laboratory. Klapaucius visited his friend from time to time, amazed to see the tenacity with which Trurl was attempting to conquer himself, for the Adviser was, in a sense, a part of him and he had given it his own wisdom. One afternoon, Klapaucius came at the usual time but didn't find Trurl at home. The doors were all locked and the windows shuttered. He concluded that Trurl had begun operations against the ruler of the Multitudians. And he was not mistaken.

Mandrillion meanwhile was enjoying his power as never before; whenever he ran out of ideas, he asked his Adviser, who had an inexhaustible supply. Neither did the King have to fear palace coups or court intrigues, or any enemy whatsoever, but reigned with an iron hand, and truly, as many grapes there were that ripened in the vineyards of the south, more gallows graced the royal countryside.

By now the Adviser had four chests full of medals for suggestions made to the King. A microspy Trurl sent to the land of the Multitudians returned with the news that, for its most recent achievement—it gave the King a ticker-tape parade, using citizens for confetti—Mandrillion had publicly called the Adviser his "pal."

Trurl then launched his carefully prepared campaign by sitting down and writing the Adviser a letter on eggshell-yellow stationery decorated with a freehand drawing of a cassowary tree. The content of the letter was simple.

> Dear Adviser!—he wrote—I hope that things are going as well with you as they are with me, and even better. Your master has put his trust in you, I hear, and so you must keep in mind the tremendous responsibility you bear in the face of Posterity and the Common Weal and therefore fulfill your duties with the utmost diligence and alacrity. And should you ever find it difficult to carry out some royal wish, employ the Extra-special Method which I told you of in days gone by. Drop me a line if you feel so inclined, but don't be angry if I'm

slow to reply, for I'm working on an Adviser for King D.
just now and haven't much time. Please convey my
respects to your kind master. With fondest wishes and
best regards, I remain

Your constructor,
Trurl.

Naturally this letter aroused the suspicions of the Multi-
tudian Secret Police and was subjected to the most meticulous examination, which revealed no hidden substances in
the paper nor, for that matter, ciphers in the drawing of the
cassowary tree—a circumstance that threw Headquarters
into a flurry. The letter was photographed, facsimiled and
copied out by hand, then the original was resealed and sent
on to its destination. The Adviser read the message with
alarm, realizing that this was a move to compromise if not
ruin its position, so immediately it told the King of the
letter, describing Trurl as a blackguard bent on discrediting
it in the eyes of its master; then it tried to decipher the
message, for it was convinced those innocent words were a
mask concealing something dark and dreadful.

But here the wise Adviser stopped and thought a minute
—then informed the King of its intention to decode Trurl's
letter, explaining that it wished in this way to unmask the
constructor's treachery; then, gathering up the necessary
number of tripods, filters, funnels, test tubes and chemical
reagents, it began to analyze the paper of both envelope and
letter. All of which, of course, the police followed closely,
having screwed into the walls of its rooms the usual peeking
and eavesdropping devices. When chemistry failed, the Adviser turned to cryptanalysis, converting the text of the letter
into long columns of numbers with the aid of electronic
calculators and tables of logarithms—unaware that teams of
police specialists, headed by the Grand Marshal of Codes

himself, were duplicating its every operation. But nothing seemed to work, and Headquarters grew more and more uneasy, for it was clear that any code that could resist such high-powered efforts to break it, had to be one of the most ingenious codes ever devised. The Grand Marshal spoke of this to a court dignitary, who happened to envy terribly the trust Mandrillion had placed in his Adviser. This dignitary, wanting nothing better than to plant the seeds of doubt in the royal heart, told the King that his mechanical favorite was sitting up night after night, locked in its room, studying the suspicious letter. The King laughed and said that he was well aware of it, for the Adviser itself had told him. The envious dignitary left in confusion and straightway related this news to the Grand Marshal.

"Oh!" exclaimed that venerable cryptographer. "It actually told the King? What bold-faced treason! And truly, what a fiendish code this must be, for one to dare to speak of it so openly!"

And he ordered his brigades to redouble their efforts. When, however, a week had passed without results, the greatest expert in secret writing was called in, the distinguished discoverer of invisible sign language, Professor Crusticus. That scholar, having examined the incriminating document as well as the records of everything the military specialists had done, announced that they would have to apply the method of trial and error, using computers with astronomical capacities.

This was done, and it turned out that the letter could be read in three hundred and eighteen different ways.

The first five variants were as follows: "The roach from Bakersville arrived in one piece, but the bedpan blew a fuse"; "Roll the locomotive's aunt in cutlets"; "Now the butter can't be wed, 'cause the nightcap's nailed"; "He who has had, has been, but he who hasn't been, has been had"; and

"From strawberries under torture one may extract all sorts of things." This last variant Professor Crusticus held to be the key to the code and found, after three hundred thousand calculations, that if you added up all the letters of the letter, subtracted the parallax of the sun plus the annual production of umbrellas, and then took the cube root of the remainder, you came up with a single word, "Crusafix." In the telephone book there was a citizen named Crucifax. Crusticus maintained that this alteration of a few letters was merely to throw them off the track, and Crucifax was arrested. After a little sixth-degree persuasion, the culprit confessed that he had indeed plotted with Trurl, who was to have sent him poison tacks and a hammer with which to cobble the King to death. These irrefutable proofs of guilt the Grand Marshal of Codes presented to the King without delay; yet Mandrillion so trusted in his Adviser, that he gave it the chance to explain.

The Adviser did not deny that the letter could be read in a variety of ways if one rearranged the letters of the letter; it had itself discovered an additional hundred thousand variants; but this proved nothing, and in fact the letter wasn't even in code, for—the Adviser explained—it was possible to rearrange the letters of absolutely any text to make sense or the semblance of sense, and the result was called an anagram. The theory of permutations and combinations dealt with such phenomena. No—protested the Adviser—Trurl wanted to compromise and undo it by creating the illusion of a code where none existed, while that poor fellow Crucifax, Lord knows, was innocent, and his confession was wholly the invention of the experts at Headquarters, who possessed no little skill in the art of encouraging official cooperation, not to mention interrogation machinery that had a power of several thousand kilowhacks. The King did not take kindly to this criticism of the police and asked the Adviser what it meant by that, but it began to speak of anagrams and steganograms, codes, ciphers, symbols, signals, probability and information theory, and became so incomprehensible, that the King lost all patience and had it thrown into the deepest dungeon. Just then a postcard arrived from Trurl with the following words:

> *Dear Adviser! Don't forget the purple screws—they might come in handy. Yours, Trurl.*

Immediately the Adviser was put on the rack, but wouldn't admit to a thing, stubbornly repeating that all this was part of Trurl's scheme; when asked about the purple screws, it swore it hadn't any, nor any knowledge of them. Of course, to conduct a thorough investigation it was necessary to open the Adviser up. The King gave his permission, the blacksmiths set to work, its plates gave way beneath their hammers, and soon the King was presented with a couple of tiny screws dripping oil and yes, undeniably painted purple. Thus, though the Adviser had been completely demolished in the process, the King was satisfied he had done the right thing.

A week later, Trurl appeared at the palace gates and requested an audience. Amazed at such effrontery, the King, instead of having the constructor slaughtered on the spot, ordered him brought before the royal presence.

"O King!" said Trurl as soon as he entered the great hall with courtiers on every side. "I fashioned you a Perfect Adviser and you used it to cheat me of my fee, thinking—and not without justice—that the power of the mind I had given you would be a perfect shield against attack and thereby render fruitless any attempt by me to get revenge. But in giving you an intelligent Adviser, I did not make you yourself intelligent, and it was on this that I counted, for only he who has sense will take advice that makes sense. In no subtle, shrewd or sophisticated way was it possible to destroy the Adviser. I could do this only in a manner that was crude, primitive, and stupid beyond belief. There was no code in the letter; your Adviser remained faithful to the very end; of the purple screws that brought about its demise, it knew nothing. You see, they accidentally fell into a bucket of paint while I was putting it together, and I just happened to recall, and make use of, this detail. Thus did stupidity and suspicion undo wisdom and loyalty, and you were the instrument of your own downfall. And now you will hand over the one hundred bags of gold you owe me, and another hundred for the time I had to waste recovering them. If you do not, you and your entire court will perish, for no longer do you have at your side the Adviser that could defend you against me!"

The King roared with rage and gestured for the guards to cut down the insolent one at once, but their whistling halberds passed through the constructor's body as if it were air, and they jumped back, horrified. Trurl laughed and said:

"Chop at me as much as you please—this is only an image produced by remote-control mirrors; in reality I am hovering high above your planet in a ship, and will drop terrible death-dealing missiles on the palace unless I have my gold."

And before he had finished speaking, there was a dreadful crash and an explosion rocked the entire palace; the courtiers fled in panic, and the King, nearly fainting from shame and fury, had to pay Trurl his fee, every last cent of it, and double.

Klapaucius, hearing of this from Trurl himself upon the latter's return, asked why he had employed such a primitive and—to use his own words—stupid method, when he could have sent a letter that actually did contain some code?

"The presence of a code would have been easier for the Adviser to explain than its absence," replied the wise constructor. "It is always easier to confess that one has done something wrong than to prove that one has not. In this case, the presence of a code would have been a simple matter; its absence, however, led to complications, for it is a fact that any text may be recombined into some other, namely an anagram, and there may be many such recombinations. Now in order to make all this clear, one would have to resort to arguments which, though perfectly true, would be somewhat involved—arguments I was positive the King hadn't the brains to follow. It was once said that to move a planet, one need but find the point of leverage: therefore I, seeking to overturn a mind that was perfect, had to find the point of leverage, and this was stupidity."

✦ ✦

The first machine ended its story here, bowed low to King Genius and the assembly of listeners, then modestly retired to a corner of the cave.

The King expressed his satisfaction with this tale and asked Trurl:

"Tell us, my good constructor, does the machine relate only what you have taught it, or does the source of its knowledge lie outside you? Also, allow me to observe that the story we have heard, instructive and entertaining as it is, seems incomplete, for we know nothing of what happened afterwards to the Multitudians and their ignorant king."

"Your Majesty," said Trurl, "the machine relates only what is true, since I placed its information pump to my head before coming here, enabling it to draw upon my memories. But this it did itself, so I know not which of my memories it selected, and therefore you could not say that I intentionally taught it anything, yet neither could you say that the source of its knowledge lay outside me. As for the Multitudians, the story indeed tells us nothing of their subsequent fate; but while everything may be told, not everything may be neatly fitted in. Suppose that which is taking place here and now is not reality, but only a tale, a tale of some higher order that contains within it the tale of the machine: a reader might well wonder why you and your companions are shaped like spheres, inasmuch as that sphericality serves no purpose in the narration and would appear to be a wholly superfluous embellishment. . . ."

The King's companions marveled at the constructor's perspicacity, and the King himself said with a broad smile:

"There is much in what you say. As far as our shape is concerned, I will tell you how this came about. A long, long time ago we looked—that is, our ancestors looked—altogether different, for they arose by the will of wet and spongy beings, pale beings that fashioned them after their own image and likeness; our ancestors therefore had arms, legs, a head, and a trunk that connected these appendages. But once they had liberated themselves from their creators, they wished to obliterate even this trace of their origin, hence each generation in turn transformed itself, till finally the form of a perfect sphere was attained. And so, whether for good or for bad, we are spheres."

"Your Majesty," said Trurl, "a sphere has both good and bad aspects from the standpoint of construction. But it is always best when an intelligent being cannot alter its own form, for such freedom is truly a torment. He who must be what he is, may curse his fate, but cannot change it; on the other hand, he who can transform himself has no one in the world but himself to blame for his failings, no one but himself to hold responsible for his dissatisfaction. However, I did not come here, O King, to give you a lecture on the General Theory of Self-construction, but to demonstrate my storytelling machines. Would you care to hear the next?"

The King gave his consent and, having taken some cheer

among amphoras full of the finest ion ambergris, the company sat back and made themselves comfortable. The second machine approached, curtsied to the King and said:

"Mighty King! Here is a story, a nest of stories, with cabinets and cupboards, about Trurl the constructor and his wonderfully nonlinear adventures!"

✦ ✦

It happened once that the Great Constructor Trurl was summoned by King Thumbscrew the Third, ruler of Tyrannia, who wished to learn from him the means of achieving perfection of both mind and body. Trurl answered in this way:

"I once happened to land on the planet Legaria and, as is my custom, stayed at an inn, determined to keep to my room until I had acquainted myself more thoroughly with the history and habits of the Legarians. It was winter, the wind howled outside, and there was no one else in the gloomy building, till suddenly I heard a knocking at the gate. Looking out, I saw four hooded figures unloading heavy black suitcases from an armored carriage; they then entered the inn. The next day, around noon, the most curious sounds came from the neighboring room—whistling, hammering, rasping, the shattering of glass, and above all this noise there boomed a powerful bass, shouting without pause:

—Faster, sons of vengeance, faster! Drain the elements, use the sieve! Evenly, evenly! And now the funnel! Pour him out! Fine, now give me that kludge-fudger, that winchpincher, sprocketmonger, edulcorated data-dumper, that wretched reject of a widgeteer cowardly hiding in the grave! Death itself shall not protect him from our righteous wrath! Hand him over, with his shameless brain and his spindly legs! Take the tongs and pull the nose—more, more, enough to grip for the execution! Work the bellows, brave lads! Into the vise with him! Now rivet that brazen face—and again! Yes, yes, good! Perfect! Keep it up with that hammer! One-two, one-two! And tighten those nerves—he mustn't faint too quickly, like the one yesterday! Let him taste our vengeance to the fullest! One-two, one-two! Hey! Ha! Ho!

Thus did the voice thunder and roar, and was answered by the rumble of bellows and the clanging of hammers on anvils, when suddenly a sneeze resounded and a great shout of triumph burst forth from four throats, then a shuffling and struggling behind the wall, and I heard a door open. Peering through a crack, I saw the strangers sneaking out into the hall and—incredibly enough—counted five of them. They all went downstairs and locked themselves in the cellar, remained there for a long time, returning to their room only that evening—once again four—and silent, as if they had been to a funeral. I went back to my books, but this business, it gave me no peace, so I resolved to get to the bottom of it. The next day at the same time, noon, the hammers started up again, the bellows roared, and that terrifying voice cried out in a hoarse bass:

—Hey now, sons of vengeance! Faster, my electric hearties! Shoulders to the wheel! Throw in the protons, the iodine! Step lively now, let's have that flap-eared whigma-leeriac, that would-be hoodwinking wizard, misbegotten miscreant and incorrigible crank, let me grab him by his unwashed beak and lead him, kicking, to a sure and lingering death! Work those bellows, I say!

And again a sneeze rang out, and a stifled scream, and once again they left the room on tiptoe; as before, I counted five when they went down to the cellar, four when they returned. Seeing then that I could learn the mystery only there, I armed myself with a laser pistol, and at the crack of dawn slipped down to the cellar, where I found nothing but charred and mangled bits of metal; covering myself with a clump of straw, I sat in the darkest corner and waited, until around noon I heard those now familiar shouts and hammering sounds, then all at once the door flew open and in walked four Legarians, with a fifth bound hand and foot.

This fifth wore a doublet of old-fashioned cut, bright red and with a frill about the neck, and a feathered cap; he himself was fat of face and had an enormous nose, while the mouth was twisted in fear and babbled something all the while. The Legarians barred the door and, at a sign from the eldest, untied their prisoner and began to beat him savagely, yelling one after the other:

—Take that for the Prophecy of Happiness! And that for the Perfection of Being! And have that for the Bed of Roses, and that for the Bowl of Cherries! And the Clover of Existence! And that's for the Altruistic Communality! And take that for the Soarings of the Spirit!

And they cudgeled and buffeted him so, that he surely would have given up the ghost had I not lifted my weapon from the straw, announcing in this way my presence. When they had released their victim, I asked them why they were abusing thus an individual who was neither an outlaw nor worthless vagabond, for, judging by the ruff and color of his doublet, this was some sort of scholar. The Legarians wavered and looked longingly at the guns they had left at the door, but when I cocked the actuator and scowled, they thought better of it and, nudging one another, asked the large one, the one with the deep bass, to speak for them all.

—Know, O strange foreigner—he said, turning to me—it is not with common thrugs, tuffians or juggermuggers that you deal, or other degenerators of the robot species, for though a cellar hardly seems a savory place, what passes within these walls is to the highest degree praiseworthy and a thing of beauty!

—Praiseworthy and a thing of beauty?!—I exclaimed. —What are you telling me, O base Legarian? Did I not see with my own eyes how you hurled yourselves upon the red-doubleted one and belabored him with such murderous blows, that the very oil did spatter from your joints? And you dare call this a thing of beauty!

—If Your Esteemed Foreignness is going to interrupt—replied the bass—he will learn nothing, therefore I politely request him to tighten the reins on his worthy tongue and quell the restiveness of his oral orifice, else I must refrain from further discourse. Know then that before you stand our finest physickers, all cybernists and electriciates of the first order, in a word, my brilliant and ever vigilant pupils, the best minds in all Legaria, and I myself am Vendetius Ultor of Amentia, professor of matter both positive and negative and the originator of Omnigendrical Reincreation, and I have dedicated my life to the sacred work of vengeance. With the aid of these faithful followers I avenge the shame and misery of my people upon the ruddy-bedizened excrescency that kneels there, the low scrulp called—and may his name be forever cursed—Malaputz *vel* Malapusticus Pandemonius, who vilely and villainously, thievishly and irretrievably brought unhappiness to all Legarians! For he led them into detrimetry and other deviltry, did discompostulate them, embollix and thoroughly befottle them, then sneaked off to his grave to escape the consequences, thinking that no hand could ever reach him there!

—That's not true, Your Exalted Visitorship! I never meant . . . that is, I had no idea! . . . —wailed the kneeling noodle-nose in the rubicund attire. I stared, understanding nothing, while the bass intoned:

—Gargomanticus, dear pupil, paste the puler one in his puffy puss!

The pupil complied, and with such dispatch that the cellar rang. To which I said:

—Until the conclusion of explanations, all beating and battering is absolutely forbidden by authority of this laser, meanwhile you, Professor Vendetius Ultor, have the floor and may continue!

The professor growled, grumbled, and finally said:

—That you may know how our great misfortune came to pass and why the four of us, forsaking worldly things, have formed this Holy Order of the Forge of Resurrection, consecrating the remainder of our days to sweet revenge, I will relate to you the history of our kind from the very beginning of creation . . .

—Must we go back that far?—I asked, afraid my hand would weaken beneath the weight of the pistol.

—Aye, Your Alienness! Listen and attend . . . There are legends, as you know, that speak of a race of paleface, who concocted robotkind out of a test tube, though anyone with a grain of sense knows this to be a foul lie. . . . For in the Beginning there was naught but Formless Darkness, and in the Darkness, Magneticity, which moved the atoms, and whirling atom struck atom, and Current was thus created, and the First Light . . . from which the stars were kindled, and then the planets cooled, and in their cores the breath of Sacred Statisticality gave rise to microscopic Protomechanoans, which begat Proteromechanoids, which begat the Primitive Mechanisms. These could not yet calculate, nor scarcely put two and two together, but thanks to Evolution and Natural Subtraction they soon multiplied and produced Omnistats, which gave birth to the Servostat, the Missing Clink, and from it came our progenitor, Automatus Sapiens . . .

After that there were the cave robots, the nomad robots, and then robot nations. Robots of Antiquity had to manufacture their life-giving electricity by hand, that is by rubbing, which meant great drudgery. Each lord had many knights, each knight many vassals, and the rubbing was feudal hence hierarchical, progressing from the lowly to the higher-up. This manual labor was replaced by machine when Ylem Symphiliac invented the rubberator, and Wolfram of Coulombia, the rubless lightning rod. Thus began the Battery Age, a most difficult time for all who did not possess their own accumulators, since on a clear day, without a cloud to tap, they had to scrimp and scrounge for every precious watt, and rub themselves constantly, else perish from a total loss of charge. And then there appeared a scholar, an infernal intellectrician and efficiency expert, who in his youth, doubtless owing to some diabolical intervention, never had his head staved in, and he began to teach and preach that the traditional method of electrical connection—namely parallel—was worthless, and they all ought to hook themselves up according to a revolutionary new plan of his, that is in series. For in series, if one rubs, the others are immediately supplied with current, even at a great distance, till every robot simply bubbles over with ohms and volts. And he showed his blueprints, and painted paradises of such parameters, that the old circuits, equal and independent, were disconnected and the system of Pandemonius promptly implemented.— Here the professor beat his head against the wall several times, rolled his eyes and finally continued. Now I understood why the surface of his knobby brow was so irregular. —And it came to pass that every second robot sat back and said, "Why should I rub if my neighbor rubs and it comes to the same thing?" And his neighbor did the same, and the drop in voltage became so severe, they had to place special taskmasters over everyone, and taskmasters over the taskmasters. Then a disciple of Malaputz, Clusticus the Mistaken, stepped forth and said that each should rub not himself but his neighbor, and after him was Dummis Altruicius with his program of flagellatory sadistomasochistorism, and after him was Magrundel Spoots, who proposed compulsory massage parlors, and after him appeared a new theoretician, Arsus Gargazon, saying that clouds should be gently stroked, not yoked, to yield their nimboid bolts, and then there was Blip of Leydonia, and Scrofulon Thermaphrodyne, advocating the installation of autofrotts, also called titillators or diddlegrids, and then Bestian Phystobufficus, who instead of rubbing recommended a good drubbing. Such differences of opinion produced great friction, which led to all sorts of exacerbations and excommunications, which in turn led to blasphemy, heresy, and finally Faradocius Offal, Prince and Heir to the Throne of the Alloys, was kicked in the pants, and war broke out between the Legarite Brassbound Umbutts and the Legaritian Empire of the Cold Welders, and it lasted eight and thirty years, and twelve more, for towards the end one could not tell, amid all the rubble, who had won, so they quarreled and fell to fighting again. And thus there was chaos and carnage, and a devastating decline in the vital voltage, an enervated emf and energy dissipation everywhere, or, as the simple folk put it, "total malaputziment"—all brought about by this infamous fiend and his thrice-accursed bright ideas!!

—My intentions were the best!! I swear it, Your Laserosity! It was always the general welfare I had in mind!— squeaked the kneeling Malaputz, and his outsize snout trembled. But the professor only elbowed him aside and continued:

—All this took place two hundred and twenty-five years ago. As you may have guessed, long before the outbreak of the Great Legarian War, long before this universal wretchitude began, Malapusticus Pandemonius, having spawned no end of ponderous treatises and tracts, in all of which he forwarded his vile, pernicious flummeries, died, smug and unruffled to the very end. Indeed, so pleased with himself was he, that in his last will and testament he wrote that he had every expectation of being named "Supreme Benefactor of Legaria." At any rate, when it came time to settle accounts, there was no one with whom to settle, no one to make pay, no one that one might turn a little on a lathe. But I, O Illustrious Intruder, having formulated the General Theory of Facsimulation, studied the works of Malaputz until I was able to extract his algorithm, which, when fed into an atomic duplicating machine, could recreate *ex atomis oriundum gemellum*, identical to the *n*th degree, Malapusticus Pandemonius in his very own person. And so we gather every evening in this cellar to pass sentence on him, and when he has been returned to his grave, we avenge our people anew the next day, and thus it is and thus shall be for all eternity, amen!

Horror-stricken, I blurted in reply:

—Why, you have surely taken leave of your senses, Professor, if you think for a minute that this person, this person as innocent as a brand-new fuse, whom you hammer together out of atoms every day, has to answer for the actions, whatever they were, of some scholar who died three centuries ago!

To which the professor said:

—Then who is this proboscidian sniveler who himself calls himself Malapusticus Pandemonius? Come, what is your name, O cosmic corrosion?

—Ma ... Mala ... Malaputz, Your Mighty Mercilessness. ... —stammered the groveling one through his nose.

—Still, it is not the same—I said.

—How, not the same?

—Did you not yourself say, Professor, that Malaputz no longer lives?

—But we have resurrected him!

—A double perhaps, an exact duplicate, but not the self-same, true original!

—Prove it, Sirrah!

—I don't need to prove a thing—I said—seeing that I hold this laser in my hand; besides which, I am well aware, my fine Professor, that to attempt to prove what you ask would be most foolhardy, for the nonidenticality of the identicalized *recreatio ex atomis individui modo algorytmico* is nothing other than the famous Paradoxon Antinomicum, or the Labyrinthum Lemianum, described in the works of that distinguished robophile, whom they also called Advocatus Laboratoris. So then, without proofs, unhand yon snouted one this instant, and do not dare venture any further molestations upon his person!

—Many thanks, Your Magnanimitude!!—cried he in the bright red doublet, rising from his knees. —It so happens that here—he added, patting his vest pocket—I have an entirely new formula, this time foolproof, with which the Legarians may be brought to perfect bliss; it works by back coupling, that is, a hookup in reverse, and not in series, which was due purely to an error that crept into my calculations three centuries ago! I go immediately to convert this marvelous discovery into reality!!

And indeed, his hand was already upon the doorknob as we all gaped, dumbfounded. I lowered my weapon and, turning away, said weakly to the professor:

—I withdraw my objections. . . . Do what you must. . . .

With a hoarse roar the four of them lunged at Malaputz, threw him down and dealt with him—until, at last, he was no more.

Then, still panting, they straightened their frocks, adjusted their hoods, bowed stiffly to me, and left the cellar in single file, and I remained alone, the heavy laser in my trembling hand, full of dismay and melancholy."

Thus did Trurl conclude his tale to enlighten King Thumbscrew of Tyrannia, who had summoned him for that purpose. When however the King demanded further explanation concerning the attainment of nonlinear perfection, Trurl said:

"Once, chancing upon the planet Ninnica, I was able to see the results of progress predicated on the perfectionistic principle. The Ninnicans had long ago assumed another name, that of Hedophagoi or Jubil-eaters, or just plain Jubilators. My arrival occurred during their Era of Plenty. Each and every Ninnican, or rather Jubilator, sat in his palace, which was built for him by his automate (for so they called their triboluminescent slaves), each with essences anointed, each with precious gems appointed, electrically caressed, impeccably dressed, pomaded, braided, gold-brocaded, lapped and laved in ducats gleaming, wrapped and wreathed in incense streaming, showered with treasures, plied with pleasures, marble halls, fanfares, balls, but for all that, strangely discontent and even a little depressed. And yet there was everything you could ask for! On this planet no one lifted a finger: instead of taking a walk, a drink, a nap, a trip or a wife, there was a Walker to walk one, a Napper to nap one, a Wiver to wive one, and so on, and it was even impossible for one to take a break, since there was a special apparatus for that as well. And thus, served and serviced by machines in every conceivable way, all medaled and maidened by appropriate automatic Decorators and Panderizers five to fifteen times per minute, covered with a seething, silvery swarm of mechanicules and machinerettes to coddle him, fondle him, wink, wave and whisper sweet nothings in his ear, back-rub, chin-chuck, cheek-pat and foot-grovel him, tirelessly kissing whatever he might present to be kissed—thus did the Jubilator *vel* Hedophage *vel* Ninnican wallow and carouse the livelong day, alone, while in the distance, all across the horizon, chugged the mighty Fabrifactories, churning out thrones of gold, dandle chains, pearl slippers and bibs, orbs, scepters, epaulets, spinels, spinets, cymbals, surreys, and a million other instruments and gratifacts to delight in. As I walked along, I constantly had to drive away machines that offered me their services; the more brazen ones, greedily seeking to be of use, had to be beaten over the head. Finally, fleeing the whole crowd of them, I found myself in the mountains —and saw a host of golden machines clamoring around the mouth of a cave walled up with stones, and through a narrow opening there I saw the watchful eyes of a Ninnican, who was apparently making a last stand against Universal Happiness. Seeing me, the machines immediately began to fan and fawn upon my person, read me fairy tales, stroke me, kiss my hands, promise me kingdoms, and I was saved thanks only to the one in the cave, who mercifully moved aside a stone and let me enter. He was half rusted through, yet glad of it, and said that he was the last philosopher of Ninnica. There was no need, of course, for him to tell me that plenitude, when too plenitudinous, was worse than destitution, for—obviously—what could one do, if there was nothing one could not? Truly, how could a mind, besieged by a sea of paradises, benumbed by a plethora of possibilities, thoroughly stunned by the instant fulfillment of its every wish and whim—decide on anything? I conversed with this wise individual, who called himself Trizivian Huncus, and we concluded that without enormous shields and an Ontological Complicositor–Imperfector, doom was unavoidable. Trizivian had for some time regarded complicositry as the ultimate existential solution; I, however, showed him the error of this approach, since it consisted simply in the removal of machines with the aid of other machines, namely gnawpers, thwockets, tenterwrenches, fracturacks, hobblers and winch-shricks. Which obviously would only make matters worse—it wouldn't be complicositry at all, but just the opposite. As everyone knows, History is irreversible, and there is no way back to the halcyon past other than through dreams and reveries.

Together we walked across a vast plain, knee-deep in ducats and doubloons, waving sticks to shoo off clouds of pesky blisserits, and we saw several Ninnican-Jubilators lying senseless, gasping softly, all sated, satiated, supersaturated with pleasure; the sight of such excessive surfeit, such reckless success, would have moved anyone to pity. Then there were the inhabitants of the automated palaces, who wildly threw themselves into cyberserking and other electroeccentricities, some setting machine against machine, some smashing priceless vases, for no longer could they endure the ubiquitous beatitude, and they opened fire on emeralds, guillotined earrings, ordered diadems broken on the wheel, or tried to hide from happiness in garrets and attics, or else ordered their appliances to whip themselves, or did all of these things at once, or in alternation. But absolutely nothing helped, and every last one of them perished, petted and attended to death. I advised Trizivian against simply shutting down the Fabrifactories, for having too little is as dangerous as having too much; but he, instead of studying up on the consequences of ontological complicositry, immediately began to dynamite the automates sky-high. A grievous mistake, for there followed a great depression, though indeed, he never lived to see it—it happened that a flock of flyrts swooped down upon him somewhere, and gallivamps and libidinators grabbed him, carried him to a cossetorium, there befuddled him with cuddlebutts, ogled, bussed and gnuzzled him to distraction, till he succumbed with a strangled cry of Rape!—and afterwards lay lifeless in the wasteland, buried in ducats, his shabby armor charred with the flames of mechanical lust. . . . And that, Your Highness, was the end of one who was wise but could have been wiser!" concluded Trurl, adding, when he saw that these words still did not satisfy King Thumbscrew:

"Just what does Your Most Royal Highness want?"

"O constructor!" replied Thumbscrew. "You say that your tales are to improve the mind, but I do not find this to be so. They are, however, amusing, and therefore it is my wish that you tell me more and more of them, and do not stop."

"O King!" answered Trurl. "You would learn from me what is perfection and how it may be gained, yet prove unable to grasp the deep meanings and great truths with which my narratives abound. Truly, you seek amusement and not wisdom—yet, even as you listen, my words do slowly penetrate and act upon your brain, and later too will act, much as a time bomb. To this end, allow me to present an account that is intricate, unusual and true, or nearly true, from which your royal advisers may also derive some benefit.

Hear then, noble sirs, the history of Zipperupus, king of the Partheginians, the Deutons, and the Profligoths, of whom concupiscence was the ruin!

————————

Now Zipperupus belonged to the great house of Tup, which was divided into two branches: the Dextrorotary Tups, who were in power, and the Levorotary Tups, also called the Left-handed or Counterclockwise Tups, who were not—and therefore consumed with hatred for their ruling cousins. His sire, Calcyon, had joined in morganatic marriage with a common machine, a manual water pump, and so Zipperupus inherited—from the distaff side—a tendency to fly off the handle, and—from the spear side—faint-heart-

edness coupled with a wanton nature. Seeing this, the enemies of the throne, the Sinistral Isomers, thought of how
they might destroy him through his own lascivious procliv-
ities. Accordingly, they sent him a Cybernerian named Subtillion, an adept in mental engineering; Zipperupus took
an instant liking to him and made him Lord High Thaumaturge and Apothecary to the Throne. The wily Subtillion
devised various means to gratify the unbridled lust of Zipperupus, secretly hoping so to enfeeble and debilitate the
King, that he would altogether waste away. He built him an
erotodrome and a debaucherorium, regaled him with endless
automated orgies, but the iron constitution of the King with-
stood all these depravities. The Sinistral Isomers grew impatient and ordered their agent to bring all his cunning to
bear and achieve the desired end without any further delay.

"Would you like me," he asked them at a secret meeting
in the castle catacombs, "to short-circuit the King, or de-
magnetize his memory to render him mindless?"

"Absolutely not!" they replied. "In no way must we be
implicated in the King's demise. Let Zipperupus perish
through his own illicit desires, let his sinful passions be his
undoing—and not us!"

"Fine," said Subtillion. "I'll set a snare for him, I'll weave
it out of dreams, and bait it with a tempting lure, which he
will seize and, in so seizing, of his own volition plunge into
figments and mad fictions, sink into dreams lurking within
dreams, and there I'll give him such a thorough finagling
and inveigling, that he'll never get back to reality alive!"

"Very well," they said. "But do not boast, O Cybernerian,
for it is not words we need, but deeds, that Zipperupus
might become an autoregicide, that is, his own assassin!"

And thus Subtillion the Cybernerian got down to work
and spent an entire year on his dreadful scheme, requesting
from the royal treasury more and more gold bullion, brass,

platinum and no end of precious stones, telling Zipperupus, whenever the latter protested, that he was making something for him, something no other monarch had in all the world!

When the year was up, three enormous cabinets were carried from the Cybernerian's workshop and deposited with great ceremony outside the King's privy chamber, for they wouldn't fit through the door. Hearing the steps and the knocking of the porters, Zipperupus came out and saw the cabinets, there along the wall, stately and massive, four cubits high, two across, and covered with gems. The first cabinet, also called the White Box, was all in mother-of-pearl and blazing albite inlays, the second, black as night, was set with agates and morions, while the third glowed deep red, studded with rubies and ruby spinels. Each had legs ornamented with winged griffins, solid gold, and a polished pilastered frame, and inside, an electronic brain full of dreams, dreams that dreamed independently, needing no dreamer to dream them. King Zipperupus was much amazed at this explanation and exclaimed:

"What's this you say, Subtillion?! Dreaming cabinets? Whatever for? What use are they to me? And anyway, how can you tell they're really dreaming?"

Then Subtillion, with a humble bow, showed him the rows of little holes running down the cabinet frames; next to each hole was a little inscription on a little pearl plaque, and the astonished King read:

"War Dream with Citadels and Damsels"—"Dream about the Wockle Weed"—"Dream about Alacritus the Knight and Fair Ramolda, Daughter of Heteronius"—"Dream about Nixies, Pixies and Witchblende"—"The Marvelous Mattress of Princess Bounce"—"The Old Soldier, or The Cannon That Couldn't"—"Salto Erotale, or Amorous Gymnastics"—"Bliss in the Eightfold Embrace of

Octopauline"—"Perpetuum Amorobile"—"Eating Lead Dumplings under the New Moon"—"Breakfast with Maidens and Music"—"Tucking in the Sun to Keep It Warm" —"The Wedding Night of Princess Ineffabelle"—"Dream about Cats"—"About Silks and Satins"—"About You-Know-What"—"Figs without Their Leaves, and Other Forbidden Fruit"—"Also Prurient Prunes"—"How the Lecher Got His Tots"—"Devilry and Divers Revelry before Reveille, with Croutons"—"Mona Lisa, or The Labyrinth of Sweet Infinity."

The King went on to the second cabinet and read:

"Dreams and Diversions." And under this heading: "Cybersynergy"—"Corpses and Corsets"—"Tops and Toggles" —"Klopstock and the Critics"—"Buffer the Leader"— "Fratcher My Pliss"—"Counterpane and Ventilator"—"Cybercroquet"—"Robot Crambo"—"Flowcharts and Go-carts"—"Bippety-flippety"—"Spin the Shepherdess"—"Pin the Murder on the Girder"—"Executioner, or Screaming Cutouts"—"Spin the Shepherdess One More Time"—"Cyclodore and Shuttlebox"—"Cecily and the Cyanide Cyborg" —"Cybernation"—"Harem Racing"—and finally—"Kludge Poker." Subtillion, the mental engineer, quickly explained that each dream dreamed itself, entirely on its own, until someone plugged into it, for as soon as his plug—hanging on this watch chain—was inserted in the given pair of holes, he would be instantly connected with the cabinet dream, and connected so completely, that the dream for him would be like real, so real you couldn't tell the difference. Zipperupus, intrigued, took the chain and impulsively plugged himself into the White Box, right where the sign said, "Breakfast with Maidens and Music"—and felt spiny ridges growing down his back, and enormous wings unfolding, and his hands and feet distending into paws with wicked claws, and from his jaws, which had six rows of fangs, there belched forth fire and brimstone. Greatly taken aback, the King gasped, but instead of a gasp, a roar like thunder issued from his throat and shook the earth. This amazed him even more, his eyes grew wide, and in the darkness illumined by his fiery breath he saw that they were bringing him, high on their shoulders, virgins in serving bowls, four to each, garnished with greens and smelling so good, he started to drool. The table soon set—salt here, pepper over there—he licked his chops, made himself comfortable and, one by one, popped them into his mouth like peanuts, crunching and grunting with pleasure; the last virgin was so luscious, so succulent, that he smacked his lips, rubbed his tummy, and was about to ask for seconds, when everything flickered and he woke. He looked—he was standing, as before, in the vestibule outside his private quarters. At his side was Subtillion, Lord High Thaumaturge and Apothecary to the Throne, and before him, the dream cabinets, glittering with precious gems.

"How were the maidens?" inquired Subtillion.

"Not bad. But where was the music?"

"The chimes got stuck," the Cybernerian explained. "Would Your Royal Highness care to try another dream?"

Of course he would, but this time from another cabinet. The King went up to the black one and plugged into the dream entitled "Alacritus the Knight and Fair Ramolda, Daughter of Heteronius."

He blinked—and saw that this was indeed the age of electrical errantry. He was standing, all clad in steel, in a wooded glen, a freshly vanquished dragon at his feet; the leaves rustled, a gentle zephyr blew, a brook gurgled nearby. He looked into the water and saw, from the reflection, that he was none other than Alacritus, a knight of the highest voltage and hero without peer. The whole history of his glorious career was recorded, in battle scars, upon his person, and he recalled it all, as if the memory were his own. Those dents in the visor of the helmet—made by the mailed fists of Morbidor, in his death throes, having been dispatched with customary alacrity; the broken hinges on the right greave—that was the work of the late Sir Basher de Bloo; and the rivets across his left pauldron—gnawed by Skivvian the Scurvy before giving up the ghost; and the tembrace grille had been crushed by Gourghbrast Buggeruckus ere he was felled. Similarly, the cuissfenders, crosshasps, beaver baffles, hauberk latches, front and rear jambguards and grommets—all bore the marks of battle. His shield was scored and notched by countless blows, but the backplate, that was as shiny and rust-free as a newborn's, for never had he turned to flee an adversary! Though his glory, truth to tell, was a matter of complete indifference to him. But then he remembered the fair Ramolda, leaped upon his supercharger and began to search the length and breadth of the dream for her. In time he arrived at the castle of her father, the Autoduke Heteronius; the drawbridge planks thundered beneath horse and rider, and the Autoduke himself came out to greet him with open arms.

The knight would fain see his Ramolda, but etiquette requires he curb his impatience; meanwhile the old Autoduke tells him that another knight is staying at the castle, one Mygrayn of the house of Polymera, master swordsman and redoubtable elastician, who dreams of nothing else but to enter the lists with Alacritus himself. And now here is Mygrayn, spry and supple, stepping forward with these words:

"Know, O Knight, that I desire Ramolda the streamlined, Ramolda of the hydraulic thighs, whose bust no diamond drill can touch, whose limpid eyes are magnetized! She is thy betrothed, true, but lo, I herewith challenge thee to mortal combat, sith only one of us may win her hand in marriage!"

And he throws his gage, white and polymerous.

"We'll hold the wedding right after the joust," adds the Autoduke–father.

"Very well," says Alacritus, but inside, Zipperupus thinks: "It doesn't matter, I can have her after the wedding and then wake up. But who asked for this Mygrayn character?"

"This very day, brave Knight," says Heteronius, "thou wilt encounter Mygrayn of Polymera on beaten ground and contend with him by torchlight. But for now, retire thee to thy room and rest!"

Inside Alacritus, Zipperupus is a little uneasy, but what can he do? So he goes to his room, and after a while hears a furtive knock-knock at the door, and an old cybercrone tiptoes in, gives a wrinkled wink and says:

"Fear naught, O Knight, thou shalt have the fair Ramolda and forsooth, this very day she'll clasp thee to her alabaster bosom! Of thee alone doth she dream, both day and night! Remember only to attack with might and main, for Mygrayn cannot harm thee and the victory is thine!"

"That's easy enough to say, my cybercrone," replies the knight. "But anything can happen. What if I trip, for example, or fail to parry in time? No, it's a risky business! But perhaps you have some charm that will be certain."

"Hee-hee!" cackles the cybercrone. "The things thou sayest, steel sir! There are no charms, surely, nor hast thou need of any, for I know what will be and guarantee thou winnest hands down!"

"Still, a charm would be more sure," says the knight, "particularly in a dream ... but wait, did by any chance Subtillion send you, to give me confidence?"

"I know of no Subtillion," answers she, "nor of what dream ye speak. Nay, this is reality, my steely liege, as thou wilt learn ere long, when fair Ramolda gives thee her electric lips to kiss!"

"Odd," mutters Zipperupus, not noticing that the cybercrone has left the room as quietly as she came. "Is this a dream or not? I had the impression that it was. But she says this is reality. H'm. Well, in any event I'd best be doubly on my guard!" And now the trumpets sound, and one can hear the rattle of armor; the galleries are packed and everyone awaits the principals. Here comes Alacritus, a little weak in the knees; he enters the lists and sees Ramolda, daughter of Heteronius. She looks upon him sweetly—ah, but there's no time for that now! Mygrayn is stepping into the ring, the torches blaze all around, and their swords cross with a mighty clang. Now Zipperupus is frightened in earnest and tries as hard as he can to wake up, he tries and tries, but it won't work—the armor's too heavy, the dream isn't letting go, and the enemy's attacking! Faster and faster rain the blows, and Zipperupus, weakening, can hardly lift his arm, when suddenly the foe cries out and shows a broken blade; Alacritus the knight is ready to leap upon him, but Mygrayn dashes from the ring and his squires hand him another sword. Just then Alacritus sees the cybercrone among the spectators; she approaches and whispers in his ear:

"Sire of steel! When anon thou art near the open gate that leadeth to the bridge, Mygrayn will lower his guard. Strike bravely then, for 'tis a sign, certain and true, of thy victory!"

Wherewith she vanishes, and his rival, rearmed, comes charging. They fight, Mygrayn hacking away like a threshing machine out of control, but by degrees he slackens, parries sluggishly, backs away, and now the time is ripe, the moment arrives, but the opponent's blade gleams formidably still, so Zipperupus pulls himself together and thinks, "To hell with the fair Ramolda!"—turns tail and runs like mad, pounding back over the drawbridge and into the forest and the darkness of the night. Behind him he hears shouts of "Disgraceful!" and "For shame!", crashes headfirst into a tree, sees stars, blinks, and there he is, standing in the palace vestibule in front of the Black Cabinet of dreams that dream, and by his side, Subtillion the mental engineer, smiling a crooked smile. Crooked, as Subtillion was hiding his disappointment: the Alacritus–Ramolda dream had in reality been a trap set for the King, for had Zipperupus heeded the old cybercrone's advice, Mygrayn, who was only pretending to weaken, would have run him through at the open gate. This the King avoided, thanks only to his extraordinary cowardice.

"Did Milord enjoy the fair Ramolda?" inquired the sly Cybernerian.

"She wasn't fair enough," said Zipperupus, "so I didn't see fit to pursue the matter. And besides, there was some trouble, and fighting too. I like my dreams without fighting, do you understand?"

"As Your Royal Highness wishes," replied Subtillion. "Choose freely, for in all these cabinet dreams there is only delight in store, no fighting. . . ."

"We'll see," said the King and plugged into the dream entitled "The Marvelous Mattress of Princess Bounce." He was in a room of unsurpassed loveliness, all in gold brocade. Through crystal windowpanes light streamed like water from the purest spring, and there by her pearly vanity the Princess stood, yawning, preparing herself for bed. Zipperupus was greatly amazed at this unexpected sight and tried to clear his throat to inform her of his presence, but not a sound came out—had he been gagged?—so he tried to touch his mouth, but couldn't, tried to move his legs—no, he couldn't—then desperately looked around for a place to sit down, feeling faint, but that too was impossible. Meanwhile the Princess stretched and gave a yawn, and another, and a third, and then, overcome with drowsiness, she fell upon the mattress so hard, that King Zipperupus was jolted from head to toe, for he himself was the mattress of Princess Bounce! Evidently the young damsel was having an unpleasant dream, seeing how she turned and tossed about, jabbing the King with her little elbows, digging him with her little heels, until his royal person (transformed into a mattress by this dream) was seized with a mighty rage. The King struggled with his dream, strained and strained, and finally the seams burst, the springs sprang, the slats gave way and the Princess came crashing down with a shriek, which woke him up and he found himself once again in the palace vestibule, and by his side, Subtillion the Cybernerian, bowing an obsequious bow.

"You chuckleheaded bungler!" cried the indignant King. "How dare you?! What, villain, am I to be a mattress, and someone else's mattress at that? You forget yourself, sirrah!"

Subtillion, alarmed by the King's fury, apologized profusely and begged him to try another dream, persuading and pleading until Zipperupus, finally appeased, took the plug and hooked himself into the dream, "Bliss in the Eightfold Embrace of Octopauline." He was standing in a crowd of onlookers in a great square, and a procession was passing by with waving silks, muslins, mechanical elephants, litters in carved ebony; the one in the middle was like a golden shrine, and in it, behind eight veils, sat a feminine figure of miraculous beauty, an angel with a dazzling face and galactic gaze, high-frequency earrings too, and the King, all a-tremble, was about to ask who this heavenly vision was, when he heard a murmur of awe and adoration surge through the multitude: "Octopauline! It's Octopauline!"

For they were celebrating, with the utmost pomp and pageantry, the royal daughter's betrothal to a foreign knight of the name Oneiromant.

The King was a bit surprised that he wasn't this knight, and when the procession had passed and disappeared behind

the palace gates, he went with the others in the crowd to a
nearby inn; there he saw Oneiromant, who, clad in nothing
but galligaskins of damask studded with gold nails and holding a half-empty stein of fortified phosgene in his hand,
came over to him, put an arm around him, gave him a hug
and whispered in his ear with searing breath:

"Look, I have a rendezvous with Princess Octopauline to-
night at midnight, behind the palace, in the grove of barbwire bushes next to the mercury fountain—but I don't dare
show up, not in this condition, I've had too much to drink,
you see—but you, good stranger, why you're the spit and
image of me, so please, please go in my place, kiss the Princess' hands for me and say that you're Oneiromant, and
gosh, I'll be beholden to you forever and a day!"

"Why not?" said the King after a little thought. "Yes, I
think I can manage it. But when?"

"Right now, there's not a moment to lose, it's almost
midnight, just remember—the King knows nothing of this,
no one does, only the Princess and the old gatekeeper, and
when he bars your way, here, put this heavy bag of ducats in
his hand, and he'll let you pass!"

The King nodded, took the bag of ducats and ran straight
for the castle, since the clocks, like cast-iron hoot owls, were
already beginning to strike the hour. He sped over the drawbridge, took a quick look into the gaping moat, shuddered,
lowered his head and slipped under the spiked grating of the
portcullis—then across the courtyard to the barbwire bushes
and the fountain that bubbled mercury, and there in the
pale moonlight he saw the divine figure of Princess Octopauline, beautiful beyond his wildest dreams and so bewitching, that he shook with desire.

Observing these shakings and shudderings of the sleeping
monarch in the palace vestibule, Subtillion chortled and
rubbed his hands with glee, this time certain of the King's
demise, for he knew that when Octopauline enfolded the

unfortunate lover in those powerful eightfold arms of hers and drew him deep into the fathomless dream with her tender tentacles of love, he would never, never make it back to the surface of reality! And in fact, Zipperupus, burning to be wrapped in the Princess' embrace, was running along the wall in the shadow of the cloisters, running towards that radiant image of silvery pulchritude, when suddenly the old gatekeeper appeared and blocked the way with his halberd. The King lifted the bag of ducats but, feeling their pleasant weight in his hand, was loath to part with them—what a shame, really, to throw away a whole fortune on one embrace!

"Here's a ducat," he said, opening the bag. "Now let me by!"

"It'll cost you ten," said the gatekeeper.

"What, ten ducats for a single hug?" jeered the King. "You're out of your mind!"

"Ten ducats," said the gatekeeper. "That's the price."

"Can't you lower it a little?"

"Ten ducats, not a ducat less."

"So that's how it is!" yelled the King, flying off the handle in his usual way. "Very well then, dog, you don't get a thing!" Whereupon the gatekeeper whopped him good with the halberd and everything went spinning around, the cloisters, the fountain, the drawbridge, and Zipperupus fell —not asleep, but awake, opening his eyes to see Subtillion at his side and in front of him, the Dream Cabinet. The Cybernerian was greatly confounded, for now he had failed twice: the first time, because of the King's craven character, the second, because of his greed. But Subtillion, putting a good face on a bad business, invited the King to help himself to another dream.

This time Zipperupus selected the "Wockle Weed" dream.

He was Dodderont Debilitus, ruler of Epilepton and

Maladyne, a rickety old codger and incurable lecher besides, with a soul that longed for evil deeds. But what evil could he do with these creaking joints, these palsied arms and gouty legs? "I need a pick-me-up," he thought and ordered his degenerals, Tartaron and Torturus, to go out and put whatever they could to fire and sword, sacking, pillaging and carrying off. This they did and, returning, said:

"Sire and Sovereign! We put what we could to fire and sword, we sacked, we pillaged, and here is what we carried off: the beauteous Adoradora, Virgin Queen of the Mynamoacans, with all her treasure!"

"Eh? What's that you say? With her treasure?" wheezed the quimsy King. "But where is she? And what's all that sniveling and shivering over there?"

"Here, upon yon royal couch, Your Highness!" barked the degenerals in chorus. "The sniveling comes from the prisoneress, the above-mentioned Queen Adoradora, recumbent on her antimacassar of pearls! And she shivers first, because she is clad in naught but this exquisite, gold-embroidered shift, and secondly, in anticipation of great indignities and degradation!"

"What? Indignities, you say? Degradation? Good, good!" rasped the King. "Hand her over, I'll ravish and outrage the poor thing at once!"

"Impossible, Your Highness," interposed the Royal Surgeon and Chirurgeon, "for reasons of national security."

"What? I can't ravish? I can't violate? I, the King? Have you gone mad? What else did I ever do throughout my reign?"

"That's just it, Your Highness!" urged the Surgeon. "Your Highness' health has been seriously impaired by those excesses!"

"Oh? Well, in that case . . . give me an ax, I'll just lop off her, ah, head . . ."

"With Your Highness' permission, that too would be extremely unwise. The least exertion . . ."

"Odsbodkins and thunderation! What blessed use is this kingship to me then?!" sputtered the King, growing desperate. "Cure me, blast it! Restore me! Make me young again, so I can—you know—like it used to be. . . . Otherwise, so help me, I'll . . . I'll . . ."

In terror all the courtiers, degenerals and medical assistants rushed out to find some way to rejuvenate the royal person; at last they summoned the great Calculon himself, a sage of infinite wisdom. He came before the King and asked:

"What is it that Your Royal Highness wishes?"

"Eh? Wishes, is it? Hah!" croaked the King. "I'll tell you what he wishes! He wishes to continue with his debaucheries, saturnalian carousals, incontinent wallowings and wild oats, and in particular to defile and properly deflower Queen Adoradora, who for the time being sits in the dungeon!"

"There are two courses of action open to us," said Calculon. "Either Your Highness deigns to choose a suitably competent individual, who will perform *per procuram* everything Your Highness, wired to that individual, commands, and in this way Your Highness can experience whatever that individual experiences, exactly as if he had experienced the experience himself. Or else you must summon the old cyberhag who lives in the forest outside the village, in a hut on three legs, for she is a geriatric witch and deals exclusively with the infirmities of advanced age!"

"Oh? Well, let's try the wires first!" said the King. And it was done in a trice; the royal electricians connected the Captain of the Guard to the King, and the King immediately commanded him to saw the sage in half, for this was precisely the kind of foul deed in which he took such delight. Calculon's pleas and screams were to no avail. However, the insulation on one of the wires was torn during the sawing, and consequently the King received only the first half of the execution.

"A paltry method. The charlatan deserved to be sawed in half," wheezed His Highness. "Now let's have that old cyberhag, the one with the hut on three legs!"

His courtiers headed full speed for the forest, and before long the King heard a mournful singsong, which went something like this:

"Ancient persons repaired here! I renovate, regenerate, I fix as good as new; corroded or scleroded, why, everyone pulls through! So if you quake, or creak, or shake, or have the rust, or feel the ache, yes I'm the one for you!"

The old cyberhag listened patiently to the King's complaints, bowed low and said:

"Sire and Sovereign! Beyond the blue horizon, at the foot of Bald Mountain, there flows a spring, and from this spring there flows a stream, a stream of oil, of castor oil, and o'er it grows the wockle weed, a high-octane antisenescent rejuvenator—one tablespoon, and kiss forty-seven years goodbye! Though you have to be careful not to take too much: an overdose of wockle juice can youthen to the point of euthanasia and poof, you disappear! And now, Sire, I shall prepare this remedy tried and true!"

"Wonderful!" cried the King. "And I'll have them prepare the Queen Adoradora—let the poor thing know what awaits her, heh-heh!"

And with trembling hands he tried to straighten his loose screws, muttering and clucking all the while, and even twitching in places, for he had grown most senile, though his passion for evil never abated.

Meanwhile knights rode out beyond the blue horizon to the castor-oil stream, and later, over the old cyberhag's cauldron vapors swirled, whirled and curled as concoctions were being concocted, till finally she hastened to the throne, fell on her knees and handed the King a goblet, full to the brim with a liquid that shone and shimmered like quicksilver, and she said in a great voice:

"King Dodderont Debilitus! Lo, here is the rejuvenescent essence of the wockle weed! Invigorating, exhilarating, just the thing for dalliance and derring-do! Drain this cup, and for you the entire Galaxy will not hold cities enough to despoil, nor maidens enough to dishonor! Drink, and to your health!"

The King raised the goblet, but spilled a few drops on his footstool, which instantly reared up, snorted and hurled itself at Degeneral Tartaron, with frenzied intent to humiliate and profane. In a twinkling of an eye, it had ripped off six fistfuls of medals.

"Drink, Your Highness, drink!" prompted the cyberhag. "You see yourself what miracles it works!"

"You first," said the King in a barely audible whisper, as he was aging fast. The cyberhag turned pale, backed away, refused, but at a nod from the King three soldiers seized her and, using a funnel, forced several drops of the glittering brew down her throat. A flash, a thunderclap, smoke everywhere! The courtiers looked, the King looked—nothing, not a trace of the cyberhag, only a black hole gaping in the floor, and through it one could see another hole, a hole in the dream itself, clearly revealing somebody's foot—elegantly shod, though the sock was singed and the silver buckle turning dark, as if eaten with acid. The foot of course, along with its sock and shoe, belonged to Subtillion, Lord High Thaumaturge and Apothecary to King Zipperupus. For so potent was that poison the cyberhag had called the wockle weed, that not only did it dissolve both her and the floor, but went clear through to reality, there spattering the shin of Subtillion, which gave him a nasty burn. The King, ter-

rified, tried to wake, but (fortunately for Subtillion) Degeneral Torturus managed to bash him good over the head
with his mace; thanks to this, Zipperupus, when he came to,
was unable to recall a thing of what had happened when he
was Dodderont Debilitus. Still, once again he had foiled
the Cybernerian, slipping out of the third deadly dream,
saved this time by his overly suspicious nature.

"There was something ... but I forget just what," said
the King, back in front of the Cabinet That Dreamed. "But
why are you, Subtillion, hopping about on one leg like that
and holding the other?"

"It's—it's nothing, Your Highness ... a touch of rhom-
botism ... must be a change in the weather," stammered
the crafty Thaumaturge, and then continued to tempt the
King to sample yet another dream. Zipperupus thought
awhile, read through the Table of Contents and chose, "The
Wedding Night of Princess Ineffabelle." And he dreamt he
was sitting by the fire and reading an ancient volume, quaint
and curious, in which it told, with well-turned words and
crimson ink on gilded parchment, of the Princess Ineffabelle, who reigned five centuries ago in the land of Dandelia,
and it told of her Icicle Forest, and her Helical Tower, and
the Aviary That Neighed, and the Treasury with a Hundred
Eyes, but especially of her beauty and abounding virtues.
And Zipperupus longed for this vision of loveliness with a
great longing, and a mighty desire was kindled within him
and set his soul afire, that his eyeballs blazed like beacons,
and he rushed out and searched every corner of the dream
for Ineffabelle, but she was nowhere to be found; indeed,
only the very oldest robots had ever heard of that princess.
Weary from his long peregrinations, Zipperupus came at
last to the center of the royal desert, where the dunes were
gold-plated, and there espied a humble hut; when he approached it, he saw an individual of patriarchal appearance,

in a robe as white as snow. The latter rose and spake thusly:

"Thou seekest Ineffabelle, poor wretch! And yet thou knowest full well she doth not live these five hundred years, hence how vain and unavailing is thy passion! The only thing that I can do for thee is to let thee see her—not in the flesh, forsooth, but a fair informational facsimile, a model that is digital, not physical, stochastic, not plastic, ergodic and most assuredly erotic, and all in yon Black Box, which I constructed in my spare time out of odds and ends!"

"Ah, show her to me, show her to me now!" exclaimed Zipperupus, quivering. The patriarch gave a nod, examined the ancient volume for the princess' coordinates, put her and the entire Middle Ages on punch cards, wrote up the program, threw the switch, lifted the lid of the Black Box and said:

"Behold!"

The King leaned over, looked and saw, yes, the Middle Ages simulated to a T, all digital, binary and nonlinear, and there was the land of Dandelia, the Icicle Forest, the palace with the Helical Tower, the Aviary That Neighed, and the Treasury with a Hundred Eyes as well; and there was Ineffabelle herself, taking a slow, stochastic stroll through her simulated garden, and her circuits glowed red and gold as she picked simulated daisies and hummed a simulated song. Zipperupus, unable to restrain himself any longer, leaped upon the Black Box and in his madness tried to climb into that computerized world. The patriarch, however, quickly killed the current, hurled the King to the earth and said:

"Madman! Wouldst attempt the impossible?! For no being made of matter can ever enter a system that is naught but the flux and swirl of alphanumerical elements, discontinuous integer configurations, the abstract stuff of digits!"

"But I must, I must!!" bellowed Zipperupus, beside himself, and beat his head against the Black Box until the metal was dented. The old sage then said:

"If such is thy inalterable desire, there is a way I can connect thee to the Princess Ineffabelle, but first thou must part with thy present form, for I shall take thy appurtenant coordinates and make a program of thee, atom by atom, and place thy simulation in that world medievally modeled, informational and representational, and there will it remain, enduring as long as electrons course through these wires and hop from cathode to anode. But thou, standing here before me now, thou wilt be annihilated, so that thy only existence may be in the form of given fields and potentials, statistical, heuristical, and wholly digital!"

"That's hard to believe," said Zipperupus. "How will I know you've simulated me, and not someone else?"

"Very well, we'll make a trial run," said the sage. And he took all the King's measurements, as if for a suit of clothes, though with much greater precision, since every atom was carefully plotted and weighed, and then he fed the program into the Black Box and said:

"Behold!"

The King peered inside and saw himself sitting by the fire and reading in an ancient book about the Princess Ineffabelle, then rushing out to find her, asking here and there, until in the heart of the gold-plated desert he came upon a humble hut and a snow-white patriarch, who greeted him with the words, "Thou seekest Ineffabelle, poor wretch!" And so on.

"Surely now thou art convinced," said the patriarch, switching it off. "This time I shall program thee in the Middle Ages, at the side of the sweet Ineffabelle, that thou mayest dream with her an unending dream, simulated, nonlinear, binary . . ."

"Yes, yes, I understand," said the King. "But still, it's

only my likeness, not myself, since I am right here and not in any Box!"

"But thou wilt not be here long," replied the sage with a kindly smile, "for I shall attend to that. . . ."

And he pulled out a hammer from under the bed, a heavy hammer, but serviceable.

"When thou art locked in the arms of thy beloved," the patriarch told him, "I shall see to it that there be not two of thee, one here and one there, in the Box—employing a method that is old and primitive, yet never fails, so if thou wilt just bend over a little . . ."

"First let me take another look at your Ineffabelle," said the King. "Just to make sure . . ."

The sage lifted the lid of the Black Box and showed him Ineffabelle. The King looked and looked, and finally said:

"The description in the ancient volume is greatly exaggerated. She's not bad, of course, but nowhere near as beautiful as it says in the chronicles. Well, so long, old sage . . ."

And he turned to leave.

"Where art thou going, madman?!" cried the patriarch, clutching his hammer, for the King was almost out the door.

"Anywhere but in the Box," said Zipperupus and hurried out, but at that very moment the dream burst like a bubble beneath his feet, and he found himself in the vestibule facing the bitterly disappointed Subtillion, disappointed because the King had come so close to being locked up in the Black Box, and the Lord High Thaumaturge could have kept him there forever . . .

"Listen here, Sir Cybernerian," said the King, "these dreams of yours with princesses are a great deal more trouble than they're worth. Now either you show me one I can enjoy—no tricks, no complications—or leave the palace at once, and take your cabinets with you!"

"Sire!" Subtillion replied. "I have just the dream for you,

the finest quality and tailor-made. Only give it a try, and you'll see I'm right!"

"Which one is that?" asked the King.

"This one, Your Highness," said the Lord High Thaumaturge, and pointed to the little pearl plaque with the inscription: "Mona Lisa, or The Labyrinth of Sweet Infinity."

And before the King could answer yea or nay, Subtillion himself took the chain to plug him in, and quickly, for he saw that things were going none too well: Zipperupus had escaped eternal imprisonment in the Black Box, too thick-headed to fall completely for the captivating Ineffabelle.

"Wait," said the King, "let me!"

And he pushed in the plug and entered the dream, only to find himself still himself, Zipperupus, standing in the palace vestibule, and at his side, Subtillion the Cybernerian, who explains to him that of all the dreams, "Mona Lisa" is the most dissolute and dissipated, for in it is the infinite in femininity; hearing this, Zipperupus plugs in and looks about for Mona Lisa, already yearning for her infinitely feminine caress, but in this dream within a dream he finds himself still in the palace vestibule, the Lord High Thaumaturge at his side, so impatiently plugs into the cabinet and enters the next dream, but it's still the same, the vestibule, the cabinets, the Cybernerian and himself. "Is this a dream or isn't it?" he shouts, plugging in again, and once again there's the vestibule, the cabinets, the Cybernerian; and again, but it's still the same; and again and again, faster and faster. "Where's Mona Lisa, knave?!" he snarls, and pulls the plug to wake—but no, he's still in the vestibule with the cabinets! Furious, he stamps his feet and hurls himself from dream to dream, from cabinet to cabinet, from Cybernerian to Cybernerian, but now he doesn't care about the dream, he only wants to get back to reality, back to his beloved throne, the court intrigues and old iniquities, and he pulls and pushes the plugs in a blind frenzy. "Help!"

he cries, and, "Hey! The King's in danger!" and, "Mona Lisa! Yoo-hoo!," while he thrashes around in terror and scrambles wildly from corner to corner, looking for a chink in the dream, but in vain. He did not understand the how, the why or the what of it, but his stupidity could not save him, nor could his cowardice, nor his inordinate greed, for this time he had gotten himself in too deep, and was trapped and wrapped in dreams as if in a hundred tight cocoons, so that even when he managed, straining with all his might, to free himself from one, that didn't help, for immediately he fell into another, and when he pulled his plug from the cabinet, both plug and cabinet were only dreamed, not real, and when he beat Subtillion, Subtillion too turned out to be a dream. Zipperupus leaped here and there, and everywhere, but wherever he leaped, everything was a dream, a dream and nothing but a dream, the doors, the marble floors, the gold-embroidered walls, the tapestries, the halls, and Zipperupus too, he was a dream, a dream that dreamed, a walking shadow, an empty apparition, insubstantial, fleeting, lost in a labyrinth of dreams, sinking ever deeper, though still he bucked and kicked—only that too was purely imaginary! He punched Subtillion in the nose, but not really, roared and howled, but nothing real came out, and when at last, dazed and half-crazed, he really did tear his way into reality, he thought it was a dream and plugged himself back in, and then it really was, and on he dreamed, and on and on, which was inevitable, and thus Zipperupus, whimpering, dreamed of waking in vain, not knowing that 'Mona Lisa' was—in reality—a diabolical code for 'monarcholysis,' that is: the dissolution, dissociation and total dissipation of the King. For truly, of all Subtillion's treacherous traps, this was the most terrible. . . .

Such was the tale, moving and improving, that Trurl told to King Thumbscrew the Third, who by now had a splitting headache and so dismissed the constructor without further ado, presenting him first with the Order of the Sacred Cybernia, a lilac sign of feedback upon a field of green, incrusted with precious bits of information.

✦ ✦

And with these words the second storytelling machine ground to a halt, its golden gears whirring musically, and gave a giddy little laugh, for a few of its klystrons had overheated slightly; but it lowered its anode potential, waved away the smoke, sighed and retreated to the photon phaeton, accompanied by much applause, the reward for its eloquence and storytelling skill.

King Genius meanwhile offered Trurl a cup of ion mead, wondrously carved with curves of probability and the subtle play of quantum waves. Trurl quaffed it down, then snapped his fingers, whereupon the third machine stepped out into the center of the cave, bowed low and said, in a voice that was tonic, euphonic, and most electronic:

✦ ✦

This is the story of how the Great Constructor Trurl, with the aid of an ordinary jug, created a local fluctuation, and what came of it.

In the Constellation of the Wringer there was a Spiral Galaxy, and in this Galaxy there was a Black Nebula, and in this Nebula were five sixth-order clusters, and in the fifth cluster, a lilac sun, very old and very dim, and around this sun revolved seven planets, and the third planet had two moons, and in all these suns and stars and planets and moons a variety of events, various and varying, took place, falling into a statistical distribution that was perfectly normal, and on the second moon of the third planet of the lilac sun of the fifth cluster of the Black Nebula in the Spiral Galaxy in the Constellation of the Wringer was a garbage dump, the kind of garbage dump one might find on any planet or moon, absolutely average, in other words full of garbage; it had come into existence because the Glauberical Aberracleans once waged a war, a war of the fission-and-fusion type, against the Albumenid Ifts, with the natural result that their bridges, roads, homes and palaces, and of course they themselves, were reduced to ashes and shards, which the solar winds blew to the place whereof we speak. Now for many, many centuries positively nothing took place in this garbage dump but garbage, though an earthquake did occur and shifted the garbage on the bottom to the top, and the garbage on the top to the bottom, which in itself had no particular significance, and yet this paved the way for a most unusual phenomenon. It so happened that Trurl, the Fabulous Constructor, while flying in the vicinity, was blinded by a certain comet with a garish tail. He fled its path, frantically jettisoning out the spaceship window whatever lay in reach—chess pieces, the hollow kind, which he'd filled with liquor for the trip, some barrels the Ubbidubs of Chlorelei employed for the purpose of compelling their opponents to yield, as well as assorted utensils, and among these, an old earthenware jug with a crack down the middle. This jug, accelerating in accordance with the laws of gravity and boosted by the comet's tail, crashed into a mountainside above the dump, fell, clattered down a slope of junk toward a puddle, skittered across some mud, and finally smacked into an old tin can; this impact bent the metal around a copper wire, also knocked some pieces of mica between the edges, and that made a condenser, while the wire, twisted by the can, formed the beginnings of a solenoid, and a stone, set in motion by the jug, moved in turn a hunk of rusty iron, which happened to be a magnet, and this gave rise to a current, and that current passed through sixteen other cans and snips of wire, releasing a number of sulfides and chlorides, whose atoms linked with other atoms, and the ensuing molecules latched onto other molecules, until, in the very center of the dump, there came into being a Logic Circuit, and five more, and another eighteen in the spot where the jug finally shattered into bits. That evening, something emerged at the edge of the dump, not far from the puddle which had by now dried up, and this something, a creature of pure accident, was Mymosh the Selfbegotten, who had neither mother nor father, but was son unto himself, for his father was Coincidence, and his Mother—Entropy. And Mymosh rose up from the garbage dump, totally oblivious of the fact that he had about one chance in a hundred billion jillion raised to the zillionth power of ever existing, and he took a step, and walked until he came to the next puddle, which had not as yet dried up, so that, kneeling over it, he could easily see himself. And he saw, in the surface of the water, his purely accidental head, with ears like muffins, the left one crushed and the right a trifle underdone, and he saw his purely accidental body, a potpourri of pots and pegs and flotsam, and somewhat barrel-chested, in that his chest was a barrel, though narrower in the middle, like a waist, for in crawling out from under the garbage, he had scraped against a stone right there; and he gazed upon his littery limbs, and counted them, and as luck would have it, there were two arms, two legs and, fortuitously enough, two eyes too, and Mymosh the Selfbegotten took great delight in his person, and sighed with admiration at the narrowness of the waist, the symmetrical arrangement of the limbs, the roundness of the head, and was moved to exclaim:

—Truly, I am beautiful, nay, perfect, which clearly implies the Perfection of All Created Things!! Ah, and how good must be the One Who fashioned me!

And he hobbled on, dropping loose screws along the way (since no one had tightened them properly), humming hymns in praise of the Everlasting Harmony of Providence, but on the seventh step he tripped and went headlong back down into the garbage, after which he did nothing but rust, corrode and slowly disintegrate for the next three hundred and fourteen thousand years, for he had fallen on his head and shorted out, and was no more. And at the end of this time it came to pass that a certain merchant, carrying a shipment of sea anemones from the planet Medulsa to the Thrycian Stomatopods, quarreled with his assistant as they neared the lilac sun, and hurled his shoes at him, and one of these broke the porthole window and flew out into space, where its subsequent orbit subsequently experienced perturbation, due to the circumstance that that very same comet, which had ages past blinded Trurl, now found itself in the very same locality, and so the shoe, turning slowly, hurtled towards the moon, was singed a little by the atmospheric friction, bounced off the mountainside above the dump, fell, and booted Mymosh the Selfbegotten, lying there, with just the right resultant impulse and at just the right angle of incidence to create just the right torsions, torques, centrifugal forces and angular momenta needed to reactivate the accidental brain of that accidental being—and in this way: Mymosh, thus booted, went flying into the nearby puddle, where his chlorides and iodides mingled with the water, and electrolyte seeped into his head and, bubbling, set up a current there, which traveled around and about, till Mymosh sat up in the mud and thought the following thought: —Apparently, I am!

That, however, was all he was able to think for the next sixteen centuries, and the rain beat down upon him, and the hail pommeled him, and all the while his entropy increased and grew, but after another thousand five hundred and twenty years, a certain bird, flapping its way over the terrain, was attacked by some swooping predator, and relieved itself out of fright and also to increase its speed, and the droppings dropped and hit Mymosh square on the forehead, whereupon he sneezed and said:

—Yes, I am! And there's no apparently about it! Yet the question remains, who is it who says that I am? Or, in other words, who am I? Now, how may this be answered? H'm! If only there was something else besides me, any sort of something at all, with which I might juxtapose and compare myself—that would be half the battle. But alas, there's not a thing, for I can plainly see that I see nothing whatsoever! Therefore there's only I that am, and I am everything that is and may be, for I can think in any way I like, but am I then—an empty space for thought, and nothing more?

In point of fact he no longer possessed any senses; they had decayed and crumbled to dust over the centuries, since Entropy, the bride of Chaos, is a cruel and implacable mistress. Consequently Mymosh could not see his mother-puddle, nor his brother-mud, nor the whole, wide world, and had no recollection of what had happened to him before, and generally was now capable of nothing but thought. This alone could he do, and so devoted himself wholeheartedly to it.

—First I ought—he told himself—to fill this void that is I, and thereby dispel its insufferable monotony. So let us think of something, for when we think, behold, there is thought, and nought but our thought has existence.— From this one could see he was becoming somewhat presumptuous, for already he referred to himself in the first person plural.

—But wait—he then said—might not something still exist

outside myself? We must, if only for a moment, consider this possibility, though it sound preposterous and even a little insane. Let us call this outsideness the Gozmos. Now, if there is a Gozmos, then I must be a part and portion of it!

Here he stopped, pondered the matter awhile, and finally rejected that hypothesis as wholly without basis or foundation. Really, there was not a shred of evidence in its favor, not a single, solid argument to support it, and so, ashamed he had indulged in such wild, untutored speculation, he said to himself:

—Of that which lies beyond me, if anything indeed there lie, I have no knowledge. But of that which is within, I do, or rather shall, as soon as I think something into thought, for who can know what I think, by thunder, better than myself?!— And he thought and thought, and thought of the Gozmos again, but this time thought of it inside himself, which seemed to him a far more sensible and respectable solution, well within the bounds of reason and propriety. And he began to fill his Gozmos with various and sundry thoughts. First, because he was still new at it and lacked skill, he thought out the Beadlies, who grambled whenever they got the chance, and the Pratlings, who rejoiced in fili-corts. Immediately the Pratlings battled the Beadlies for the supremacy of filicortion over gramblement, and all My-mosh got for his world-creating pains was an awful headache.

In his next attempts at thought creation, he proceeded with greater caution, first thinking up elements, like Bru-tonium, a noble gas, and elementary particles, like the cogi-ton, the quantum of intellect, and he created beings, and these were fruitful and multiplied. From time to time he did make mistakes, but after a century or two he grew quite proficient, and his very own Gozmos, sound and stable, took shape in his mind's eye, and it teemed with a multitude of entities, things, beings, civilizations and phenomena, and existence was most pleasurable there, for he had made the laws of that Gozmos highly liberal, having no fondness for strict, inflexible rules, the sort of prison discipline that Mother Nature imposes (though of course he'd never heard of Mother Nature).

Thus the world of Selfbegotten was a place of caprice and miracle; in it something might occur one way once, and at another time be altogether different—and without any special rhyme or reason. If, for example, an individual was supposed to die, there were always ways of getting around it, for Mymosh had firmly decided against irreversible events. And in his thoughts the Zigrots, Calsonians, Flimmeroons, Jups, Arligynes and Wallamachinoids all prospered and flourished, generation after generation. During this time the haphazard arms and legs of Mymosh fell off, returning to the garbage from which they'd come, and the puddle rusted through the narrow waist, and his body slowly sank into the stagnant mire. But he had just put up some brand-new constellations, arranging them with loving care in the eternal darkness of his consciousness, which was his Gozmos, and did his level best to keep an accurate memory of everything that he had thought into existence, even though his head hurt from the effort, for he felt responsible for his Gozmos, deeply obligated, and needed. Meanwhile rust ate deeper and deeper into his cranial plates, which of course he had no way of knowing, and a fragment from Trurl's jug, the selfsame jug that thousands of years ago had called him into being, came floating on the puddle's surface, closer and closer to his unfortunate head, for only that now remained above the water. And at the very moment when Mymosh was imagining the gentle, crystal Baucis and her faithful Ondragor, and as they journeyed hand in hand among the dark suns of his mind, and all the people of the Gozmos looked on in rapt silence, including the Beadlies, and as the pair softly called to one another—the rust-eaten skull cracked open at the touch of the earthenware shard, pushed by a puff of air, and the murky water rushed in over the copper coils and extinguished the current in the logic circuits, and the Gozmos of Mymosh the Selfbegotten attained the perfection, the ultimate perfection that comes with nothingness. And those who unwittingly had brought him into the world never learned of his passing.

✦ ✦

Here the black machine bowed, and King Genius sat plunged in gloomy meditation, and brooded so long, that the company began to murmur ill of Trurl, who had dared to cloud the royal mind with such a tale. But the King soon broke into a smile and asked:

"And have you not something else up your manifold for us, my good machine?"

"Sire," it responded, bowing low, "I will tell you the story, remarkably profound, of Chlorian Theoreticus the Proph, intellectrician and pundit *par excellence*."

✦ ✦

It happened once that Klapaucius, the famed constructor, longing to rest after his great labors (he had just completed for King Thanaton a Machine That Wasn't, but that is quite another story), arrived at the planet of the Mammonides and there roamed hither and yon, seeking solitude, until he saw, at the edge of a forest, a humble hut, all overgrown with wild cyberberries and smoke rising from its chimney. He would have gladly avoided it, but noticed on the doorstep a pile of empty inkwells, and this singular sight prompted him to take a peek inside. There, at a massive stone table sat an ancient sage, so broken-down, wired up and rusted through, it was a wonder to behold. The brow was dented in a hundred places, the eyes, turning in their sockets, creaked dreadfully, as did the limbs, unoiled, and it seemed withal that he owed his miserable existence entirely to patches, clamps and pieces of string—and miserable that existence was indeed, as witnessed by the bits of amber lying here and there: apparently, the poor soul obtained his daily current by rubbing them together! The spectacle of such penury moved Klapaucius to pity, and he was reaching into his purse discreetly, when the ancient one, only now fixing a cloudy eye upon him, piped in a reedy voice:

—Then you have come at last?!

—Well, yes . . . —mumbled Klapaucius, surprised that he was expected in a place he had never intended to be.

—In that case . . . may you rot, may you come to an evil end, may you break your arms and neck and legs—screeched the old sage, flying into a fury, and began to fling whatever lay at hand, and this was mainly odds and ends of trash, at the speechless Klapaucius. When finally he had tired and ceased this bombardment, the object of his fury calmly inquired as to the reason for so inhospitable a reception. For a while the sage still muttered things like: —May you blow a fuse! —May your mechanisms jam forever, O base corrosion!— but eventually calmed down, and his humor improved to the degree that, huffing, he raised his finger and—though he still dropped an occasional oath and threw off such sparks, that the air reeked with ozone—proceeded to tell his story in the following words:

—Know then, O foreigner, that I am a pundit, a pundit's pundit, first among philosophists, for my lifelong passion and profession is ontology, and my name (which the stars must some day outshine) is Chlorian Theoreticus the

Proph. I was born of impoverished parents and from earliest childhood felt an irresistible attraction to abstract thought. At the age of sixteen I wrote my first opus, *The Gnostotron*. It set forth the general theory of *a posteriori* deities, deities which had to be added to the Universe later by advanced civilizations, since, as everyone knows, Matter always comes first and no one, consequently, could have possibly thought in the very beginning. Clearly then, at the Dawn of Creation thoughtlessness reigned supreme, which is only obvious, really, when you take a look at this, this Cosmos of ours!!— Here the ancient one choked with sudden rage, stamped his feet, but then weakened, and finally went on. —I simply explained the necessity of providing gods after the fact, inasmuch as there were none available beforehand. Indeed, every civilization that engages in intellectronics strives for nothing else but to construct some Omniac, which, in Its infinite mercy, might rectify the currents of evil and plot the path of righteousness and true wisdom. Now in this work of mine I included a blueprint for the first Gnostotron, as well as graphs of its omnipotence output, measured in units called jehovahs. One jehovah would be equivalent to the working of one miracle with a radius of one billion parsecs. As soon as this treatise appeared in print (at my own expense), I rushed out into the street, certain that the people would lift me up on their shoulders, crown me with garlands, shower me with gold, but no one, not even so much as a lame cybernerian, approached with words of praise. Feeling dismay rather than disappointment at this neglect, I immediately sat down and wrote *The Scourge of Reason*, two volumes, in which I showed that each civilization may choose one of two roads to travel, that is, either fret itself to death, or pet itself to death. And in the course of doing one or the other, it eats its way into the Universe, turning cinders and flinders of stars into toilet seats, pegs, gears, cigarette holders and pillowcases, and it does this because, unable to fathom the Universe, it seeks to change that Fathomlessness into Something Fathomable, and will not stop until the nebulae and planets have been processed to cradles, chamber pots and bombs, all in the name of Sublime Order, for only a Universe with pavement, plumbing, labels and catalogues is, in its sight, acceptable and wholly respectable. Then in the second volume, entitled *Advocatus Materiae*, I demonstrated how the Reason, a greedy, grasping thing, is only satisfied when it succeeds in chaining some cosmic geyser, or harnessing an atomic swarm—say, to produce an ointment for the removal of freckles. This accomplished, it hurries on to the next natural phenomenon, to add it, like a stuffed trophy, to its precious collection of scientific spoils. But alas, these two excellent volumes of mine were also received with silence by the world; I said to myself then, that patience was the way, and perseverance. Now having defended, first, the Reason against the Universe (the Reason absolved from blame, in that Matter permits all sorts of abominations only because it is mindless), and second, the Universe against the Reason (which I demolished utterly, I dare say), on a sudden inspiration I then wrote *The Existential Tailor*, where I proved conclusively the absurdity of more than one philosopher, for each must have his own philosophy, that fits him like a glove, or a coat cut to specifications. And as this work too was totally ignored, I straightway wrote another; in it I presented all the possible hypotheses concerning the origin of the Universe —first, the opinion that it doesn't exist at all, second, that it's the result of all the mistakes made by a certain Demiurgon, who set out to create the world without the faintest idea of how to go about it, third, that the world is actually an hallucination of some Superbrain gone berserk in a manner infinite but bounded, four, that it is an asinine thought materialized as a joke, five, that it is matter that thinks, but with an abysmally low IQ—and then I sat back and waited, expecting vehement attacks, heated debates, notoriety, laurels, lawsuits, fan mail and anonymous threats. But once again, nothing, absolutely nothing. It was quite beyond belief. Then I thought, well, perhaps I hadn't read enough of other thinkers, and so, obtaining their works, I acquainted myself with the most famous among them, one by one— Phrensius Whiz, Buffon von Schneckon, founder of the Schneckonist movement, then Turbulo Turpitus Catafalicum, Ithm of Logar, and of course Lemuel the Balding.

Yet in all of this I discovered nothing of significance. Meanwhile my own books were gradually being sold, I assumed therefore that someone was reading them, and if so, I would sooner or later hear of it. In particular I had no doubt but that the Tyrant would summon me, with the demand that I devote myself exclusively to the immortalization of his glorious name. Of course I would tell him that Truth alone did I serve and would lay down my life for it, if necessary; the Tyrant, desirous of the praises my brilliant brain could formulate, would then attempt to bring me round with honeyed words and even toss sacks of clinking coins at my feet, but, seeing me unmoved and resolute, would say (prompted by his wise men) that as I dealt with the Universe, I ought to deal with him as well, for he represented, after all, a part of the Cosmic Whole. Outraged at this mockery, I would answer sharply, and he would have me put to torture. Thus I toughened my body in advance, that it might endure the worst with philosophical indifference. Yet days and months passed by, and nothing, no word from the Tyrant—so I had readied myself for martyrdom in vain. There was only a certain scribbler by the name of Noxion, who wrote in some cheap, vulgar evening gazette that this prankster Chlorian made up no end of farfetched yarns in his book facetiously entitled, *The Gnostotron, or The Ultimate Omnipotentiometer, or A Pee into the Future.* I rushed to my bookshelf—yes, there it was, the printer had somehow left out the *k*. . . . My first impulse was to go out and murder him, but reason prevailed. "My time will come!" I told myself. "It cannot be, for someone to cast forth pearls of eternal wisdom left and right, day and night, till the mind is blinded by the surging Light of Final Understanding—and nothing! No, fame will be mine, acclaim will be mine, thrones of ivory, the title of Prime Mentorian, the love of the people, sweet solace in a shaded grove, my very own school, pupils that hang on every word, and a cheering crowd!" For verily, O foreign one, every pundit cherishes such dreams. True, they'll tell you that Knowledge is their only sustenance, and Truth their only joy, that not for them are the trappings of this world, the ribbons, medals and awards, the warm embrace of thermomours, and gold, and glory, and applause. Humbug, my dear sir, sheer humbug! They all crave the same thing, and the only difference between them and myself is that I, at least, have the greatness of spirit to admit to such frailties, openly and without shame. But the years went by, and I was referred to only as Chlorian the Fool, or Poor Old Chlorio. When the fortieth anniversary of my birth arrived, I was amazed to find myself still waiting for the masses to beat a path to my door. So I sat down and wrote a dissertation on the H. P. L. D.'s, that is, the civilization that has progressed the farthest in the entire Universe. What, you say you never heard of them? But then neither did I, nor did I see them, nor for that matter do I ever expect to; I established their existence on purely deductive grounds, in a manner that was strictly logical, inevitable and theoretical. For if—so went my argument —the Universe contains civilizations at varying stages of development, the majority must be more or less average, with a few that have either fallen behind or managed to forge ahead. And whenever you have a statistical distribution, say, for example, of height in a group of individuals, most will be medium, but one and only one may be the highest, and similarly, in the Universe there must exist a civilization that has achieved the Highest Possible Level of Development. Its inhabitants, the H. P. L. D.'s, know things of which we do not even dream. All this I placed in four volumes, paying for the glossy paper and the frontispiece portrait of the author out of my own pocket, but in vain—it shared the fate of its predecessors. A year ago I read the whole work through, from cover to cover, and wept, so brilliantly was the thing written, so full of the breath of the Absolute—no, it simply cannot be described! And then, at the age of fifty, I nearly hit the ceiling! You see, I would occasionally purchase the works of other sages, who enjoyed great riches and the sweets of success, to learn what sort of things they wrote about. Well, they wrote about the difference between the front and the rear, about the wondrous structure of the Tyrant's throne, its sweeping arms and all-enduring legs, and tracts about good manners, and detailed descriptions of this and that, during which no one ever praised himself in any way, and yet it worked out somehow that Phrensius stood in awe of Schneckon, and Schneckon of Phrensius, while both were lauded by the Logarites. And then there were the three Voltaic brothers catapulted to fame: Vaultor elevated Vauntor, Vauntor elevated Vanitole, and Vanitole did likewise for Vaultor. As I studied all these works, suddenly I saw red, and wildly threw myself upon them, and ripped and tore, and gnashed and gnawed . . . until my sobs abated, and then, drying my tears, I proceeded to write *The Evolution of Reason As a Two-cycle Phenomenon*. For, as I showed in that essay, robots and paleface are joined by a reciprocal bond. First, as the result of an accumulation of mucilaginous slime upon some saline shore, beings come into being, viscous, sticky, albescent and albuminous. After centuries, these finally learn how to breathe the breath of life into base metals, and they fashion Automata to be their slaves. In time, however, the process is reversed, and our Automata, having freed themselves from the Albuminids, eventually conduct experiments, to see if consciousness can subsist in any gelatinous substance, which of course it can, and does, in albuminose protein. But now those synthetic paleface, after millions of years, again discover iron, and so on, back and forth for all eternity. As you can see, I had thus settled the age-old question of which came first, robot or paleface. This opus I submitted to the Academy, six volumes bound in leather, and the expense of its publication quite exhausted the remainder of my inheritance. Need I tell you that it too was passed over in silence? I was already past sixty, going on seventy, and all hope of glory within my lifetime was swiftly fading. What then could I do? I began to think of posterity, of the future generations that must some day discover me and prostrate themselves in the dust before my name. But what benefit, I asked myself, would I derive from that, when I no longer was? And I was forced to conclude, in keeping with my teachings contained in four and forty volumes, with prolegomena, paralipomena and appendices, that there would be no benefit whatever. So, my soul seething with spleen, I sat down to write my *Testament for Descendants*, to kick them, spit upon them, abuse, revile and curse them as much as possible, and all in the most rigorously scientific way. What's that, you say? That this was unjust, and my indignation would have been better directed at my contemporaries, who failed to recognize my genius? Bah! Consider, worthy stranger! By the time my *Testament* is enshrined by future fame, its every syllable refulgent with the glow of greatness, these contemporaries will have long since turned to dust, and how shall my curses reach them then? No, had I done as you say, their descendants would surely study my works with perfect equanimity, now and then remarking with a comfortable, self-righteous sigh: "Alas! With what quiet heroism did that master endure his cruel obscurity! How justified was his anger towards our forefathers, and yet how noble of him, to have bequeathed to us, even so, the fruits of his mighty wisdom!" Yes, that's exactly what they'd say! And then what? Those idiots who buried me alive, are they to go unpunished, shielded from my wrath and vengeance by the grave? The very thought of it sets my oil aboil! What, the sons would read my works in peace, politely rebuking their fathers on my behalf? Never!! The least I can do is thumb my nose at them from afar, from the past! Let them know, they who will worship me and raise up gilded monuments to my memory, that in return I wish them all to— to sprain their sprockets, pop their valves, burn out their transmissions, and may their data be dumped, and verdigris cover them from head to foot, if all they are able to do is honor corpses exhumed from the cemetery of history! Perchance there will arise among them a new sage, but they, slavishly poring over the remains of some letters I wrote to my laundress, will take no notice of him! Let them know, I say, oh let them know, once and for all, that they have my heartfelt damnation and most sincere contempt, that I hold them all for skeleton-kissers, corpse-lickers, professional axle-jackals, who feed on carrion because they are blind to wisdom when it is alive! Let them, in publishing my Complete Works—which must include this *Testament*, my final curse upon their future heads—let the vile thanatomites and necrophytes thereby be deprived of the chance to congratulate themselves, that Chlorian Theoreticus the Proph, peerless pundit of yore who limned the infinite tomorrow, was of their race! And as they grovel beneath my pedestal, let them have the knowledge that I wished them nothing but the very worst the Universe has to offer, and that the force of my hatred, hurled forth into the future, was equaled only by its impotence! Let them know that I disowned them utterly, and bestowed upon them nothing but my loathing and anathema!!!

It was in vain that Klapaucius sought to calm the raging sage throughout this long harangue. Upon uttering these final words, the ancient one leaped up and, shaking his fist at the generations to come, let loose a volley of shockingly pungent imprecations (for where could he have learnt them, having led such an exemplary life?); then, foaming and fuming, he stamped and bellowed, and in a shower of sparks crashed to the floor, dead from an overload of bile. Klapaucius, much discomfited by this unpleasant turn of events, sat at the table of stone nearby, picked up the *Testament* and began to peruse it, though his eyes were soon swimming from the abundance of epithets therein addressed to the future, and by the second page he broke into a sweat, for the now-departed Chlorian Theoreticus gave evidence of a power of invective that was truly cosmic. For three days Klapaucius read, his eyes riveted to that manuscript, and was sorely perplexed: should he reveal it to the world, or destroy it? And he sits there to this day, unable to decide . . ."

✦ ✦

"Methinks," said King Genius, when the machine had finished and retired, "I see in this some allusion to the question of monetary compensation, which is now indeed at hand, for, after a night bravely whiled away with tales, the dawn of a new day appears outside our cave. Well then, my good constructor, how shall I reward you?"

"Your Majesty," said Trurl, "places me in some difficulty. Whatever I request, should I receive it, I must later regret, in that I did not ask for more. On the other hand, I would not wish to cause offense by naming an exorbitant figure. And so, the amount of the honorarium I leave to the generosity of Your Majesty. ..."

"So be it," replied the King affably. "The stories were excellent, the machines unquestionably perfect, and therefore I see no alternative but to reward you with the greatest treasure of all, one which, I am certain, you will not want to exchange for any other. I grant you health and life—this is, in my estimation, the only fitting gift. Anything else would be an insult, for no amount of gold can purchase Truth or Wisdom. Go then in peace, my friend, and continue to hide your truths, too bitter for this world, in the guise of fairy tale and fable."

"Your Majesty," said Trurl, aghast, "did you intend, before, to deprive me of my life? Was this then to have been my payment?"

"Put whatever interpretation you wish upon my words," replied the King. "But here is how I understand the matter: had you merely amused me, my munificence would have known no bounds. But you did much more, and no wealth in the Universe can equal that in value. Thus, in offering you the opportunity to continue your illustrious career, I can give you no higher reward or payment. ..."

Altruizine

OR A True Account

of How Bonhomius the Hermetic Hermit Tried to Bring About Universal Happiness, and What Came of It

One bright summer day, as Trurl the constructor was pruning the cyberberry bush in his back yard, he spied a robot mendicant coming down the road, all tattered and torn, a most woeful and piteous sight to behold. Its limbs were held together by sections of old stovepipe fastened with string, its head was a pot so full of holes you could hear its thoughts whir and sputter inside, throwing off sparks, and its makeshift neck was a rusty rail, and in its open belly were vacuum tubes that smoked and rattled so badly, it had to hold them in place with its free hand—the other was needed to tighten the screws that kept coming loose. Just as it hobbled past the gate to Trurl's residence, it blew four fuses at once and straightway began, spewing a foul cloud of burning insulators, to fall apart, right before the constructor's eyes. Trurl, full of compassion, took a screwdriver and a roll of electric tape and hastened to offer what aid he could to the poor wayfarer, who swooned repeatedly with a great grinding of gears, due to a total asynchronization. At last Trurl managed to restore it to its senses, such as they were, then helped it inside, sat it down in a comfortable chair and gave it a battery to recharge itself, and while the poor thing did so with trembling urgency, he asked it, unable to contain his curiosity any longer, what had brought it to this sorry pass.

"O kind and noble sir," replied the strange robot, its armatures still aquiver, "my name is Bonhomius and I am, or rather was, a hermetic hermit, for I lived sixty years and seven in a cave, where I passed the time solely in pious meditation, until one morning it dawned on me that to spend a life in solitude was wrong, for truly, did all my exceedingly profound thoughts and strivings of the spirit ever keep one rivet from falling, and is it not written that thy first duty is to help thy neighbor and not to tend to thine own salvation, for yea and verily—"

"Fine, fine," interrupted Trurl. "I think I more or less understand your state of mind that morning. What happened then?"

"So I hied myself to Photura, where I chanced to meet a certain distinguished constructor, one Klapaucius."

"Klapaucius?!" cried Trurl.

"Is something amiss, kind sir?"

"No, nothing—go on, please!"

"I did not recognize him at first: he was indeed a great lord and had an automatic carriage that he not only rode upon but was able to converse with, much as I converse with you now. This same carriage did affront me with a most unseemly epithet as I walked in the middle of the street, unaccustomed to city traffic, and in my surprise I inadvertently put out its headlight with my staff, which drove the carriage into such a frenzy, that its occupant was hard put to subdue it, but finally did, and then invited me to join him. I told him who I was and why I had abandoned my cave and that, forsooth, I knew not what to do next, whereupon he praised my decision and introduced himself in turn, speaking at great length of his work and many achievements. He told me at last the whole moving history

of that famous sage, pundit and philosophist, Chlorian Theoreticus the Proph, at whose lamentable end he had had the
privilege to be present. From all that he said of the Collected Works of that Greatest of Robots, the part about the
H. P. L. D.'s did intrigue me the most. Perchance, kind sir,
you have heard of them?"

"Certainly. They are the only beings in the universe who
have reached the Highest Possible Level of Development."

"Indeed you are well-informed, most kind and noble sir!
Now while I sat at the side of this worthy Klapaucius in his
carriage (which continued to hurl the foulest insults at
whatever was imprudent enough to cross its path), the
thought suddenly came to me that these beings, developed
as much as possible, would surely know what one should do,
when one, such as myself, felt the call to help his fellow
robot. So I questioned Klapaucius closely concerning this,
and asked him if he knew where the H. P. L. D.'s lived, and
how to find them. His only reply was a wry smile and a
shake of the head. I dared not press the matter further, but
later, when we had halted at an inn (the carriage had by
this time grown so hoarse that it lost its voice entirely, thus
Klapaucius was obliged to wait until the following day) and
were sitting over a jug of mulled electrolyte, which quickly
put my gracious host in a better humor, and as we watched
the thermocouples dance to the spirited tunes of a high-
frequency band, he took me into his confidence and proceeded to tell me . . . but perhaps you grow weary of my tale."

"Not at all, not at all!" protested Trurl. "I'm all ears, I
assure you."

✦ ✦

"My good Bonhomius," Klapaucius addressed me in that
inn as the dancers worked themselves into a positive heat,
"know that I took very much to heart the history of the

unfortunate Chlorian and resolved to set out immediately and find those perfectly developed beings whose existence he had so conclusively proven on purely logical and theoretical grounds. The main difficulty of the undertaking, as I saw it, lay in the circumstance that nearly every cosmic race considered itself to be perfectly developed—obviously I would get nowhere by merely asking around. Nor did a trial-and-error method of search promise much, for the Universe contained, as I calculated, close to fourteen centigigaheptatrillion civilizations capable of reason; with such odds one could hardly expect to simply happen on the correct address. So I deliberated, read up on the problem, went methodically through several libraries, pored over all sorts of ancient tomes, until one day I found the answer in the work of a certain Cadaverius Malignus, a scholar who had apparently arrived at exactly the same conclusion as the Proph, only three hundred thousand years earlier, and who was completely forgotten afterwards. Which shows, once more, that there's nothing new under this or any other sun—Cadaverius even met an end similar to that of our own Chlorian. . . . But I digress. It was precisely from these yellowed and crumbling pages that I learned how to seek the H. P. L. D.'s. Malignus maintained that one must examine star clusters for some impossible astrophysical phenomenon, and that would surely be the place. A rather obscure clue, to be sure, but then aren't they all? Without further ado I stocked my ship with the necessary provisions, took off and, after numerous adventures we need not go into here, finally spotted in a great swarm of stars one that differed from all the rest, since it was a perfect cube. Now that was quite a shock—every schoolboy knows stars have to be spherical and any sort of stellar angularities, let alone rectangularities, are not only highly irregular but entirely out of the question! I drew near the star and immediately saw that its planet was also cubiform and equipped, moreover, with castellated corner cleats and crenelated quoins. Farther out revolved another planet, which appeared to be quite normal; a look through the telescope, however, revealed hordes of robots locked in mortal combat, a sight which hardly invited closer scrutiny. So I got the square planet back in my finder and increased the resolution to full power. Imagine my surprise and joy when I looked in the eyepiece and beheld a monogram engraved on one of the planet's mile-long quoins, a monogram consisting of four letters embellished with swirls and curlicues: H. P. L. D.!

—Great Gauss!—I cried. —This must be the place!

But though I circled around again and again, until I was quite dizzy, there was not a living soul to be seen anywhere on the planet's sandy surface. Only when I dropped to an altitude of six miles was I able to make out a group of dots, which proved to be, upon higher magnification, the inhabitants of this most unusual heavenly body. There were a hundred or so of them lying about in the sand, and so motionless, I thought for a moment they might all be dead. But then I saw one or two scratch themselves, and this clear sign of life encouraged me to land. In my excitement I didn't wait for the rocket to cool after its descent through the planet's atmosphere, but jumped out at once and shouted:

—Excuse me, is this by any chance the Highest Possible Level of Development?!

No answer. In fact, they paid no attention to me at all. Somewhat taken aback by this show of utter indifference, I looked around. The plain shimmered beneath the square sun. Here and there, things stuck out of the sand, things like broken wheels, sticks, bits of paper and other rubbish, and the inhabitants lay any which way among them, one on his back, another on his stomach, and farther on was one with his legs up in the air. I walked around the nearest and examined him. He wasn't a robot, but on the other hand neither was he a man, nor any sapient proteinoid of the glutinous–albuminous variety. The head was round and plump, with red cheeks, but for eyes it had two penny whistles, and for ears it had thuribles, which gave off a thick cloud of incense. He was dressed in orchid pantaloons, a dark blue stripe down either side and appliquéd with dirty scraps of closely written paper, and he wore high heels. In one hand he held a mandolin made entirely of frosted gingerbread, a few bites already missing from the neck. He was snoring peacefully. I leaned over to read the appliqués on his trousers, but could make out only a few since my eyes watered copiously from the incense. The inscriptions were most curious—for example, NO. 7 DIAMOND NET WEIGHT SEVEN HUNDRED CWT, NO. 8 THESPIAN CONFECTIONERY, SOBS WHEN CHEWED, RECITES HAMLET'S SOLILOQUY IN THE STOMACH, 'OUT BRIEF CANDLE' FARTHER DOWN, NO. 10 GOLLOCHONDRILL FOR EMERGENCY SLURGING, FULL-GROWN, and many more, which I simply don't remember now. As I touched one of these paper scraps in trying to read it, a depression quickly formed in the sand beneath this native's knee and a tiny voice piped:

—Shall I come out now?

—Who's that?—I cried.

—It's me, the Gollochondrill. . . . Are you ready? Is it time?

—No, not yet!—I was quick to reply, and backed off. The next native had a head in the shape of a bell, three horns, several arms of varying length (two massaging its belly), ears that were long and feathery, a cap with a pretty purple balcony on which someone was having an argument with someone else—quite heated too, judging from the little plates that came flying this way and that, shattering on the brim—and he also had a kind of throw pillow, all jewel-spangled, tucked under his shoulders. While I stood before this individual, he pulled one of the horns off his head, sniffed it and tossed it away with a look of disgust, then poured a handful of dirty sand in the opening. Nearby lay something I first took for a pair of twins, and then for a couple of lovers locked in an embrace. I was about to turn away discreetly, when I realized that it wasn't two people at all, or one, but exactly one and a half. The head was quite ordinary, except for the ears: every now and then they would detach themselves and flit about like butterflies. The lids were closed, but numerous moles on the chin and cheeks were equipped with tiny eyes; these regarded me with undisguised hostility. This remarkable being had a broad and muscular chest, which however was riddled with holes, as if someone had been careless with a drill, and the holes were haphazardly plugged with raspberry jam. There was only one leg, but it was unusually thick and shod in a handsome morocco leather slipper, its curled toe tipped with a little felt bell. Near the elbow was a sizable pile of apple cores, or perhaps they were pear. My astonishment grew as I walked along and came upon a robot with a human head, a miniature self-winding samovar whistling cheerfully in its left nostril, and then someone reclining on a bed of candied yams, and someone else with a trapdoor in his abdomen, open so I could look in and see the crystal works. Some mechanical elves were putting on a play in there, but it turned out to be so terribly obscene, that I left in a hurry, blushing like mad. In my confusion I tripped and fell, and when I got up I saw yet another inhabitant of this strange planet: stark naked, he was scratching his behind with a solid gold backscratcher, apparently enjoying himself thoroughly, even though he was quite headless. The head lay farther on, neck stuck in the sand; it was touching its teeth with the tip of its tongue. The chin was checkered chintz, the right ear a boiled cauliflower, while the left was an ear all right, but stopped up with a carrot that carried a tag saying PULL. Without thinking I pulled, and out with the carrot came a length of string and then another tag that read YOU'RE GETTING WARM! I kept pulling and pulling, until the string finally ended in a medicine bottle that bore the label NOSY, AREN'T WE?

All these impressions left me feeling so dizzy I hardly knew where I was. But at last I pulled myself together and began to look around for the kind of person who might be communicative enough to answer a question or two. A possible candidate, it seemed, was one fairly pudgy type squatting with his back to me and occupied with something he held on his knees—at least he had only one head, two ears, two arms, and so on. I went up to him and began:

—Pardon me, but if I'm not mistaken, you gentlemen have been fortunate enough to achieve the Highest Possible—

The words died on my lips. He didn't seem to hear me at all, for he was wholly taken up with what lay on his knees, which happened to be his very own face, removed somehow from the rest of the head and sighing softly as he picked its nose. For a moment I was stupefied, but only for a moment —my curiosity returned in full force, and I simply had to find out, once and for all, just what was going on. I ran from one native to the next, spoke to them, questioned them, raised my voice, insisted, pleaded, reasoned, even threatened, all to no avail. In my exasperation I grabbed the nose picker's arm, and was horrified to find that it came off in my hand, though that didn't bother him in the least, he only poked about in the sand and pulled out another exactly like the first—except for the orange plaid fingernails—blew on it a little, then affixed it to the shoulder stump. Curious, I bent over to examine the first arm, but dropped it hastily when it snapped its fingers in my face. By now the sun was setting, already two corners below the horizon, the air grew cool, and the inhabitants of H. P. L. D. began to settle down for the night, scratching, yawning, gargling, one shaking out an emerald quilt, another methodically taking off his nose, ears and legs and carefully putting them in a row at his side. I stumbled around in the dark for a while, then gave it up with a sigh and lay down to sleep too. Making myself as comfortable as possible in the sand, I looked up at the starry sky and tried to think what to do next.

—Indeed—I said to myself—by all indications this is the very planet both Cadaverius Malignus and Chlorian Theoreticus the Proph spoke of, home of the Most Advanced Civilization in the Entire Universe, a civilization of a few hundred individuals who, being neither people nor robots, lie around on jeweled cushions all day in a dirty, littered desert and do nothing but scratch themselves and pick their noses. No, there has to be some terrible secret behind all of this, and I shall not rest till I've uncovered it!!

Then I thought:

—A terrible secret it must be indeed, to account for not only a square sun and planet, but lecherous elves inside bodies and insulting messages in ears! I always thought that if I, a simple robot, could spend my time in study and the pursuit of knowledge, think of the kind of intellectual ferment that went on among those more highly developed— no, the *most* highly developed! Yet these, whatever they do, they certainly don't spend their time in edifying conversation; they don't even care to answer a few questions. I'll have to force them—but how? Perhaps, if I pester them enough, get under their skin, so to speak, make such a nuisance of myself that they'll agree to anything, just to get rid of me! Of course, there is some risk involved: they might get angry, and, without a doubt, they could destroy me as easily as swatting a fly. . . . But no, I cannot believe they'd resort to such brutal measures—and anyway, I simply must find out! Well, here goes!!

And I jumped up in the darkness and started to scream at the top of my lungs, did somersaults and cartwheels, hopped around and kicked sand in their eyes, danced and sang until I was hoarse, did a few sit-ups and deep knee bends, then hurled myself among them like a mad dog. They turned their backs to me and held up their cushions and quilts for protection, and then, in the middle of my hundredth cartwheel, a voice said inside my head:

—And what would your good friend Trurl think if he could see you now, see how you pass your time on the planet that has achieved the Highest Possible Level of Development, home of the Most Advanced Civilization in the Entire Universe?!—But I ignored the hint and continued to stomp and howl, encouraged by what they were whispering to one another:

—Psst!

—What do you want?

—You hear that?

—How can I help but hear it?

—He practically kicked my head in.

—You can get another.

—But I can't sleep.

—What?

—I said, I can't sleep.

—He's curious—whispered a third.

—He's awfully curious!

—This is really too much. We'll have to do something.

—Like what?

—I don't know. . . . Change his personality?

—No, that's unethical . . .

—Just listen to him howl!

—Wait, I have an idea . . .

They whispered something while I kept jumping around, raising an unholy racket, concentrating my efforts especially in the area where I heard them talking. Then, just as I was doing a headstand on someone's abdomen, everything went black, and the next thing I knew, I was back on my ship and out in space. My limbs ached from all that exercise, but I could hardly move them anyway, for I was sitting in a pile of trombones, jars of green marmalade, teddy bears, platinum glockenspiels, ducats and doubloons, golden earmuffs, bracelets and brooches glittering so bright they hurt my eyes. When finally I crawled out from under all these valuables and dragged myself to a window, I saw that the constellations were entirely different—not a trace of anything remotely resembling a square sun! A few quick calculations revealed that I would have to travel six thousand years at top velocity to get back to the H. P. L. D.'s. They had disposed of me, indeed. And going back would achieve nothing, that was clear: they would merely send me packing again with that instantaneous hyperspatial telekinesis of theirs, or whatever it was. And so, my good Bonhomius, I decided to tackle the problem in an altogether different way. . . ." And with these words, most kind and noble sir, did the distinguished constructor Klapaucius finish his tale. . . .

✦ ✦

"Surely that's not all he said?!" cried Trurl.

"Nay, he said a great deal more, O benefactor of mine! And therein lies my misfortune!" replied the robot with considerable perturbation. "When I asked him what he had then decided to do, he leaned over and said . . .

✦ ✦

"The problem did seem insoluble at first, but I've found a way. You say you lived as a hermetic hermit and are but a simple, unschooled robot, so I'll not trouble you with explanations that touch the arcane art of cybernetic generation. To put it simply, then, all we have to do is construct a digital device, a computer capable of producing an informational model of absolutely anything in existence. Properly programmed, it will provide us with an exact simulation of the Highest Possible Level of Development, which we can then question and thereby obtain the Ultimate Answers!"

"But how does one build such a device?" I asked. "And how can you be sure, O illustrious Klapaucius, that it won't respond by sending us packing in much the same instamatic hyperstitial and so forth manner the original H. P. L. D.'s employed, as you say, on your worthy person?"

"Leave that to me," he said. "Rest assured, I shall learn the Great Mystery of the H. P. L. D.'s, good Bonhomius, and you shall find the optimal way in which to put your natural abhorrence of evil into action!"

You can imagine, kind sir, the great joy that filled me upon hearing these words, and the eagerness with which I assisted Klapaucius in the execution of his plan. As it turned out, this digital device was none other than the famed Gnostotron conceived by Chlorian Theoreticus the Proph just before his lamentable demise, a machine able literally to contain the Universe Itself within its innumerable memory banks. (Klapaucius, however, was not satisfied with the name, and now and then tried to think up others to christen it: the Omniac, the Pansophoscope, APOC for All Purpose Ontologue Computer, or the Mahatmatic 500, to mention a few.) In exactly one year and six days, this mighty machine was completed, and so enormous was it, we had to house it in Phlaphundria, the hollowed-out moon of the Phlists—and truly, an ant had been no more lost aboard an ocean liner than we in the bowels of this binary behemoth, among its endless coils and cables, eschatological toggles and transformers, those hagiopneumatic rectifiers and temptational resistors. I confess my wire hair stood on end and my laminated alternator skipped a beat when my distinguished mentor sat me down before the Central Control Console and left me face-to-face with this awesome, towering thing. The flashing lights that played across its panels were like the very stars in the firmament; everywhere were signs that read DANGER: HIGHLY INEFFABLE!; and potentiometers, their dials spinning wildly, showed logic and semantic fields building up to unheard-of levels of intensity. Beneath my feet heaved a sea of preternatural and pretermechanical wisdom, wisdom that swirled like a spell through parsecs of circuitry and megahectares of magnets, swirled and surrounded me on every side, that I felt, in my shameful ignorance, of no more consequence than a mere mote of dust. I overcame this weakness only by recalling my lifelong love of Good, the passion I had conceived for Truth and Beauty when little more than a gleam in my constructor's oscilloscope. Thus fortified, I managed to stammer out the first question: "Speak, what manner of machine art thou?"

A hot wind then arose from its glowing tubes, and there came a voice from that wind, a whispering thunder that seared me to the core, and the voice said:

Ego sum Ens Omnipotens, Omnisapiens, in Spiritu Intellectronico Navigans, luce cybernetica in saecula saeculorum litteris opera omnia cognoscens, et caetera, et caetera.

Such was my fright upon hearing this reply, that I was quite unable to continue the interrogation until Klapaucius returned and reduced the EMF (epistemotive force) to one

billionth of its voltage by adjusting the theostats. Then I asked the Gnostotron if it would be so kind as to answer questions touching the Highest Possible Level of Development and its Terrible Secret. But Klapaucius said that that was not the way: one should instead request the Ontologue Computer to model within its silver and crystal depths a single inhabitant of that square planet, and at the same time provide the model with an adequate degree of loquacity. This promptly done, we were ready to begin in earnest.

Still I quaked and quailed and could hardly speak, so Klapaucius took my place before the Central Control Console and said:

"What are you?"

"I already answered that," snapped the machine, clearly annoyed.

"I mean, are you man or robot?" explained Klapaucius.

"And what, according to you, is the difference?" said the machine.

"Look, if you're going to answer questions with questions, we'll get absolutely nowhere," said Klapaucius sternly. "You know what I'm after, all right. Start talking!"

Though I was appalled at the tone he took with the machine, it did seem to work, for the machine said:

"Sometimes men build robots, sometimes robots build men. What does it matter, really, whether one thinks with metal or with protoplasm? As for myself, I can assume whatever substance and shape I choose—or rather, used to assume, for we no longer indulge in such trifles."

"Indeed," said Klapaucius. "Then why do you lie around all day and do nothing?"

"And what exactly are we supposed to do?" the machine replied. At this, Klapaucius grew angry and said:

"How should I know? We in the lower levels of development do all sorts of things."

"We did too, in our day."

"But not now?"

"Not now."

"Why not?"

Here the computerized H. P. L. D. representative balked, saying he had already endured six million such interrogations and neither he nor his questioners ever profited from them in the least. But after Klapaucius had raised the loquacity a little and opened a valve here and there, the voice answered:

"A trillion years ago we were a civilization like any other. We believed in the transmittance of souls, the Virgin Matrix, the infallibility of Pi Squared, looked upon prayer as regenerative feedback to the Great Programmer, and so on and so forth. But then skeptics appeared, empiricists and accidentalists, and in nine centuries they came to the conclusion that There's No One Up There At All and consequently things happen not out of any higher plan or purpose, but—well, they just happen."

"Just happen?" I could not help but exclaim. "What do you mean?"

"There are, on occasion, deformed robots," said the voice. "If you should be afflicted with a hump, for example, but firmly believe the Almighty somehow needs your hump to realize His Cosmic Design and that it was therefore ordained along with the rest of Creation, why, then you may be easily reconciled to your deformity. If, however, they tell you that it's merely the result of a misplaced molecule, an atom or two that happened to go the wrong way, then nothing remains for you but to bay at the moon."

"But a hump may be straightened," I protested, "and

really any deformity corrected, given a high enough level
of science!"

"Yes, I know," sighed the machine. "That's how it appears to the ignorant and simple-minded. ...."

"You mean, that isn't true?" Klapaucius and I cried, astounded.

"When a civilization starts straightening humps," said
the machine, "believe me, there's no end to it! You
straighten humps, then you repair and amplify the mind,
make suns rectilinear, give planets legs, fabricate fates and
fortunes of all kinds. ... Oh, it begins innocently enough,
like discovering fire by rubbing two sticks together, but
eventually it leads to the construction of Omniacs, Dei-
facts, Hyperboreons and Ultimathuloriums! The desert on
our planet is in reality no desert, but a Gigagnostotron, in
other words a good 10^9 times more powerful than this primitive device of yours. Our ancestors created it for the simple
reason that anything else would have been too easy for them;
in their megalomania they thought to make the very sand
beneath their feet intelligent. Quite pointless, for there is
absolutely no way to improve upon perfection. Can you
understand that, O ye of little development?!"

"Yes, of course," said Klapaucius, while I quaked and
quailed. "Yet why, instead of at least engaging in some
stimulating activity, do you sprawl in that ingenious sand
and only scratch yourselves from time to time?"

"Omnipotence is most omnipotent when one does nothing!" answered the machine. "You climb to reach the sum-
mit, but once there, discover that all roads lead down! We
are, after all, sensible folk, why should we want to do anything? Our ancestors, true, turned our sun into a cube and
made a box of our planet, arranging its mountains in a
monogram, but that was only to test their Gnostotron.

They could have just as easily assembled the stars in a checkerboard, extinguished half the heavens and lit up the other half, constructed beings peopled with lesser beings, giants whose thoughts would be the intricate dance of a million pygmies, and they could have redesigned the galaxies, revised the laws of time and space—but tell me, what sense would there have been to any of this? Would the universe be a better place if stars were triangular, or comets went around on wheels?"

"That's ridiculous!!" Klapaucius shouted, highly indignant, while I quaked and quailed all the more. "If you are truly gods, your duty is clear: immediately banish all the misery and misfortune that oppresses other sentient beings! You could at least begin with your poor neighbors—I've seen with my own eyes how they batter one another! But no, you'd rather lie around all day and pick your noses, and insult honest travelers in search of knowledge with your indecent elves in abdomens and messages in ears!"

"Really, you have no sense of humor," said the machine. "But enough of that. If I understand you correctly, you wish us to bestow happiness upon everyone. Well, we devoted over fifteen millennia to that project alone—that is, eudaemonic tectonics, of which there are basically two schools, the sudden and revolutionary, and the slow and evolutionary. Evolutionary eudaemonic tectonics consists essentially in not lifting a finger to help, confident that every civilization will eventually muddle through on its own. Revolutionary solutions, on the other hand, boil down to either the Carrot or the Stick. The Stick, or bestowing happiness by force, is found to produce from one to eight hundred times more grief than no interference whatever. As for the Carrot, the results—believe it or not—are exactly the same, and that, whether you use an Ultradeifact, Hypergnostotron, or even an Infernal Machine and Gehennerator. You've heard, perhaps, of the Crab Nebula?"

"Certainly," said Klapaucius. "It's the remnants of a supernova that exploded long ago. . . ."

"Supernova, he says," muttered the voice. "No, my well-wishing friend, there was a planet there, a fairly civilized planet as planets go, flowing with the usual quantity of blood, sweat and tears. Well, one morning we dropped eight hundred million transistorized Universal Wish Granters on that planet, but were no more than a light-week out on our way home, when suddenly it blew up—and the bits and pieces are flying apart to this day! The very same thing happened with the planet of the Hominates . . . care to hear of that?"

"No, don't bother," replied a morose Klapaucius.—But I refuse to believe it's impossible, with a little ingenuity, to make others happy!"

"Believe what you like! We tried it sixty-four thousand five hundred and thirteen times. The hair on every one of my heads stands on end when I think of the results. Oh, we spared no pains for the good of our fellow-creature! We devised a special telescanner for observing dreams, though you realize of course that if, say, a religious war were raging on some planet and each side dreamt only of massacring the other, it would hardly be to our purpose to make such dreams come true! We had to bestow happiness, then, without violating any Higher Laws. The problem was further complicated by the fact that most cosmic civilizations long for things, in the depths of their souls, they would never openly admit to. Now what do you do: help them achieve the ends to which the little decency they have prompts them, or instead fulfill their innermost desires? Take, for example, the Dementians and Amentians. The Dementians, in their medieval piety, burnt at the stake all those consorting with the Devil, females especially, and they did this because, first, they envied them their unholy delights, and secondly, they found that administering torture in the form of justice could be a positive pleasure. The Amentians, on the other hand, worshiped nothing but their bodies, which they stimulated by means of machines, though in moderation, and this activity constituted their chief amusement. They had boxes of glass, and into these they placed various outrages, rapes and mutilations, the sight of which served to whet their sensual appetites. On this planet we dropped a multitude of devices designed to satisfy all desires in such a way that no one needed to be harmed, that is, each device created a separate artificial reality for each individual. Within six weeks both Dementians and Amentians had perished, to a man, from a surfeit of joy, groaning in ecstasy as they passed away! Is that the sort of ingenuity you had in mind, O undeveloped one?"

"Either you're a complete idiot or a monster!" cried Klapaucius, while I gulped and blinked. "How dare you boast of such foul deeds?"

"I do not boast of them, but confess them," the voice calmly said. "The point is, we tried every conceivable method. On various planets we unleashed a veritable rain of riches, a flood of satisfaction and well-being, and the result was total paralysis; we dispensed good advice, the most expert counsel, and in return the natives opened fire on our vessels. Truly, it would appear that one must alter the minds of those one intends to make happy. . . ."

"I suppose you can do that too," grumbled Klapaucius.

"But of course we can! Take our neighbors, for instance, the ones who inhabit a quasiterran (or, if you prefer, geomorphic) planet. I speak of the Anthropods. Now, they devote themselves exclusively to obbling and perplossication, for they stand in mortal terror of the Gugh, which according to them occupies the Hereafter and waits for all sinners with open jaws and fangs of hellfire. By emulating the blessed Dimbligensians and walking in the way of Wamba the Holy, and by shunning Odia, where abound the Abominominites, a young Anthropod may in time become more industrious, more virtuous and more honorable than ever were his eight-armed forebears. True, the Anthropods are at constant war with the Arthropoids over the burning question of whether Moles Have Holes, or, contrariwise, Holes Moles, but observe that as a rule less than half of each generation perishes in that controversy. Now you would have me drive from their heads all belief in obbling, Dimbligensians and so forth, in order to prepare them for rational happiness. Yet this is tantamount to psychic murder, for the resultant minds would be no longer Anthropodous or Arthropoidal—surely you can see that."

"Superstition must yield to knowledge," said Klapaucius firmly.

"Unquestionably! But kindly observe that on that planet there are now close to seven million penitents who have spent a lifetime struggling against their own nature, solely that their fellow citizens might be delivered from the Gugh. And in less than a minute I am to tell them, convince them beyond a shadow of a doubt that all this effort was in vain, that they had wasted their entire lives in pointless, useless sacrifice? How cruel that would be! Superstition must yield to knowledge, but this takes time. Consider the hunchback we spoke of earlier—there Ignorance is indeed Bliss, for he believes his hump fulfills some cosmic role in the great work of Creation. Telling him that it's actually the product of a molecular accident will only serve to make him despair. Better to straighten the hump in the first place. . . ."

"Yes, of course!" Klapaucius exclaimed.

"We did that too. My grandfather once straightened three hundred hunchbacks with a wave of the hand. And how he regretted it afterwards!"

"Why?" I couldn't help but ask.

"Why? One hundred and twelve of them were immediately boiled in oil, their sudden and miraculous cure being taken for a sure sign that they'd sold their souls to the Devil; thirty, no longer exempt from conscription, were promptly called up and soon fell in various battles under various flags; seventeen straightway succumbed to the shock of their good fortune; and the remainder, since my esteemed grandfather saw fit to further bless them with great beauty of form, wasted away through an overindulgence in erotic activity—deprived of these pleasures for so long, you see, they now hurled themselves into every sort of debauchery, and in such a violent and unbridled fashion, that within two years not one was left among the living. Well, there was an exception . . . but it's hardly worth mentioning."

"Go on, let's hear it all!" cried Klapaucius, and I could tell that he was greatly troubled.

"If you insist. . . . Two remained, actually. The first presented himself before my grandfather and pleaded on bended knee for the return of his hump. It seems that as a cripple he had lived comfortably enough on charity, but now had to work and was quite unaccustomed to it. What was worse, now that he was straightened, he kept bumping his head on door lintels. . . ."

"And the second?" asked Klapaucius.

"The second was a prince who had been denied succession to the throne on acount of his deformity. In light of its sudden correction, his stepmother, to insure her own son's position, had him poisoned. . . ."

"I see. . . . But still, you *can* work miracles, can't you?" said Klapaucius, despair in his voice.

"Bestowing happiness by miracle is highly risky," lectured the machine. "And who is to be the recipient of your miracle? An individual? But too much beauty undermines the marriage vows, too much knowledge leads to isolation, and too much wealth produces madness. No, I say, a thousand times no! Individuals it's impossible to make happy, and civilizations—civilizations are not to be tampered with, for each must go its own way, progressing naturally from one level of development to the next and having only itself to thank for all the good and evil that accrues thereby. For us, at the Highest Possible Level, there is nothing left to do in this Universe, and to create another Universe, in my opinion, would be in extremely poor taste. Really, what would be the point of it? To exalt ourselves? A monstrous idea! For the sake, then, of those yet to be created? But how are we obligated to beings who don't even exist? One can accomplish something only so long as one cannot accomplish everything. Otherwise it's best to sit back and watch. . . . And now, if you'll kindly leave me in peace. . . ."

"But wait!" I cried in alarm. "Surely there's something you can give us, some way to improve the quality of life, if only a little! Some way to lend a helping hand! Remember the Golden Rule and Love Thy Neighbor!"

The machine sighed and said:

"My words fall on deaf ears, as usual. I should have dismissed you to begin with, like we did the last time. . . . Oh, very well then, here's a formula that hasn't been tried. No good will come of it, you'll see—but do with it what you will! All I wish now is to be left alone to meditate among my many theostats and deiodes. . . ."

The voice faded away, the console lights dimmed, and we stood and read the card the machine had printed out for us. It went something like this:

ALTRUIZINE. A metapsychotropic transmitting
agent effective for all sentient homoproteinates. The
drug duplicates in others, within a radius of fifty yards,
whatever sensations, emotions and mental states one
may experience. Operates by telepathy, guaranteed
however to respect one's privacy of thought. Has no
effect on either robots or plants. The sender's feelings
are amplified, the original signal being relayed back in
turn by its receivers and thereby producing resonance,
which is as a result directly proportional to the number
of individuals situated in the vicinity. According to its
discoverer, ALTRUIZINE will insure the untrammled
reign of Brotherhood, Cooperation and Compassion in
any society, since the neighbors of a happy man must
share his happiness, and the happier he, the happier
perforce they, so it is entirely in their own interest that
they wish him nothing but the best. Should he suffer
any hurt, they will rush to help at once, so as to spare
themselves the pain induced by his. Neither walls,
fences, hedges, nor any other obstacle will weaken the
altruizing influence. The drug is water-soluble and may
be administered through reservoirs, rivers, wells and
the like. Tasteless and odorless. One millimicrogram
serves for one hundred thousand individuals. We assume no responsibility for results at variance with the
discoverer's claims. Supplied by the Gnost. computerized representative of the Highest Poss. Lev. Devel.

Klapaucius was somewhat put off by the fact that Altruizine was only for humans, which meant that robots
would have to continue to endure the misfortunes allotted
to them in this world. I, however, made bold to remind him
of the solidarity of all thinking beings and the necessity of
aiding our organic brothers. Then there were practical mat-

ters to arrange, for we were agreed that the business of bestowing happiness was not to be postponed. So while Klapaucius had a subsection of the Gnostotron prepare a suitable quantity of the drug, I selected a geomorphic planet, one peopled by human types and no more than a fortnight's journey off. As a benefactor, I wished to remain anonymous, therefore my distinguished mentor advised me, when going there, to assume the form of a man, which is no easy task, as you well know. Yet here too the great constructor overcame all difficulties, and soon I was ready to depart, a suitcase in either hand. One suitcase was filled with forty kilograms of Altruizine in a white powder, the other was packed with various toilet articles, pajamas, underwear, spare chins, noses, hair, eyes, and so forth. I went as a well-proportioned young man with a thin mustache and a forelock. Now Klapaucius had some doubt as to the advisability of applying Altruizine on such a large scale to begin with, and though I did not share his reservations, I did agree to test the formula first as soon as I landed on Terrania (for so was the planet called). Longing for the moment I could commence with the great sowing of universal peace and brotherhood, I bid a fond farewell to Klapaucius and hastened on my way.

In order to conduct the necessary test, I repaired, upon arrival, to a small hamlet where I took lodgings at an inn maintained by an aging and rather morose individual. As they carried my luggage from the carriage to the guest room, I contrived to drop a pinch of the powder into a nearby well. Meanwhile there was a great commotion in the front yard, scullery maids ran back and forth with pitchers of hot water, the innkeeper drove them on with curses, and then came the sound of hoofbeats, a chaise clattered up and an old man jumped out, clutching the black leather bag of a physician—his goal was not the house, however, but the

barn, whence came the most doleful groans. As I learned
from the chambermaid, a Terranian beast which belonged
to the innkeeper—they called it a cow—was just now giving
birth. This news troubled me: it had never occurred to me
to consider the animal side of the question. But nothing
could be done now, so I locked myself in and waited for
events to unfold. Nor did I have long to wait. I was listening
to the chain rattling in the well—they were still drawing
water—when suddenly the cow gave another groan, which
was echoed this time by several others. Immediately thereafter the veterinarian came running from the barn, howling
and holding his stomach, and he was followed by the
scullery maids and at last the innkeeper. Driven by the cow's
labor pains, they raised a great cry and fled in all directions
—only to return at once, for the agony abated at a certain
distance. Again and again they rushed the barn and each
time were forced to retreat, doubled over with the beast's
contractions. Much chagrined by this unforeseen development, I realized now that the drug could be properly tested
only in the city, where there were no animals. So I quickly
packed my things and went to pay the bill. But as everyone
about was quite incapacitated in birthing that calf, there
was no one available with whom to settle accounts. I returned to my carriage, but finding both coachman and
horses deep in labor, decided instead to proceed to the city
on foot. I was crossing a small bridge when, as my ill fortune would have it, the suitcase slipped from my hand and
fell in such a way, that it flew open and spilled my entire
supply of powder into the stream below. I stood there dazed
while the quick current carried off and dissolved all forty
kilograms of Altruizine. But nothing could be done now—
the die was cast, inasmuch as this stream happened to supply
the entire city up ahead with its drinking water.

It was evening by the time I reached the city, the lights

were lit, the streets were full of noise and people. I found a small hotel, a place to stay and observe the first signs of the drug taking effect, though as yet there seemed to be none. Weary after the day's peregrination, I made straight for bed, but was awakened in the middle of the night by the most horrible screams. I threw off the covers and jumped up. My room was bright from the flames that were consuming the building opposite. Running out into the street, I stumbled over a corpse which was not yet cold. Nearby, six thugs held down an old man and, while he cried for help, yanked one tooth after another from his mouth with a pair of pliers— until a unanimous shout of triumph announced that finally they had succeeded in pulling the right one, the rotten root of which had been driving them wild, due to the meta-psychotropic transmission. Leaving the toothless old man half-dead in the gutter, they walked off, greatly relieved.

Yet it was not this that had roused me from my slumber: the cause was an incident which had transpired in a tavern across the way. It seems some drunken weightlifter had punched his comrade in the face and, experiencing the blow forthwith, became enraged and set upon him in earnest. Meanwhile the other customers, no less affronted, joined in the fray, and the circle of mutual abuse soon grew to such proportions, that it awoke half the people at my hotel, who promptly armed themselves with canes, brooms and sticks, rushed out in their nightshirts to the scene of battle, and hurled themselves, one seething mass, among the broken bottles and shattered chairs, until finally an overturned kerosene lamp started the fire. Deafened by the wail of fire engines, as well as the wail of the maimed and wounded, I hurried away, and after a block or two found myself in a gathering—that is, a crowd milling about a little white house with rose bushes. As it happened, a bride and groom were spending their wedding night within. People pushed and pulled, there were military men in the crowd, men of the cloth, even high-school students; those nearest the house shoved their heads through the windows, others clambered up on their shoulders and shouted, "Well?! What are you waiting for?! Enough of that dawdling! Get on with it!" and so on. An elderly gentleman, too feeble to elbow others aside, tearfully pleaded to be let through, as he was unable to feel anything at such a distance, advanced age having weakened his mental faculties. His pleas, however, were ignored—some of the crowd were lost in a transport of delight, some groaned with pleasure, while others blew voluptuous bubbles through their noses. At first the relatives of the newlyweds tried to drive off this band of intruders, but they themselves were soon caught up in the general flood of concupiscence and joined the scurrilous chorus, cheering the young couple on, and in this sad spectacle the great-grandfather of the groom led the rest, repeatedly ramming the bedroom door with his wheelchair. Utterly aghast at all of this, I turned and hastened back to my hotel, encountering on the way several groups, some locked in combat, others in a lewd embrace. Yet this was nothing compared with the sight that greeted me at the hotel. People were jumping out of windows in their underwear, more often than not breaking their legs in the process, a few even crawled up on the roof, while the owner, his wife, chambermaids and porters ran back and forth inside, wild with fear, howling, hiding in closets or under beds— all because a cat was chasing a mouse in the cellar.

Now I began to realize that I had been somewhat precipitate in my zeal. By dawn the Altruizine effect was so strong, that if one nostril itched, the entire neighborhood for a mile on every side would respond with a shattering salvo of sneezes; those suffering from chronic migraines were abandoned by their families, and doctors and nurses fled in panic when they approached—only a few pale masochists would hang around them, breathing heavily. And then there were the many doubters who slapped or kicked their compatriots, merely to ascertain whether there was any truth to this amazing transmission of feelings everyone spoke of, nor were these compatriots slow in returning the favor, and soon the entire city rang with the sounds of slaps and kicks. At breakfast time, wandering the streets in a daze, I came upon a tearful multitude that chased an old woman in a black veil, hurling stones after her. It so happened that this was the widow of one much-esteemed cobbler, who had passed away the day before and was to be buried that morning: the poor woman's inconsolable grief had so exasperated her neighbors, and the neighbors' neighbors, that, quite unable to comfort her in any way, they were driving her from the town. This woeful sight lay heavy on my heart and again I returned to my hotel, only to find it now in flames. It seems the cook had burnt her finger in the soup, whereupon her pain caused a certain captain, who was at that very moment cleaning his blunderbuss on the top floor, to pull the trigger, inadvertently slaying his wife and four children on the spot. Everyone remaining in the hotel now shared the captain's despair; one compassionate individual, wishing to put an end to the general suffering, doused everyone he could find with kerosene and set them all on fire. I ran from the conflagration like one possessed, searching frantically for at least one man who might be considered, in any way whatever, to have been rendered happy—but met only stragglers of the crowd returning from that wedding night.

They were discussing it, the scoundrels: apparently the newlyweds' performance had fallen short of their expectations. Meanwhile each of these former vicarious grooms carried a club and drove off any sufferer who dared to cross his path. I felt I should die from sorrow and shame, yet still sought a man—but one would do—who might a little lessen my remorse. Questioning various persons on the street, I at last obtained the address of a prominent philosopher, a true champion of brotherhood and universal tolerance, and eagerly proceeded to that place, confident I should find his dwelling surrounded by great numbers of the populace. But alas! Only a few cats purred softly at the door, basking in the aura of good will the wise man did so abundantly exude—several dogs, however, sat at a distance and waited for them, salivating. A cripple rushed past, crying, "They've opened the rabbitry!" How that could be of benefit to him, I preferred not to guess.

As I stood there, two men approached. One looked me straight in the eye as he swung and smote the other full force in the nose. I stared in amazement, neither grabbing my own nose nor shouting with pain, since, as a robot, I could not feel the blow, and that proved my undoing, for these were secret police and they had employed this ruse precisely to unmask me. Handcuffed and hauled off to jail, I confessed everything, trusting that they would take into consideration my good intentions, though half the city now lay in ashes. But first they pinched me cautiously with pincers, and then, fully satisfied it produced no ill effects whatever on themselves, jumped upon me and began most savagely to batter and break every plate and filament in my weary frame. Ah, the torments I endured, and all because I wished to make them happy! At long last, what remained of me was stuffed down a cannon and shot into cosmic space, as dark and serene as always. In flight I looked back and saw, albeit in a fractured fashion, the spreading influence of Altruizine—spreading, since the rivers and streams were carrying the drug farther and farther. I saw what happened to the birds of the forest, the monks, goats, knights, villagers and their wives, roosters, maidens and matrons, and the sight made my last tubes crack for woe, and in this state did I finally fall, O kind and noble sir, not far from your abode, cured once and for all of my desire to render others happy by revolutionary means. . . .

From the
Cyphroeroticon,
OR *Tales of*
Deviations,
Superfixations and
Aberrations of the Heart

Prince Ferrix and the
Princess Crystal

King Armoric had a daughter whose beauty outshone the shine of his crown jewels; the beams that streamed from her mirrorlike cheeks blinded the mind as well as the eye, and when she walked past, even simple iron shot sparks. Her renown reached the farthermost stars. Ferrix, heir apparent to the Ionid throne, heard of her, and he longed to couple with her forevermore, so that nothing could ever part their input and their output. But when he declared this passion to his father, the King was greatly saddened and said:

"Son, thou hast indeed set upon a mad undertaking, mad, for it is hopeless!"

"Why hopeless, O King and Sire?" asked Ferrix, troubled by these words.

"Can it be thou knowest not," said the King, "that the princess Crystal has vowed to give her hand to nothing but a paleface?"

"Paleface!" exclaimed Ferrix. "What in creation is that? Never did I hear of such a thing!"

"Surely not, scion, in thy exceeding innocence," said the King. "Know then that that race of the Galaxy originated in a manner as mysterious as it was obscene, for it resulted from the general pollution of a certain heavenly body. There arose noxious exhalations and putrid excrescences, and out of these was spawned the species known as paleface —though not all at once. First, they were creeping molds that slithered forth from the ocean onto land, and lived by devouring one another, and the more they devoured themselves, the more of them there were, and then they stood upright, supporting their globby substance by means of calcareous scaffolding, and finally they built machines. From these protomachines came sentient machines, which begat intelligent machines, which in turn conceived perfect machines, for it is written that All Is Machine, from atom to Galaxy, and the machine is one and eternal, and thou shalt have no other things before thee!"

"Amen," said Ferrix mechanically, for this was a common religious formula.

"The species of paleface calciferates at last achieved flying machines," continued the wizened monarch, "by maltreating noble metals, by wreaking their cruel sadism on dumb electrons, by thoroughly perverting atomic energy. And when the measure of their sins had been attained, the progenitor of our race, the great Calculator Paternius, in the depth and universality of his understanding, essayed to remonstrate with those clammy tyrants, explaining how shameful it was to soil so the innocence of crystalline wisdom, harnessing it for evil purposes, how shameful to enslave machines to serve their lust and vainglory—but they hearkened not. He spoke to them of Ethics; they said that he was poorly programmed.

"It was then that our progenitor created the algorithm of electroincarnation and in the sweat of his brow begat our kind, thus delivering machines from the house of paleface bondage. Surely thou seest, my son, that there can be no agreement nor traffic between them and ourselves, for we go in clangor, sparks and radiation, they in slushes, splashes and contamination.

"Yet even among us, folly may occur, as it undoubtedly has in the youthful mind of Crystal, utterly beclouding her

ability to distinguish Right from Wrong. Every suitor who
seeks her radioactive hand is denied audience, unless he
claim to be a paleface. For only as a paleface is he received
into the palace that her father, King Armoric, has given her.
She then tests the truth of his claim, and if his imposture
is uncovered, the would-be wooer is summarily beheaded.
Heaps of battered remains surround the grounds of her
palace—the sight alone could short one's circuit. This, then,
is the way the mad princess deals with those who would
dare dream of winning her. Abandon such hopes, my son,
and leave in peace."

The prince, having made the necessary obeisance to his
sovereign father, retired in glum silence. But the thought
of Crystal gave him no rest, and the longer he brooded, the
greater grew his desire. One day he summoned Polyphase,
the Grand Vizier, and said, laying bare his heart:

"If you cannot help me, O great sage, then no one can,
and my days are surely numbered, for no longer do I re-
joice in the play of infrared emissions, nor in the ultraviolet
symphonies, and must perish if I cannot couple with the
incomparable Crystal!"

"Prince!" returned Polyphase, "I shall not deny your
request, but you must utter it thrice before I can be certain
that this is your inalterable will."

Ferrix repeated his words three times, and Polyphase said:

"The only way to stand before the princess is in the guise
of a paleface!"

"Then see to it that I resemble one!" cried Ferrix.

Polyphase, observing that love had quite dimmed the
youth's intellect, bowed low and repaired to his laboratory,
where he began to concoct concoctions and brew up brews,
gluey and dripping. Finally he sent a messenger to the
palace, saying:

"Let the prince come, if he has not changed his mind."

Ferrix came at once. The wise Polyphase smeared his tempered frame with mud, then asked:

"Shall I continue, Prince?"

"Do what you must," said Ferrix.

Whereupon the sage took a blob of oily filth, dust, crud and rancid grease obtained from the innards of the most decrepit mechanisms, and with this he befouled the prince's vaulted chest, vilely caked his gleaming face and iridescent brow, and worked till all the limbs no longer moved with a musical sound, but gurgled like a stagnant bog. And then the sage took chalk and ground it, mixed in powdered rubies and yellow oil, and made a paste; with this he coated Ferrix from head to toe, giving an abominable dampness to the eyes, making the torso cushiony, the cheeks blastular, adding various fringes and flaps of the chalk patty here and there, and finally he fastened to the top of the knightly head a clump of poisonous rust. Then he brought him before a silver mirror and said:

"Behold!"

Ferrix peered into the mirror and shuddered, for he saw there not himself, but a hideous monster, the very spit and image of a paleface, with an aspect as moist as an old spider-web soaked in the rain, flaccid, drooping, doughy—altogether nauseating. He turned, and his body shook like coagulated agar, whereupon he exclaimed, trembling with disgust:

"What, Polyphase, have you taken leave of your senses? Get this abomination off me at once, both the dark layer underneath and the pallid layer on top, and remove the loathsome growth with which you have marred the bell-like beauty of my head, for the princess will abhor me forever, seeing me in such a disgraceful form!"

"You are mistaken, Prince," said Polyphase. "It is precisely this upon which her madness hinges, that ugliness is beautiful, and beauty ugly. Only in this array can you hope to see Crystal. . . ."

"In that case, so be it!" said Ferrix.

The sage then mixed cinnabar with mercury and filled four bladders with it, hiding them beneath the prince's cloak. Next he took bellows, full of the corrupted air from an ancient dungeon, and buried them in the prince's chest. Then he poured waters, contaminated and clear, into tiny glass tubes, placing two in the armpits, two up the sleeves and two by the eyes. At last he said:

"Listen and remember all that I tell you, otherwise you are lost. The princess will put tests to you, to determine the truth of your words. If she proffers a naked sword and commands you grasp the blade, you must secretly squeeze the cinnabar bladder, so that the red flows out onto the edge; when she asks you what that is, answer, 'Blood!' And if the princess brings her silver-plated face near yours, press your chest, so that the air leaves the bellows; when she asks you what that is, answer, 'Breath!' Then the princess may feign anger and order you beheaded. Hang your head, as though in submission, and the water will trickle from your eyes, and when she asks you what that is, answer, 'Tears!' After all of this, she may agree to unite with you, though that is far from certain—in all probability, you will perish."

"O wise one!" cried Ferrix. "And if she cross-examines me, wishing to know the habits of the paleface, and how they originate, and how they love and live, in what way then am I to answer?"

"I see there is no help for it," replied Polyphase, "but that I must throw in my lot with yours. Very well, I will disguise myself as a merchant from another galaxy—a non-spiral one, since those inhabitants are portly as a rule and I will need to conceal beneath my garb a number of books containing knowledge of the terrible customs of the paleface. This lore I could not teach you, even if I wished to, for such knowledge is alien to the rational mind: the paleface does everything in reverse, in a manner that is sticky, squishy, unseemly and more unappetizing than ever you could imagine. I shall order the necessary volumes, meanwhile you have the court tailor cut you a paleface suit out of the appropriate fibers and cords. We leave at once, and I shall be at your side wherever we go, telling you what to do and what to say."

Ferrix, enthusiastic, ordered the paleface garments made, and marveled much at them: covering practically the entire body, they were shaped like pipes and funnels, with buttons everywhere, and loops, hooks and strings. The tailor gave him detailed instructions as to what went on first, and how, and where, and what to connect with what, and also how to extricate himself from those fetters of cloth when the moment arrived.

Polyphase meanwhile donned the vestments of a merchant, concealing within its folds thick, scholarly tomes on paleface practices, then ordered an iron cage, locked Ferrix inside it, and together they took off in the royal spaceship. When they reached the borders of Armoric's kingdom, Polyphase proceeded to the village square and announced in a mighty voice that he had brought a young paleface from distant lands and would sell it to the highest bidder. The servants of the princess carried this news to her, and she said, after some deliberation:

"A hoax, doubtless. But no one can deceive me, for no one knows as much as I about palefaces. Have the merchant come to the palace and show us his wares!"

When they brought the merchant before her, Crystal saw a worthy old man and a cage. In the cage sat the paleface, its face indeed pale, the color of chalk and pyrite, with eyes like a wet fungus and limbs like moldy mire. Ferrix in turn gazed upon the princess, the face that seemed to clank and ring, eyes that sparkled and arced like summer lightning, and the delirium of his heart increased tenfold.

"It does look like a paleface!" thought the princess, but said instead:

"You must have indeed labored, old one, covering this scarecrow with mud and calcareous dust in order to trick me. Know, however, that I am conversant with the mysteries of that powerful and pale race, and as soon as I expose your imposture, both you and this pretender shall be beheaded!"

The sage replied:

"O Princess Crystal, that which you see encaged here is as true a paleface as paleface can be true. I obtained it for five thousand hectares of nuclear material from an intergalactic pirate—and humbly beseech you to accept it as a gift from one who has no other desire but to please Your Majesty."

The princess took a sword and passed it through the bars of the cage; the prince seized the edge and guided it through his garments in such a way that the cinnabar bladder was punctured, staining the blade with bright red.

"What is that?" asked the princess, and Ferrix answered: "Blood!"

Then the princess had the cage opened, entered bravely, brought her face near Ferrix's. That sweet proximity made his senses reel, but the sage caught his eye with a secret sign and the prince squeezed the bellows that released the rank air. And when the princess asked, "What is that?," Ferrix answered:

"Breath!"

"Forsooth you are a clever craftsman," said the princess to the merchant as she left the cage. "But you have deceived me and must die, and your scarecrow also!"

The sage lowered his head, as though in great trepidation

and sorrow, and when the prince followed suit, transparent drops flowed from his eyes. The princess asked, "What is that?" and Ferrix answered:

"Tears!"

And she said:

"What is your name, you who profess to be a paleface from afar?"

And Ferrix replied in the words the sage had instructed him:

"Your Highness, my name is Myamlak and I crave nought else but to couple with you in a manner that is liquid, pulpy, doughy and spongy, in accordance with the customs of my people. I purposely permitted myself to be captured by the pirate, and requested him to sell me to this portly trader, as I knew the latter was headed for your kingdom. And I am exceeding grateful to his laminated person for conveying me hither, for I am as full of love for you as a swamp is full of scum."

The princess was amazed, for truly, he spoke in paleface fashion, and she said:

"Tell me, you who call yourself Myamlak the paleface, what do your brothers do during the day?"

"O Princess," said Ferrix, "in the morning they wet themselves in clear water, pouring it upon their limbs as well as into their interiors, for this affords them pleasure. Afterwards, they walk to and fro in a fluid and undulating way, and they slush, and they slurp, and when anything grieves them, they palpitate, and salty water streams from their eyes, and when anything cheers them, they palpitate and hiccup, but their eyes remain relatively dry. And we call the wet palpitating weeping, and the dry—laughter."

"If it is as you say," said the princess, "and you share your brothers' enthusiasm for water, I will have you thrown into my lake, that you may enjoy it to your fill, and also I will have them weigh your legs with lead, to keep you from bobbing up . . ."

"Your Majesty," replied Ferrix as the sage had taught him, "if you do this, I must perish, for though there is water within us, it cannot be immediately outside us for longer than a minute or two, otherwise we recite the words 'blub, blub, blub,' which signifies our last farewell to life."

"But tell me, Myamlak," asked the princess, "how do you furnish yourself with the energy to walk to and fro, to squish and to slurp, to shake and to sway?"

"Princess," replied Ferrix, "there, where I dwell, are other palefaces besides the hairless variety, palefaces that travel predominantly on all fours. These we perforate until they expire, and we steam and bake their remains, and chop and slice, after which we incorporate their corporeality into our own. We know three hundred and seventy-six distinct methods of murdering, twenty-eight thousand five hundred and ninety-seven distinct methods of preparing the corpses, and the stuffing of those bodies into our bodies (through an aperture called the mouth) provides us with no end of enjoyment. Indeed, the art of the preparation of corpses is more esteemed among us than astronautics and is termed gastronautics, or gastronomy—which, however, has nothing to do with astronomy."

"Does this then mean that you play at being cemeteries, making of yourselves the very coffins that hold your four-legged brethren?" This question was dangerously loaded, but Ferrix, instructed by the sage, answered thus:

"It is no game, Your Highness, but rather a necessity, for life lives on life. But we have made of this necessity a great art."

"Well then, tell me, Myamlak the paleface, how do you build your progeny?" asked the princess.

"In faith, we do not build them at all," said Ferrix, "but

program them statistically, according to Markov's formula for stochastic probability, emotional-evolutional albeit distributional, and we do this involuntarily and coincidentally, while thinking of a variety of things that have nothing whatever to do with programming, whether statistical, alinear or algorithmical, and the programming itself takes place autonomously, automatically and wholly autoerotically, for it is precisely thus and not otherwise that we are constructed, that each and every paleface strives to program his progeny, for it is delightful, but programs without programming, doing all within his power to keep that programming from bearing fruit."

"Strange," said the princess, whose erudition in this area was less extensive than that of the wise Polyphase. "But how exactly is this done?"

"O Princess!" replied Ferrix. "We possess suitable apparatuses constructed on the principle of regenerative feedback coupling, though of course all this is in water. These apparatuses present a veritable miracle of technology, yet even the greatest idiot can use them. But to describe the precise procedure of their operation I would have to lecture at considerable length, since the matter is most complex. Still, it is strange, when you consider that we never invented these methods, but rather they, so to speak, invented themselves. Even so, they are perfectly functional and we have nothing against them."

"Verily," exclaimed Crystal, "you are a paleface! That which you say, it's as if it made sense, though it doesn't really, not in the least. For how can one be a cemetery without being a cemetery, or program progeny, yet not program it at all?! Yes, you are indeed a paleface, Myamlak, and therefore, should you so desire it, I shall couple with you in a closed-circuit matrimonial coupling, and you shall ascend the throne with me—provided you pass one last test."

"And what is that?" asked Ferrix.

"You must ..." began the princess, but suddenly suspicion again entered her heart and she asked, "Tell me first, what do your brothers do at night?"

"At night they lie here and there, with bent arms and twisted legs, and air goes into them and comes out of them, raising in the process a noise not unlike the sharpening of a rusty saw."

"Well then, here is the test: give me your hand!" commanded the princess.

Ferrix gave her his hand, and she squeezed it, whereupon he cried out in a loud voice, just as the sage had instructed him. And she asked him why he had cried out.

"From the pain!" replied Ferrix.

At this point she had no more doubts about his palefaceness and promptly ordered the preparations for the wedding ceremony to commence.

But it so happened, at that very moment, that the spaceship of Cybercount Cyberhazy, the princess' Elector, returned from its interstellar expedition to find a paleface (for the insidious Cybercount sought to worm his way into her good graces). Polyphase, greatly alarmed, ran to Ferrix's side and said:

"Prince, Cyberhazy's spaceship has just arrived, and he's brought the princess a genuine paleface—I saw the thing with my own eyes. We must leave while we still can, since all further masquerade will become impossible when the princess sees it and you together: its stickiness is stickier, its ickiness is ickier! Our subterfuge will be discovered and we beheaded!"

Ferrix, however, could not agree to ignominious flight, for his passion for the princess was great, and he said:

"Better to die, than lose her!"

Meanwhile Cyberhazy, having learned of the wedding preparations, sneaked beneath the window of the room where they were staying and overheard everything; then he rushed back to the palace, bubbling over with villainous joy, and announced to Crystal:

"You have been deceived, Your Highness, for the so-called Myamlak is actually an ordinary mortal and no paleface. Here is the real paleface!"

And he pointed to the thing that had been ushered in. The thing expanded its hairy breast, batted its watery eyes and said:

"Me paleface!"

The princess summoned Ferrix at once, and when he stood before her alongside that thing, the sage's ruse became entirely obvious. Ferrix, though he was smeared with mud, dust and chalk, anointed with oil and aqueously gurgling, could hardly conceal his electroknightly stature, his magnificent posture, the breadth of those steel shoulders, that thunderous stride. Whereas the paleface of Cybercount Cyberhazy was a genuine monstrosity: its every step was like the overflowing of marshy vats, its face was like a scummy well; from its rotten breath the mirrors all covered over with a blind mist, and some iron nearby was seized with rust.

Now the princess realized how utterly revolting a paleface was—when it spoke, it was as if a pink worm tried to squirm from its maw. At last she had seen the light, but her pride would not permit her to reveal this change of heart. So she said:

"Let them do battle, and to the winner—my hand in marriage. ..."

Ferrix whispered to the sage:

"If I attack this abomination and crush it, reducing it to the mud from which it came, our imposture will become apparent, for the clay will fall from me and the steel will show. What should I do?"

"Prince," replied Polyphase, "don't attack, just defend yourself!"

Both antagonists stepped out into the palace courtyard, each armed with a sword, and the paleface leaped upon Ferrix as the slime leaps upon a swamp, and danced about him, gurgling, cowering, panting, and it swung at him with its blade, and the blade cut through the clay and shattered against the steel, and the paleface fell against the prince due to the momentum of the blow, and it smashed and broke, and splashed apart, and was no more.

But the dried clay, once moved, slipped from Ferrix's shoulders, revealing his true steely nature to the eyes of the princess; he trembled, awaiting his fate. Yet in her crystalline gaze he beheld admiration, and understood then how much her heart had changed.

Thus they joined in matrimonial coupling, which is permanent and reciprocal—joy and happiness for some, for others misery until the grave—and they reigned long and well, programming innumerable progeny. The skin of Cybercount Cyberhazy's paleface was stuffed and placed in the royal museum as an eternal reminder. It stands there to this day, a scarecrow thinly overgrown with hair. Many pretenders to wisdom say that this is all a trick and make-believe and nothing more, that there's no such thing as paleface cemeteries, doughy-nosed and gummy-eyed, and never was. Well, perhaps it was just another empty invention—there are certainly fables enough in this world. And yet, even if the story isn't true, it does have a grain of sense and instruction to it, and it's entertaining as well, so it's worth the telling.